Dangerous
Journey

NOVELS BY JOHN CREASEY

Bruce Murdoch, Mary Dell and The Withered Man Saga

DANGEROUS JOURNEY
I AM THE WITHERED MAN
THE WITHERED MAN
WHERE IS THE WITHERED MAN?
UNKNOWN MISSION

Superintendent Folly Mysteries

THE GALLOWS ARE WAITING
CLOSE THE DOOR ON MURDER
FIRST A MURDER

Dangerous
Journey

John Creasey

David McKay Company, Inc.
Ives Washburn, Inc.
New York

DANGEROUS JOURNEY

First American Edition, 1974

LIBRARY OF CONGRESS CATALOG CARD NUMBER: 73-81177

ISBN 0-679-50485-0

MANUFACTURED IN THE UNITED STATES OF AMERICA

6

581296

1 : Idyll Disturbed

The journey would never have been started but for the weak roots of the old elms at the bottom of the tiny garden, and the out-of-season gale which swept the South of England in early September. The wind whistled, howled and whined, cold enough to warrant that blazing log-fire Percy Briggs had been inspired to build. But the newly-fitted windows kept out the draughts, and the small lounge was warm and snug. Which was another triumph for Bruce Murdoch and Mary Dell, whose friends had been convinced that the dilapidated little old cottage near Lulworth Cove could never be made comfortable.

From the outside, it was a gem of that early Elizabethan architecture which only reached Dorset a few months before the death of Good Queen Bess—for new styles in architecture, like most other innovations in the fashionable world, started near London in those days and travelled slowly. But, said the critics, the oak beams were worm-eaten and the bricks crumbling to dust, and Mary and Murdoch were poor, benighted fools for wasting time and money on it. And anyway, it was hardly decent.

Had Bruce and Mary been married, it would have been bad enough. But to go into ecstasies over that broken-down little rabbit-hutch and brazenly plan its rebuilding and talk about the two months they would spend down there, without any prior visit to registry office or church—no, it was too bad!

None of which worried the two conspirators.

Murdoch was tall and broad and almost flaxen-haired; Scottish-born and English-bred. Mary, tall for a woman, was slim and dark and very lovely. Neither were given to quick

5

enthusiasms, but both had set their hearts on the cottage from the first.

Of the few who believed that they used different bed-rooms and observed the proprieties—while cursing the clause in their contracts which prevented their marrying—Percy Briggs, Murdoch's man, was one. He confessed to an occasional crony that he couldn't understand it, but deep down in his loyal Cockney heart he was glad. And Bruce and Mary were simply intent upon wringing the last shred of enjoyment out of a holiday that might be interrupted any day.

A week before, Sir Robert Holt—that incredibly large, incredibly pink man—had paid them a flying visit, admired the elms and the medley of stock and aster and antirrhinums. dahlias and late roses, and said:

'All very nice and pretty—I expect Mary did most of the work, as usual? But—sorry, and all that—I might have to break this idyll, soon. So keep some things packed.'

He had stayed long enough to partake of tea, with strawberry jam and Dorset cream—which rarely gets full justice—then driven off at the wheel of his open tourer, the sun shining down on that bald, pink head that never seemed to tan. They had watched him out of sight with mixed feelings.

'If he calls us before this weather breaks,' Mary had threatened, 'I'll . . .'

'Catch the first train,' Bruce had completed for her, even as he smiled in sympathetic accord.

Then the storm had come, rising in the middle of the night and lulling towards dawn. They had spent the morning clearing up the wind's wreckage in the garden, but the afternoon brought the real force of the gale.

It was just after four o'clock when they heard the crash, and went out to inspect the damage. One of the elms had been up:ooted: luckily, it had fallen into the paddock at the side of the cottage.

'Logs for the winter,' Murdoch soothed, but Percy sniffed. 'H'elm don't burn safe, Mr. Bruce. 'Ot as 'ell, but cracks and splits all over the shop.' He glanced suspiciously at the other big trees, then at the sky. 'Crikey, ain't it blowin'?'

They had to struggle against the storm to reach the cot-

6

tage, and their last sight from the small porch was of dark streaks of rain blustering into the grey stretches of the Channel. Then tea— Mary's cakes, Mary's jam, and Lulworth bread and cream. Afterwards, Bruce settled in one armchair with the book he was reading, and Mary snuggled deep in another with hers. While, unknown to either of them, efforts were being made to reach the cottage by telephone. . . .

The call that should have disturbed their tranquillity lost itself somewhere near the fallen elm in the wires it had taken down with it. In a large room in a small house in Sloane Square, Sir Robert Holt was growing pinker by the moment —finally achieving a shade of outraged strawberry when the operator said:

'I'm sorry, sir, but the line is broken. We can get Lulworth, but no further.'

'What the blazes broke it?' roared Sir Robert.

The operator attended the lines of a number of prominent Whitehall figures, whose tantrums on the telephone she had learned to bear with patience. She explained calmly:

'There's a gale blowing off the coast, sir.'

'Goddamit!' bellowed Sir Robert. 'You mean your perishing engineers can't make a cable strong enough to . . .' He broke off, mopping a perspirating forehead with a large silk square. 'All right, all right!' he muttered. 'Put me on to Telegrams.'

Five minutes later a large, pleasant-faced man at the small village post office scratched his head, tried to get Cliff Cottage although he had been assured that the line was down, then went to the door of his shop. As he opened it the wind whipped in, sending the whole paraphernalia of a general store hammering and clattering and blowing about the two square yards cleared for customers and the twenty square yards crammed with stock.

'Tommy can't go out there on a bike, that's a fact,' he murmured, and called: 'Lizzie! *Lizzie!*'

His wife opened the door leading to the small parlour.

'Did you call, dear?'

'Important telegram to deliver to Cliff Cottage,' said the postmaster, phlegmatically. 'I'll have to take the car.'

7

Lizzie scowled her disapproval.

'Those people there don't deserve you should go out on a night like this! Not so much as a ring to *pretend* they . . .'

The postmaster liked Mary Dell.

'Got to be done, Lizzie—I won't be long.'

Thus disruption in the form of that large, placid man and his battered Morris forced its way through the gale towards Cliff Cottage, four miles away, as Bruce and Mary grew more deeply immersed in their books and what for them was the unbelievable luxury of that shared peaceful solitude.

Came a knock at the front door, Percy's sharp footsteps, a howl of wind, a bang, and then voices from the tiny hall.

Percy opened the door.

'Tellygram—urgent—sir.'

Bruce scowled, and Mary looked up abruptly as he took the envelope, tore it open, and glanced at the contents.

'No answer, Percy,' he said, crisply.

'Okey-doke, sir.'

'What is it?' asked Mary, as the door closed.

He handed her the telegram, and she read:

Both report at once catch six o'clock from Dorchester if possible wire if you miss it. H.

'So it's come!' She gave him a lopsided smile. 'We've been lucky to have so long. Can we make the train '

'It's half-past five now. I doubt it, but we'll try. Percy!' he called, adding as that worthy appeared with remarkable promptitude: 'Get the car out, we're going in five minutes.'

'Okay, sir.' Percy's battered, pugnacious and comical face showed no surprise as he disappeared again, and five minutes later he was driving as furiously as the heavy wind would allow. But at five to six, they still had four miles to go and Bruce shrugged.

'It'll be quicker by road, now, I expect.'

In Dorchester, ten minutes later, he phoned Holt. The result was that they filled up with petrol, and Percy settled back to drive as fast as he could to London.

'I wonder if it's in England?' Bruce mused.

'Not likely.'

8

'No . . .'

Had the gale not blown, had the elm not fallen, had the postmaster driven at thirty miles an hour instead of fifteen, they would have caught the six o'clock, been in London soon after eight, with Holt at eight-thirty and at Mere House in Surrey two hours later—and they would not have started on that dangerous journey.

But while Percy was driving through the wind and rain, things were happening in London and Mere House. . . .

In London, Sir Robert Holt—called affectionately by all the agents of the Secret Service 'the Pink 'Un'—was in conference with the Foreign Secretary, the Rt. Hon. Vernon Glennister, the War Minister, Dalby, and Paddon, Minister for the Co-ordination of Home Defence. The three ministers were saying the same thing, but Glennister put it more tersely than the others.

'Von Romain must not leave the country for twenty-four hours, Holt. You've got to find some pretext for keeping him here.'

'All very well!' snapped Holt. 'Man's a diplomatic representative of a friendly state, isn't he? I've two men watching Mere House, but they can't shanghai him. Or can they?' He glared.

Dalby reproved him. 'There's no reason to lose your temper. Surely a small matter like the accidental detention of von Romain should not strain your resources unnecessarily.'

'I haven't got any resources!' Holt's opinion of Dalby and the other members of the Cabinet—with Glennister the chief exception—was low. 'You don't give me enough money. Your blasted pin-pricking regulations stop my men doing what they could, and . . .' his sudden roar contained all the pent-up fury of the last few hours: 'on this night of all nights the blasted telephone wires break. I can't get the two people who could hold von Romain. I can't even . . .'

'All the same,' said Paddon—a tall, thin, white-haired man whose habitual expression was one of dignified disapproval, and whose retorts discourteous in the House had frequently brought Opposition members to their feet in protest—'you must stop von Romain, Holt.'

9

Holt looked like a pink-painted Easter egg as he glared. 'Oh, I must, must I? Maybe you'll tell me how? If he gets out of the country, I'll have him followed: I can't do more. Is that plain enough?'

'He mustn't go!' Dalby spoke with rare emphasis, and the Pink 'Un grew visibly pinker.

'Von Romain must not . . .' began Paddon, in the same breath.

'Holt will do all he can,' remonstrated Glennister. He knew that Sir Robert was reaching his limit, and that if they stayed together for another five minutes it would bring down a vitriolic condemnation of the Cabinet, its methods and its members—and two of its dimmer lights in particular.

.   .   .   .   .

Alone, Holt sat at his desk, staring at the wall and scribbling on a writing-block.

While Percival Briggs negotiated a fallen tree-branch with skill, and Bruce and Mary wondered if they would reach London alive—and, if they did, what Holt would have for them to do.

And Herr Kurt von Romain, at Mere House in Surrey, systematically burned incriminating papers and prepared to depart.

2 : They Learn of Things

The Daimler pulled up outside a small house in a side street near Sloane Square. The tail-end of the wind whipped drearily past a man and a girl eating chips out of newspaper and a hopeful dog following their trail. The big car was as out of place in that dingy thoroughfare as an orchid in a cabbage-patch.

'The flat, Percy. We'll join you there, or phone you.'

'Yessir.'

'And you'd better fix something to eat,' said Bruce.

'A man and his stomach,' murmured Mary, as he led the way to the door with its flaking paint and unpolished knocker and general air of seedy decay, which so improbably masked the elegant splendour of Sir Robert's actual environment.

The door was opened by a large and stately man who blocked most of the narrow passage. He pressed back to let Bruce and Mary squeeze through.

'Hallo, Gordon? He's in, I hope?'

'Yes, sir, and expecting you.'

There was no hint of a smile on Gordon's solemn face, nor suggestion of amusement in his voice, but Murdoch glanced at him sharply and Mary said a dry:

'Like that, is it?'

Up a flight of dingy stairs and along another narrow passage, was another door in need of a coat of paint. Gordon opened it—and they stepped into a room which would have been a credit to Claridges. It was spacious and high-ceilinged, quietly but exquisitely decorated and furnished.

In one corner, at a desk piled high with papers, Sir Robert sat—scribbling still, as he regarded them: he had a disconcerting habit of looking anywhere but at his pad, when writing. Mary sat down, and Bruce followed her example. Without preamble, and still scribbling, Holt snapped:

'Of all the blundering lunatics, I warned you not to go down there, didn't I? And when you can't even see to it that the telephone wire's all right!'

'It was a tree,' said Bruce, and Sir Robert snorted.

He stopped writing, tore off the sheet of paper, screwed it up and threw it into a waste-paper basket. Most of what he wrote went there; his best friends knew that he only put words on paper to make them more vivid in his mind. 'All right—sorry,' he growled. 'How are you, Mary? Look here, we haven't much time, so listen hard. There's a man named von Romain, Kurt von Romain—sounds all wrong, I know, but it's a real one—at Mere House, in Surrey—near Guildford. Road-map and route indication here.' He banged a great hand on the pile of papers. 'Von Romain is Under-Secretary to the German Ambassador. They said. We doubt it. He was two years secretary to Otto Grandt, their economic big-shot.

You know him? Man immediately responsible for the trade drive in the Balkans—we found him out a couple of years after he'd started. Well, now. We're beginning a counter-drive. Secret. Big concessions to the right people, but—not so secret.' Holt rubbed his hand over his bald dome, and every word came out as though the next was pressing hard for utterance. Although this was his normal manner of speech, there was an undercurrent of tension which both Murdoch and Mary recognised.

'It appears von Romain's picked up some ideas of what we're going to do. More, he knows we've been negotiating agreements with most of the small European countries. Also, he knows we've offered armaments on the strict understanding that in a war they'll join us. Been fine if it had been secret. Something sprang a leak. So von Romain's off, hard as he can go, to put counter-offers before these lovely governments. Goverments!' repeated the pink Sir Robert, as though he would gladly wither them all. He glared. 'Following?'

'Yes,' said Bruce, and Mary nodded.

'I wonder!' growled Holt. 'You look too cold and hungry. Have to eat on the way, sorry. Well, now—we've found something. I told those fat-headed, blithering nincompoops who call themselves . . .' He snorted again then plunged on, his voice sharper: 'I told the Cabinet about this a week ago. They've just believed me now. Von Romain is going to offer our prospective allies what we propose, with a difference. A big difference. Arms,' he elaborated, gruffly, 'virtually for nothing, *but*—stored and controlled by Nazi agents! And he's going to threaten them, in all likelihood. Do it, or else— you know the attitude. No one believes we'd start in, if there was a scrap. We've given way so much they don't believe we'd reach a limit. But we will. We have. Understand this: if any one of five countries accepts the German offer, it's a fight. We daren't let them get farther in Europe; it's got to stop. But we don't want war . . .' Holt's eyes were hard. 'And of course this is all being beautifully arranged. Secret meetings, secret agreements. On the surface everything's lovely; Hitler made a speech last night—you may have heard it: holding out his hand of friendship. Everything's set pretty, but we're doing our best to cut each other's throats and we each know it.'

Behind the welter of words there was a depth of feeling which worried both Murdoch and Mary. Holt rarely took a thing as grimly as this; and they, knowing the cut-throat policy of totalitarian goverments, knowing the knife-edge on which peace swayed so perilously, felt deep apprehension.

'Now,' he went on, 'we've got to stop von Romain starting until our own man is off. Cardyce is going for us, and if any man can pull off the agreements, he will. Face von Romain and what he stands for with *fait accompli*, and Germany either has to swallow it, or fight. They'll know then, that we will fight. But if they get in first, they'll take the usual advice; they'll believe we won't. In short Germany's making this offer on the basis of British appeasement. If he gets in first he thinks we'll just grin and bear it or . . .' Holt sneered—'make a protest. Only we won't. I've had Dalby and Paddon here this evening, and if that pair are prepared to make a stand, it's a stand, all right. So von Romain's got to be delayed—and you've got to delay him.'

Murdoch stirred. Mary's hands tightened.

'Don't sit there looking like dummies,' roared Holt. 'We can't have him stopped officially—it would create an uproar, make the difference between "friendly relations" and damned hostile ones! It's got to be done quietly: there's got to be no proof that the British Government is stopping him. If there is, it'll probably light the bonfire. This is important: war materials, trade—everything depends on it. If he gets in first —flare up. If he doesn't, there's a ghost of a chance of getting the balance of power on our side. We've got the prejudice of years of shilly-shallying to overcome—the smaller countries won't be easily persuaded. But Cardyce is going to make offers that they can't turn down—unless they're accepted the German offers, first.'

He stood up, suddenly, and took a wallet from the desk. He had lost much of his natural ebullience, and looked tired to a point of exhaustion.

'A year ago, propositions like this would have been referred to the various Cabinets. Today, the authority is vested

13

in a few individuals, and decisions can be made overnight. At a few hours' notice, generally. So Cardyce needs just twenty-four lead on von Romain—and—*he's—got—to—have—it!* If you can't keep him in England, get after him. Don't know his first port of call, but it's likely to be Luthia. Call on whoever you like for help, but you're in this as private citizens. No Government support—I needn't tell you that. I've spent twenty minutes talking,' Holt added, grimly, 'and that's twenty more you've got to make up. No use giving you half a story, you know the essence now. There's the road directions, and one or two other things that might help you.'

He gave Mary a wry smile.

'Sorry, m'dear. But I know you like working together. 'Bye, and all the luck in the world!'

He shook hands with each in turn. and Bruce said slowly:

'You're leaving this entirely to us?'

'I can't send a tank corps after von Romain, can I?'

'No. If we hit trouble, who'll replace us?'

'Angell and Fuller. They'll be at hand.'

'Good!' Bruce's face cleared. 'Now I'd just like to phone the flat.'

Five minutes later, Percy Briggs was driving again towards Sloane Square, a packet of sandwiches and flasks of coffee on the seat beside him. Ten minutes later, one of the five telephones on Holt's desk rang, and he broke off in the middle of a sentence to answer it.

'Hallo? Yes . . . all right, Angell . . . yes, they'll be there in an hour . . . Hold or follow v R . . .'bye.'

He banged down the receiver, his triple chins quivering, and his eyes very wide.

'Von Romain's due to leave in half an hour! Angell has got at his car, so he'll be delayed a bit. Frankly I don't think you'll be in time to do much over here, but you can try. You've two advantages. Von Romain makes the inevitable German mistake—he under-estimates us, so he won't suspect he's being followed. And to make his jaunt less apparent, he's likely to leave England by a sea-route—a flight would be too ostentatious.'

'All right. We'll do all we can.' Bruce smiled fleetingly.

'Violent death objected to, I take it?'

'Pull a hair of his head,' barked Holt, 'and the chances are that he'll identify you. Once he knows we're on the hunt, there'll be the devil to pay! You've got to keep delaying him and play possum yourselves. Of course I'm asking a lot. I'd say I was asking the impossible, but you've got just one chance in a thousand.'

'And that,' said Bruce as he settled back in the car, with Percy phlegmatically obeying his terse order to make for Guildford, 'was an over-estimate. If we've a chance in ten thousand, that's all. Of all the . . .'

'The luck might break our way,' Mary murmured, but without much confidence. This was likely to be a bitter fight against hopeless odds.

And risks.

If they were caught, they knew what would happen. In dictator states spies went to the same place, in peace or war. It was an appalling prospect and it added to Bruce's depression—made him want to shout from the roof-tops of the stupidity which had brought the world to the borders of war.

But at least now the Government knew that it was fighting desperately against the general upheaval; that war was a hard-and-fast probability. Holt had merely given them a precis of the truth.

It would have taken a dozen full-length books for any man to sum up the international situation as it was that night. Twenty-one short years since the Armistice, twenty-odd short years since the last man had died in battle for democracy, since when the blunders of men and the nations they stood for had brought the world close to chaos.

Like ghosts, the tragedies of aggression stalked the lands. Treaties had been broken only to be rebuilt and broken again. The debris of Versailles littered a dozen countries. A hundred 'incidents' which would have meant war twenty-five years before, had been allowed to pass almost unchallenged.

No one believed in promises of help.

There was no faith in the lands.

But in most countries there was a small organisation, like Sir Robert Holt's, with one aim and one concern: fighting

15

the battle for peace and supporting their Governments' efforts to get the balance of power where they felt it should be.

Holt was right: individuals counted today more than at any time in modern history. Even the democratic countries—other than France—were controlled by Governments with such overwhelming majorities that they could dictate policy and not submit it to the people's ballot.

Of the welter of intrigue and lies and profit-making, little seeped through into the Press. More, much more, reached Holt's agents, and Murdoch knew the weight of the responsibility on his shoulders and Mary's. A single false move—and they were over the edge. At best, it would be the end for themselves; at worst it would be the end for millions.

If the world ever learned this story it would be of Cardyce, that shrewd, clever and unscrupulous general-utility member of the Cabinet. Cardyce and the Goverment would be blamed or praised, whatever the result.

Murdoch and Mary had to allow Cardyce to get ahead and keep ahead of Kurt von Romain.

3 : First Report

'There's the A.A. box,' said Bruce, leaning forward and speaking through the open glass partition. 'Next turning right, Percy, and the second drive gates on the left.'

'Yessir.'

'Exactly what are you thinking of doing?' asked Mary.

Bruce shrugged.

'Angell will be there, I hope, and he'll know what's happened. We'll work it out from that point. At the moment I haven't the faintest idea of what to do or how to do it.'

'Where's there's a will there's a way, sir,' chirped Percy.

'Oh, you're listening, are you? You look for those turnings, Percy, and say some prayers.'

'Okey-doke, sir.'

Murdoch grinned. Percy could be calculated to relieve

16

depression more thoroughly than any man of his acquaintance. He had been with Murdoch for seven years. Before that he had been in the Army: in Flanders at sixteen, a sergeant at eighteen, and after the general demobilisation, had enlisted again and spent most of the next ten years in India. Finally out of the Army in nineteen-twenty-nine, he had won two thousand pounds—by choosing an outsider with a pin—squandered it in twelve months, and been virtually starving when he had inflicted himself on Murdoch.

On the actual night of their first meeting, Murdoch had been twenty-two, and comparatively unused to liquor. A night with friends and a considerable mixing of drinks had sent him staggering into the cold November air, almost into the arms of Percy.

Percy had inspected his wallet, found a card, and led him to the Clarges Street address on it. In the morning—after his own first substantial breakfast for months—he had read a homily on the evils of drink. At the time, Bruce had been too thick-headed to be amused, but had recited the event with gusto afterwards. Tenaciously Percy had stayed, and his Army training, including a spell as batman, qualified him for the rank of gentleman's gentleman.

Only a few months before buying the cottage, Murdoch had been introduced to Holt.

The uncovering of an armament ring and the saving of military secrets had made Murdoch one of Holt's best agents. Mary had worked with the Department for years and had topped the list before Murdoch arrived. After the affair which had been Bruce's baptism,* they had worked together, making three trips to Europe before their holiday. It was a combination founded on mutual respect and now strengthened by mutual love, and was so effective that Holt had come to rely on them to achieve the impossible.

Nevertheless, as Percy slowed down by the drive gates of Mere House, they wondered whether the Pink 'Un had not asked too much, this time.

·   ·   ·   ·   ·

* *Secret Errand* by John Creasey.

In the glare of the headlights, the figure of a man showed clearly. He had darted from the hedge and as Percy braked hard, he snatched the door open. A dark, tall, good-looking and hefty customer, his teeth flashed as he grinned a greeting.

'Hi, folks! Come to join the party?'

'What's happened?' Bruce snapped.

'Von Romain's likely to start any time,' reported Edward Angell. 'I fitted a brace of dud carburettors to his Mercedes—it's the only car he's got, and he had to send a man on a bike to the nearest garage.'

Mary asked: 'How many men are with him?'

'Three.'

'Any women?'

'One. And oh my, is she...'

'She'll keep,' said Bruce, briefly. 'Listen, Ted. It's probable that he'll aim for Folkestone—there's a night crossing there. If he hits the Folkestone Road, get ahead of him, and we'll see you at the harbour.'

'Right, old man,' Ted Angell nodded. 'All the best.'

As he slipped away Bruce said:

'Up to the house, Percy.'

'Yessir.' Percy had kept the engine running, and he let in the clutch promptly. The drive was little more than three hundred yards long, and the headlights picked out almost at once the massive neo-Georgian structure that was Mere House. From the large windows on the right of the front door, lights shone out, silhouetting two men and a woman.

In the list of 'information' Holt had provided was the fact that Kurt von Romain called himself, at Mere House, Carl Lenster. He had a passport in that name, and the house had been bought by him five years before.

As far as Murdoch could judge, von Romain would leave on the night-boat from Folkestone. Or try to. The steamer left the Kentish port at half past one, to connect with the changed Boulogne-Paris train times. At the back of his mind, a plan was forming. . . .

The Daimler pulled up outside Mere House at half past eleven: von Romain would have to travel fast to make that Folkestone run.

Mary huddled in her furs and pressed back out of sight in the dark interior, as Murdoch climbed from the car. Percy closed the door after him, then stood rigidly to attention beside it while Murdoch mounted the broad granite steps and knocked heavily on the massive front door.

There was a moment of silence, then quiet footsteps. The door opened and a heavy-jowled man in a belted overcoat stood there, slate-grey eyes glittering as he snapped a bad-tempered:

'Yes?'

'May I see Mr. Lenster, please?'

'He is not here, and...'

'Surely,' Murdoch protested mildly, 'my eyes did not betray me? I could have sworn I saw him through the window.'

Thick lips tightened as Murdoch looked past him. The door to the right was ajar, and the light from the room threw shadows half-way across the hall. Two people were standing near the door, listening.

'He is not in!' the man rasped. 'Understand that! I have no time...'

Murdoch stepped deliberately across the threshold.

'I'm sure,' he said softly, 'that Herr von Romain will wish to see me.'

The name had all the effect he could have hoped. The other man stepped back startled, while from the door a voice spoke—deep, touched with a guttural harshness, yet in excellent English.

'I shall, of course, be delighted.'

Murdoch had seen photographs of von Romain, but they had not done the man justice. Here was a perfect example of the Teuton. Tall, big-boned, fair-haired, he had the clear, light blue eyes of his race, the heavy features which seemed carved from pale granite. His hair was cropped, Prussian fashion, and he had a stiffness of movement which told of military training.

His pale eyes swept Murdoch up and down as he ordered:

'Close the door, Mettink—it is cold. May I ask whom I have the pleasure of addressing...?'

'Morely,' said Murdoch, promptly. 'You'll have to forgive me calling so late, Mr. Lenster . . .'

'Need we keep up the pretence?'

Murdoch felt the soft menace in that voice, and knew in that moment that he was facing a man as unscrupulous as any he was likely to meet.

'Much better not to, I agree. If you can spare me five minutes . . .'

'Five at the most. Three, preferably,' said the German, quickly and coldly. 'I am going out—an unexpected call to London.'

'Oh.' 'Mr. Morely' looked put out. 'That's a pity, I—anyhow, better not waste time. You won't know me, of course, but . . .'

'Bring the car round, Mettink,' von Romain ordered, sharply. 'Come in here, Mr. Morely.'

He led the way into the large drawing-room he had just left. It was apparently empty. But in the air was a faint scent of perfume, and there was no other door. At least three pieces of the heavy, old-fashioned furniture could have hidden the woman he had glimpsed through the window.

Von Romain closed the door.

'Now, Mr. Morely?'

'It's a damned shame you've got to go,' said Murdoch, naïvely. 'I know you'd be interested, and . . .'

'May I ask you to get to the point?'

'Oh, yes, of course.' In a dying fire, Murdoch saw the litter of white and black ash; needed no telling that papers had been burned in the past hour. But five minutes had passed: von Romain had less than two hours to reach Folkestone. 'You must be surprised that I know your name, sir.'

'Very.' Von Romain's pale gaze did not leave his own.

'Naturally. It is a delicate subject—I had hoped for a little more time. I . . .' He saw the glitter in the German's eyes, and decided that verbiage now would do more harm than good. 'I come, indirectly you understand, from Clayton and Company, of Birmingham. You know . . .'

There was a subtle change in von Romain's manner.

'You should have said so at once, Mr. Morely. Now let me be frank. I am going to Folkestone, not to London, on urgent business, and I have no time to discuss the matter of Clayton and Company here. Can you travel down with me?'

Murdoch's eyes widened.

'Well, I—yes, right-ho. The chauffeur won't overhear, will he?'

'He can be trusted,' said von Romain.

'And my bus can follow,' Murdoch suggested.

'I would prefer that you returned from Folkestone by train,' said von Romain, 'and send your car back, Mr. Morely. A little precaution . . .' He shrugged, and Murdoch knew better than to argue.

He blessed the little wallet from Holt.

In it had been a report of von Romain's known efforts to negotiate with Clayton and Company, the Birmingham aeroplane manufacturers whose engineers had recently evolved plans for a high-speed bomber with unquestioned advantages over any yet on the market. It did not appal Murdoch that the English concern might exchange—for a substantial consideration—the essentials of the new plane to Germany: the object of armament firms was to make money. But he wished Holt had been able to give him more information: he had to sit with von Romain for the better part of two hours, and he had to make his presentation of Clayton and Company's suggestions seem convincing.

He was in no doubt of what von Romain would do if he discovered—or even seriously suspected—that he was a fraud. Somewhere behind von Romain's Mercedes, Ted Angell and Mick Fuller would be following. But if the German came to the right conclusion on the road. . . .

Mentally, Murdoch shrugged. It was a risk that had to be taken, and his opportunities for delaying the journey were considerable. Cardyce had already started on that flying trip. If von Romain missed the night boat, it would be a substantial help.

'Right-ho,' he said. 'I'll tell my man.'

Mettink, glowering by the closed front door, opened it as Murdoch appeared. Outside, Briggs still stood at attention.

'Briggs—get back to London and wait for word from me.'

'Yessir,' said Briggs, and climbed smartly into the driving-seat. Behind the Daimler, the Mercedes stood waiting and

Murdoch wondered fleetingly whether the man who had brought it round could possibly see Mary through the window. Then as the Daimler swept off down the drive, he saw with relief that the rear window-blind was pulled down. He turned back to the hall—and had a shock.

Von Romain was standing there, clad in ulster and black Homburg. At his side, wrapped in chinchilla so that only her face and legs showed, was a woman. A woman of such vivid beauty that he could only stare; while Mettink passed him, and the Daimler turned right at the drive gates, its passage clearly marked by the swaying beam of its powerful headlights.

4 : Fräulein Weissman

'This is Fräulein Weissman, who will travel with us.' von Romain spoke with stiff courtesy. 'Fräulein, Mr. Morley.'

She nodded slightly, her chin burying itself still farther into her collar. Vivid violet eyes met Murdoch's without any expression beyond curiosity. Von Romain hurried to the porch, waited for them both to pass him, and pulled the door to. Mettink was holding the car door open and despite the heavy furs, Fräulein Weissman stepped in quickly, gracefully.

There was ample room for the three of them.

Murdoch, in the middle, wished the woman a thousand miles away. It would be more difficult to talk with the knowledge that two people were listening, two people on the alert for any false note. The car moved off smoothly and when it reached the road, turned left with a roar. Mettink drove as if he knew the narrow, twisting lanes by heart; at that speed Murdoch devoutly hoped he did.

'And now,' said von Romain. 'your message, Mr. Morely.'

'I must ask the Fräulein to forgive me,' said Murdoch, stiffly, 'but I was instructed to talk only with you, sir.'

'It is all right; you have my word for it.'

Murdoch shrugged.

'The responsibility, Herr von Romain, is entirely yours.'

'Yes, yes!' Von Romain sounded impatient, and Murdoch

saw the woman's lips curve, as though in amusement. He plunged into his imaginary message, and all the time he was praying that he would not be suspected—and wondering how he could best cause further delay.

.   .   .   .   .

'Turn right, Percy,' Mary had said, as the Daimler reached the end of the drive. 'Make it look as if we are heading for London.' She straightened up thankfully. 'Then get on to the west road for Folkestone as soon as you can. If we sight the Mercedes, try to pass it.'

'Okey-doke,' said Percy, and swung the wheel.

If Mary felt worried, she did not show it. Bruce had not expected to go with von Romain, but apparently he had started the journey of his own free will, and she believed he was capable of handling any emergency. Her chief problem was whether to try to delay the Mercedes, or whether to leave it to Bruce. Within twenty minutes, she had decided to interfere if the opportunity came.

Driving was easier, now. What wind there was drove north-west, immediately behind them. They reached Dorking and travelled fast through the town, on the main road to Tonbridge. There was no sign of the Mercedes which, if it had started within five minutes of them, would have had a six miles' start by taking the shorter route to Dorking.

Percy pushed back the partition.

'Better keep straight on, Miss. Maidstone and Ashford will be quickest.'

'Fine. And keep an eye open for the Mercedes.'

There was little traffic on the road and as the miles flew, she watched more tensely for signs of the other car. Then at half past twelve, three miles beyond Maidstone, she saw it pulled up outside a garage. She did not glimpse the occupants, and Percy did not slow down.

Lenham, Charing, Ashford. Once, they passed three men working on a telephone wire which was down, and further south, she saw the debris blown about by the storm. An idea came, unprompted.

'Stop if you see a tree down, Percy. Or a big branch.'

'Right-ho, Miss.'

They were three miles beyond Willesborough, with about twelve to go and half an hour to do it in—which meant that the Mercedes, minutes behind them, would have little time to spare—when they saw the huge branch dragged to one side out of harm's way. The brakes squealed as Percy slowed down, and Mary said quickly:

'We'll shift it into the road, Percy. You stand on that side and stop traffic that way: I'll stop it this way. But first, change the number-plates.'

The branch was heavy, but there was a slope to the grassy bank, and they soon had it accross the road sufficiently to hold up any vehicle. Percy was sweating and Mary breathing very hard, when they finished—just as the glare of headlights came.

The Mercedes?

Mary, waving a flash-lamp, stood at the roadside, her heart thumping. If von Romain was desperate to catch the boat, he might ignore her warning—and she dared not think what could happen to Bruce, if he did. The great car came on, and the speed did not seem to slacken. But the headlights bathed the width of the road in a brilliant glow—reached the Daimler, the branch, Percy on the far side. Brakes squealed as the powerful car veered out and pulled up, just past the Daimler.

The driver opened his door sharply.

'What's all this?'

'Oh, please—can you help my man? This branch . . .'

As Mettink came hurrying forward, the rear doors opened and von Romain jumped out. Bruce followed him, flinging Mary a polite apology for their haste. She watched them straining to get the branch moved, and knew that Bruce was making it seem twice as heavy. Precious seconds grew into minutes. . . .

They had it aside at last, and four minutes after the stoppage, they were on the way again. Mary knew from Bruce's expression that she had helped his plans, and felt a sharp relief at the knowledge that he was free and safe.

The Mercedes was out of sight when Percy clambered back to his seat. But he was a driver in a thousand, and they ran into Folkestone with seven minutes to spare.

Three minutes to reach the station. . . .

From there to the harbour was usually an eight or nine-minute walk. The Daimler pulled up behind the Mercedes, and Mary saw the four racing towards the station entrance. A voice at her elbow made her jump.

'No luck, Mary?'

It was Ted Angell, looking very tall in the gloom.

'They'll catch it?'

'Seems so.'

'Can't we do anything?'

'Short of creating a riot, no. Mick's waiting for them, but if the ship hasn't started, the officials will hold it long enough if they see them coming.' He was hurrying with her, now, along the station platform. 'Have you got the tickets?'

'No.'

'I've some spares,' he told her. 'Come on, Percy. A Channel crossing in a gale—once lived through, never forgotten!' Percy grinned back, but Mary's heart was heavy. She knew that Sir Robert had not seriously expected them to be able to stop von Romain leaving Folkestone, but it was damnable to think they had been within mere minutes of doing so!

Then they heard a sudden cry, from somewhere along the platform.

'Nice work!' Angell grunted, as they ran on. 'But we hurry past.'

It was as much as she could do. Bruce was down on the line, and von Romain with him. The woman was standing and shouting at them, while Mettink was trying to haul von Romain back to the platform.

As Mary and the others pushed past, a struggling Bruce slipped awkwardly back against von Romain, and Mettink's hold was loosened.

They reached the barrier. As Angell showed tickets, a short, chunky man with an enormous chin emerged from the shadows.

'It's just off.' A blast from the ship's siren confirmed the fact, and Mary gasped:

'Tell Bruce we've caught it. You come with me, Ted. Daren't stay here—von Romain might guess . . .'

'Right!' flashed the chunky man, and they flew on. Porters were beginning to lift the gangway, but held it for them. As they reached the deck and turned, they saw Bruce and von Romain at the final barrier, below, saw the chunky man approach them and guessed he was telling them it was too late. Mick Fuller, in the guise of a harbour official!

The gap between quay and ship was widening and as Mary turned away, she heard Angell chuckle, and Percy gloat:

'*That's* put 'em back a bit! Nice work, like you said, sir! But 'ere, Miss—wot are *we* goin' ter do?'

5: Suspicion?

'I really am most dreadfully sorry,' gasped Bruce. 'I slipped, I didn't realise—hang it, you've missed the boat!'

'Yes,' said von Romain slowly, and his expression was not pleasant. 'Thanks to you, Mr. Morely.'

'No, but hang it . . .'

'Need we discuss it?' Fräulein Weissman spoke sharply. The only moment she had lost her self-control had been when she had stood raving at them to hurry, while Bruce was doing his best to stop von Romain reaching the platform. But he was afraid that in the last desperate effort he had seriously overplayed his hand.

Yet there was a chance that von Romain was not yet suspicious.

His actual call had meant a delay, but not an unnatural one. No one could have blamed Murdoch for the hold-up on the road, or the trouble with the carburettors. The only direct delay he had caused had been in his fall from the platform—and to suggest its genuineness, he had a bruise on his cheek which was swelling rapidly.

26

He blessed Mary and Ted and Mick.

Angell had made it possible for him to get to Mere House before the German left. But for that branch across the road, all of them would have been on the Channel now. And Fuller's last-moment interference in the guise of an official had finally wrecked their chances.

Fräulein Weissman's sharp interruption had silenced von Romain—and considerably heightened Bruce's curiosity about her. Mettink was striding at their side, glowering.

'Astonishing chapter of accidents!' Bruce exclaimed, as they reached the Mercedes. 'But after all . . .' he forced a smile, while von Romain looked at him without speaking— 'you'll be in Folkestone, and my principals will be able to reach you. I can phone them tonight—they'll travel at once, I'm sure.'

Von Romain's eyes were expressionless.

'If they are to see me, they must be here before nine-thirty tomorrow. The morning boat leaves an hour later. You will talk with them at once?'

'By Jove, I will!' Murdoch's face brightened. He had spent half the journey down pleading with von Romain to stay in England long enought to meet his 'principals'. He had bluffed in the hope that the opportunity would not be presented. Now that it was, he had to contact quickly with Holt, and leave it to him to find a way out.

The game had started.

He had his—or Cardyce's—head in front of von Romain. The thrill of the chase, heightened by this first-round victory, was thawing his earlier pessimism. He had been slow in starting this time, but he would make the running.

And for the time being it had to be as the somewhat ingenuous Mr. Morely. . . .

'They'll come rushing down,' he asserted, as they climbed into the Mercedes. 'I—but where shall they come to?'

'We shall stay at the Regal,' said von Romain.

'Regal? Don't know it, myself. Have you stayed there before?'

'Yes,' said von Romain, so curtly that even the naïve Mr. Morely took the hint and remained silent.

Except for that sharp reproof at the quayside, Fräulein Weissman had said no word, and Mettink appeared to be carrying on a savage conversation with himself. As the car pulled up at an unpretentious hotel near the sea-front, a Frazer-Nash two-seater in need of repairs to its silencer hummed past.

In it sat Mick Fuller.

The sight of him warned Murdoch. Holt's men had a remarkable habit of turning up exactly when wanted, and remaining discreetly in the background at all other times. The Regal would be under observation—and Holt would learn of that first-round result.

Murdoch's problem was to telephone, himself, without one of the trio overhearing.

A tired night-porter wilted under von Romain's manner— 'Mr. Lenster' was not likely to be popular—and found them four rooms. He protested that a meal was impossible, but went off grumbling to make arrangements. In his room, a small one between Mettink's and von Romain's, Murdoch said with admiration:

'By the Lord Harry, you can handle 'em, sir!'

'I am used to handling people.'

'Oh, of course.' Murdoch beamed. 'I'll put a call through at once—I should have some news in ten minutes or so.'

'You can tell your principals,' said the German, slowly, 'that I shall expect them here at nine o'clock sharp, Mr. Morely.'

He went out, and Murdoch wiped his forehead. Had there been a threat in that statement?

He pushed the query aside, and put through a call to Sloane Square.

.   .   .   .   .

In the room on the other side of von Romain's, Fräulein Katerina Weissman—as she was known—had flung the chinchilla coat over her bed. Von Romain tapped, and she called sharply:

'Come in!'

As the German bowed from the waist, she glared like a

wild-cat. Eyes blazing, she snapped:'

'So, this is what happens when you arrange the passage?
I will have you understand, my friend, it is not good enough
—a long way from good enough! What will be said in Berlin, when this is known!'

'My dear Katerina. I...'

'Ach—as always, you will say it is not your fault! Then
whose? Did I not complain at the delay? Was I not urging
you to hurry? And now—when I am expected to send the
good news to Berlin...!'

'We have no knowledge that Cardyce has yet started,' von
Romain reminded her, suavely, 'and we shall lose only nine or
ten hours, Fräulein.' His manner was a combination of urbanity and apprehension. He knew the result of failing to obey
orders; knew that excuses fell on deaf ears. And this devil of
a woman had the ear of those who mattered. He knew that
she could make or break him, and he was afraid of her. But
he must not let her realise it.

'Nine or ten hours is too much!' She took a cigarette from
her case, lit it, and flicked the match towards the coal fire.

'It can be made up, Fräulein. At the moment, I have a
greater concern.'

'Greater?'

'I am wondering if the man Morely is all he seems.'

'Ach, the excuse!'

'I wonder,' said von Romain, knowing that he had her
interest, 'whether Morely knew anything about the trouble
with the car at Mere House.'

'What?'

'And whether he fell from the platform accidentally, or
not?' Von Romain's pale blue eyes did not leave her face. 'He
was so anxious to arrange that his principals saw us, Fräulein: it would not be impossible that he made sure they did.
The tree was another matter; but the rest is too much for
coincidence.'

He saw the sudden change of her mood.

'So! It could be.... This business with Clayton, it is important?'

'Very,' von Romain said, drily. 'If he will deal with us,

and we can send the aeroplane designs to Berlin, it will be of considerable value. And you can help with the men, when they come tomorrow.'

'Yes.' She flashed a smile at him now, and patted the bed. 'Sit down, Kurt; we will talk. Now, of greatest importance ...'

Next door, Bruce was speaking in undertones to the Pink 'Un. Mettink was downstairs, still stirring the night staff into activity. And in a small hotel almost opposite, in a room facing the Regal's entrance, was the chunky Mick Fuller.

. . . . .

The only Cabinet Ministers for whom the Pink 'Un had any real regard were Cardyce, at that moment in Paris arranging for an interview with the Chancellor of Luthia next day, and Glennister. Now, on their direct private lines, Glennister was saying:

'My dear Bob. I can't order Cayton about like that.'

'You've got to!' snapped Holt. 'Got to get him to Folkestone by nine o'clock in the morning—and he's got to pretend to be considering von Romain's offer. Damn and blast, I've already presented you with a miracle! You must back me up now.'

'Can't you send someone else, as Clayton?'

'Now don't be all of a damned fool!' implored Holt. 'Murdoch's sure he's suspected of delaying them, *but,* so far, von Romain's only linked it up with the Clayton business. Look here—ring Clayton and tell him I'm going to talk to him. I'll put a call through in ten minutes.'

'Very well,' said the Secretary for Foreign Affairs.

In a large house near Birmingham, a short, tubby man was awakened at a quarter past two that morning by the telephone next to his bed. Sleepily, he answered, and after a pause said:

'*What's* that?'

Another pause, and:

'All right, I'll talk to him. Yes, yes, I'll do what I can. Goodbye.'

The little man helped himself to a weak whisky-and-soda before the second call came through. He looked more absurd in his colourful pyjamas than he did in normal dress—and even in that, he had a reputation for looking comic. But in Roland Clayton was invested the supreme control of Clayton and Company, whose aircraft production was one of the key factors in the rearmament campaign. Behind the porcine eyes and receding, wrinkled forehead, was a mind which knew the international situation from A to Z. Roland Clayton had been glad to accept orders from the Government and promise quick delivery, and he was giving it—at a price.

He had built a thousand planes before he allowed the Government to know that in the person of Matthew Hawsman, in his designing department, he had an aeronautical genius who had evolved something in the way of bombers twenty per cent speedier than any known aircraft. Mr. Clayton professed himself amazed that the German, Italian, French and American Governments discovered the fact within twenty-four hours of Whitehall.

Naturally, he had been pestered with inquiries. Naturally, he had answered them all vaguely. Naturally—because he was Roland Clayton, and his god was himself—he was interested in the call from Sir Robert Holt.

Holt talked for five minutes, and received only grunted responses. Five more minutes, and Clayton said:

'Sorry, Holt, I can't do it. I've an important conference here in the morning.'

Holt talked for another five minutes.

'My dear Holt,' said Mr. Clayton. 'I would be delighted. But this is hardly my sphere, you know—rather the Government's concern. I'm sorry, but ...'

'All right!' snapped the Pink 'Un, and rang off.

Mr. Clayton had been asleep for ten minutes when the telephone rang again. He swore as he lifted it and announced himself. Thirty seconds afterwards, he said:

'My dear Prime Minister, I'll be delighted to oblige you! Delighted.'

At the other end of the wire, Sir Robert Holt wrote swiftly on his blotting pad:

'Tell Glennie I told Clayton I was the P.M. *After* ten o'clock tomorrow.'

And then he went back to bed.

31

6: Mr. Clayton Plays Up

Murdoch took an instant dislike to Roland Clayton. His expressionless little eyes created immediate distrust. Although the September warmth had come again, Clayton stepped out of his Rolls-Royce huddled in a coat with an astrakhan collar, and a too-large black Homburg. He walked sharply into the Regal and a few seconds later Murdoch's telephone rang.

'A Mr. Clayton to see you, sir.'

'I'll come down,' said Murdoch.

He wanted to get the meeting with Clayton over without company. He could hear von Romain and Mettink in the room on his right, but not the Fräulein. He went out quietly and slowed down as he passed her door. There was no sound.

The foyer of the Regal had been a place of splendour in the early days of Queen Victoria's reign. The chairs and settees were either the original models, or exact replicas. The red plush carpet was thick in places and nearly threadbare in others. But what Murdoch disliked most was the clutter of palms, aspidistras and ferns. They helped to make the foyer smell fusty—and they provided too many hiding-places.

Clayton was standing with his hat and coat on, still, although the hall was stuffy. As Murdoch hurried towards him, he heard a rustle behind a palm—and saw Fräulein Weissman, sitting in an easy chair with a magazine. Her neat costume served to emphasise her figure and silk-sheathed legs.

'*Blast* the woman!' thought Murdoch, and his heart was thumping as he approached the little industrialist. But he had a pleasant shock.

'Hallo, Morley.' Clayton spoke as if he had known him for years. 'Was this night run necessary?'

There was the right hint of annoyance, the perfect manner from employer to employed. Murdoch was compelled to admire him.

'I assure you it was, Mr. Clayton.'

32

'Well, all right. Where is he?'

'Upstairs, I ...'

'I've got exactly half an hour,' said Clayton, sharply. 'No more! You've taken things as far as you can?'

'I've gone every inch I dared, sir.'

'H'mph. All right: let's get up.' As Clayton moved towards the lift, he looked at Fräulein Weissman. She glanced up disinterestedly, then back at her magazine. She had no change out of that five minutes, thought Murdoch with satisfaction, as the lift door clanged behind them.

Clayton fidgeted until they reached the first floor. Then as they stepped into the passage, he said sharply:

'Who was that woman?'

'Which ...'

'The one with the legs—don't be a fool. Know her?'

'She's with von R.'

'*Is* she?' Clayton sucked his teeth. 'Odd. All right: talk about it later. Where's the room?'

Murdoch would have liked a five minutes' conversation before they saw the German. The question about the Fräulein startled him. But he forced back his curiosity.

'Here we are, sir.' He spoke loudly enough for von Romain to hear, and tapped sharply on the door. Mettink opened it, and let them in, then went out.

'Herr von Romain, may I introduce . . .' began Murdoch.

'Don't waste time,' said Clayton, roughly. 'We know each other by name. Well, Herr von Romain. Morely tells me you're particularly anxious to see me.'

The German smiled coldly.

'I understood the anxiety was yours, Mr. Clayton.'

Clayton's smile was a quick quirk of the lips. His deep little eyes showed no amusement.

'All right, we needn't fence—I know what you want, and I'm ready to tell you what I want. A quarter of a million pounds, Herr von Romain.'

Murdoch stifled a gasp: the German, used to the intricacies and subterfuges of diplomacy and espionage, was taken off-guard completely.

'My dear sir ... !' he demurred.

33

'No need to beat about the bush,' Clayton growled. 'Morely knows what you want; so do I. The Hawsman Bomber. I'll repeat—I'm prepared to give you the designs on prior payment of a quarter of a million pounds. The money must be drafted through New York, and the deal can be completed immediately New York has the credit. Any bank you like. They'll hold it until word from you. Well, sir?'

Von Romain had regained his self-control.

'An admirably plain statement, Mr. Clayton, and my Government will appreciate your frankness. I hold out every hope that they will accept the offer . . .'

'Up to them.' Clayton shrugged. 'I wanted to see you myself—you might not have considered the offer genuine, through an agent. I've heard your proposition; now you've got mine. Anything else?'

Murdoch came to von Romain's rescue with cigarettes, and Clayton took one also.

'I think that every detail is now settled,' said von Romain stiffly. 'With one exception, perhaps.'

'What's that?'

'Did you give Mr. Morely instructions to delay me until such time as you could arrive?'

Clayton laughed: it was a mirthless sound, more like a cackle, and his little eyes turned towards Murdoch: bright, penetrative, glinting with a sardonic amusement.

'No flies on Morely,' he declared. 'Got his job to do. How and where he does it is no business of mine, Herr von Romain. All I'm interested in are results. Well . . .'

'I assure you,' Bruce protested lamely, 'that such a thought did not enter my head, sir! I did my best to dissuade Herr von Romain from leaving until you had seen him. But as for any active effort to delay him, most certainly not.'

Clayton deliberately winked.

'Can talk, can't he?' he said. 'Morely, I want a drink—ring for it.' He had the manner of a dictator, and von Romain's eyes were beginning to show respect.

Murdoch was completely satisfied. By innuendo Clayton had suggested that he believed 'Mr. Morely' had deliberately contrived that delay. Any notion von Romain might have had

34

of Intelligence Service interference must have disappeared completely. This was the second round, and it was Murdoch's all the way.

'Well,' Clayton announced after he had been in the room twenty minutes. 'I must go. Come down to the car with me, Morely. Goodbye. Herr von Romain, I hope to hear from you soon.'

As they reached the passage, Fräulein Weissman was walking to her room.

Her eyes, large, smoky-violet, looked anywhere but at Clayton. Murdoch felt his heart miss a beat: she really was quite staggeringly beautiful. Clayton passed her without comment, and turned to the stairs.

'We can't talk in the lift,' he growled. 'Listen, Morely, or whatever-your-name-is—if you ever want work, come to me: I can use you. Now about that woman. She's with von Romain, you say?'

'Yes.'

'Odd,' Clayton repeated. 'Last time I saw her . . .'

He broke off, for immediately behind them, Mettink appeared. Clayton paused to light a cigarette, and Mettink passed in a hurry. The glint of sardonic amusement which made Clayton seem more human, came again.

'Trouble with Germans, Morely,' he murmured, 'they do everything too thoroughly. Carried too far, it's a weakness. Now, that woman—what does she call herself?'

'Weissman.'

'H'mm. It was Wellinkov, last time. In Moscow. Supposed to be Stalin's mistress. I wonder . . .'

Murdoch's eyes widened.

'She's a beauty, of course.'

Clayton grunted. 'Mongol type: nose too broad, eyes too big. Can be cunning and cruel—watch out for her. You'll handle von Romain all right, but she—well, do your best!'

They had reached the foyer, and Mettink was at the reception desk, apparently in earnest conversation with the clerk.

Out at the car, Murdoch was surprised when the little armaments millionaire extended a hand.

'Goodbye and good luck! Don't forget—if you're ever

looking for something to do, come and see me.'

For a moment those porcine eyes held his, and despite the affability of words and manner, Murdoch's dislike took a turn for the worse. Clayton grinned, and stepped into his car. Murdoch waited with apparent servility as the pale-faced chauffeur tucked rugs about the fat body and thin knees of his lord and master.

'All right, Race!' Clayton said harshly, and as the chauffeur turned to the driving seat beckoned to Murdoch.

'Ask yourself,' he suggested, 'why Fräulein Weissman was once Madame Katrina Wellinkov, what she was doing with Stalin, and what she is doing with von Romain.'

'Katrina,' thought Murdoch, as Clayton added:

'A celebrated beauty, my dear Morely. Beauty does what brains can't. Be like me, take no notice of it.' Without another word, he wound up the window.

Murdoch, alone on the pavement, reflected wryly on the things he had heard about Clayton. The Armaments Commission, which sat in 1933, had spoken sharply of the Birmingham manufacturer. Clayton was known to have engineered several small revolutions and was suspected of graver intrigues. But he had enabled Bruce to scrape out of what might have been a nasty corner, and that suggested he had the welfare of Great Britain at heart.

Still musing, he turned back towards the hotel—seeing, without really noticing, the gorgeous array of palms, ferns and flowers on the verandah immediately above the entrance. Then suddenly there was a sharp, cracking noise, and a man's voice called:

'*Look out!*'

He glanced up—and jumped.

A window-box with three shrubs in gaily painted tubs was falling, the earth spattering about him. As he plunged forward, one of the tubs hit his shoulder a glancing blow. He reached the foyer as the tubs crashed one after the other, and a porter and a clerk, equally startled, were rushing forward.

'Are you all right, sir?'

'Blimey, that was a close one!'

At the end of the foyer—calm and expressionless, Murdoch noted—the Fräulein was standing, eyeing him. Not by word or look must he let her think he believed von Romain had arranged for those tubs to fall.

But if it were true, was von Romain merely taking revenge on Mr. Morely? Or did his suspicions go deeper—did he expect to be followed?

7: What's in a Name?

Von Romain's regrets were formal but polite. He thanked Mr. Morely for enabling him to meet Roland Clayton, and hinted that if the deal was completed satisfactorily Mr. Morely's part in it would not be forgotten by his principals. He stressed the word 'principals'. Mr. Morely was very naïve in his delight at the satisfactory development of negotiations and proposed seeing von Romain and his party safely off. It was not necessary, said von Romain, but Murdoch insisted. A 'Mr. Morely' might be expected to insist.

Clayton had left at ten o'clock, and Mettink had instructions to have the car at the hotel at ten past. Those ten minutes had gone by the time the Regal's staff had recovered from the accident. Murdoch cut short the manager's shocked apologies and back in his room hurriedly flung his clothes into a case. He intended to travel third-class and to keep out of sight of the German party once he had slipped them at the quay. It would have been a hundred times better to have let von Romain to go on alone, but he could not connect with Mary, and he had to have the man followed from Boulogne . . .

The phone rang suddenly, and he lifted the receiver.

'Hallo?'

'Mick,' said Fuller's voice. 'The servant pushed the boxes —I saw him. Keep that in mind. Now there's word from Holt: he wants to see you—you're to fly to Croydon at once. You'll find a private plane waiting for you at the airport here. I'm going on the boat—Mary and Ted'll be the other side, anyhow. No time for more, old man. Good hunting!'

'Thank you—I'm much obliged,' said Bruce, in his Morely manner. 'Goodbye.'

He replaced the receiver, pleased in two ways. He could have von Romain off from the quayside, now: the party would have no possible reason for thinking he might be following them—and Mary was safe. The whole business had gone off considerably better than might have hoped.

He heard the faintest of clicks from the door.

He stiffened, and saw the handle move slightly. In three strides he was across the room. Listening intently, he heard soft footsteps along the passage. He opened the door—and saw Fräulein Weissman at the end of the passage.

'Yes,' he murmured. 'She's dangerous . . .'

Mettink was at the car, when he followed her out and climbed into the back. Von Romain was in the middle, this time. The impersonal gaze of the woman was uncanny. She had not once allowed herself to thaw: apart from the barest politeness, no word had passed between them.

At the quayside, von Romain extended his hand.

'Good of you to have taken so much trouble, Mr. Morely.'

'Oh, no trouble at all—only too glad everything went off all right!' Murdoch wrung the German's hand, beamed, and turned to the Fräulein. Startled, he saw her smile. 'I—er—goodbye, Fräulein Weissman.'

'It has been a great pleasure,' she assured him. Her eyes were dancing. Her grip was light but firm. 'And, please, be careful with your shoulder.'

'Oh, rather!'

As she walked steadily up the gangway, Murdoch reflected on her words. He could not imagine her gibing at him in such a way as to make him suspicious of the origin of the accident. The Mr. Morely of her acquaintance would hardly look beneath the surface of what would normally have been a friendly remark. But he was puzzled, the more so when he saw her stand by the rail, wave and smile, before she turned and went below.

He waited until Mick Fuller took her place at the rail, then turned and made his way back to the station yard.

'You know the airport?' he asked a taxi driver.

38

The man grimaced.

'If you could call it that, sir!'

'Take me there, please,' said Murdoch, and settled back in the corner, able to relax for the first time since the arrival of the telegram the previous day.

The steep streets of the town were so spacious that he was surprised when the cabby turned down one which was little more than a lane. But a moment later he frowned, for a second taxi had taken the same turning. He leant forward.

'Are we going straight to the airport, driver?'

'A short cut,' the man assured him. 'May Street, then ...'

'Pull up outside a hairdresser's, will you?'

In three minutes the cab had slowed down, and as Murdoch climbed out, he saw the second cab pass him and pull up ten yards farther along. A display of corsetry in the window opposite it suggested that the driver had merely been instructed to pass the first cab and stop.

He drew out some silver.

'But I thought ...' began the driver.

'I've changed my mind,' smiled Murdoch.

He waited long enough for change to see the tall, thin man, who left the other cab, then he waved the change away.

'I'm going to walk ahead of you, cabby, and you'll start off. Just in front of the cab standing there I'm jumping aboard. Understand?'

'Right, sir! Follerin' you, was he?'

'A pound if you get me to the airfield without him,' said Murdoch, and the cabby grinned like a conspirator.

Standing in front of an impressive display of lingerie was the tall man. Thin, lantern, with a pendulous underlip, he had the appearance of a foreigner and Murdoch fancied his clothes were German-cut.

The cab came sluggishly up.

The whole manœuvre was so quickly completed that the thin man had no chance to get to his cab before Murdoch's had turned the first corner. The cabby glanced round, grinning widely, and took another turn quickly. Murdoch was bewildered in the next three minutes by the twists and turns as they sped along, but he was satisfied that the man would earn his bonus.

The airport was little more than a joy-flight field, and the only modern plane—a small dual-control Hawker—was standing well way from the hangars. By it, stood two mechanics and the pilot; the only people in sight.

'Mr. Morely?' said the pilot.

'That's right.' Murdoch paid the cabby his pound.

'How long shall we be, can you tell me?'

'Oh, we'll manage Birmingham in that time easily, sir,' said the pilot, glibly.

Thank the Lord, thought Murdoch, for men quick on the uptake. He climbed aboard while the mechanics pulled the chocks away. Not until they were airborne did the pilot turn his head to reassure him:

'Croydon, isn't it, sir?'

'So long as you know,' said Murdoch, relaxing.

'All I know,' grinned the pilot, a youthful man with almost flaxen hair. 'I was told to bring a bag—and that we might be going to Luthia.'

'I wouldn't be surprised,' conceded Murdoch.

He reflected that the man could be trusted, or he would not have been given that information in advance. Holt, as always, was planning well ahead. . . .

They reached Croydon almost before he realised they were well in the air. The pilot smiled round.

'That flip's soon over, sir. I hope the long trip's on—I'm rather looking forward to it.'

The plane was met by a uniformed official, who also addressed Murdoch as Morley, and led him to the offices. In a small one next the manager's stood Sir Robert, his pink face shining.

'Come in, my boy, come in! Glad to see you—damned glad.' The door closed, and Holt chuckled, his chins quivering. 'Wonderful piece of work, Bruce, I hand it to you. How'd you manage it?'

Bruce explained briefly. Holt interrupted by nodding and grunting and occasionally chuckling. At the recital of the flower-box incident, he said:

'I needn't tell you to be careful. Now, then: Mary phoned me, last night. She'll pick them up at Boulogne with Angell, and Fuller will follow them. But two things, Bruce. First. this woman: Fuller gave me a rough description. What's your feeling about her?'

'She's dangerous, beyond doubt. And Clayton knew her.'

'Did he, though! Name?'

'She called herself Weissman here, but Clayton claims . . .'

Bruce told him, quickly.

'Yes.' Holt was nodding, thoughtfully. 'Yes. Just a minute.' He delved into his breast-pocket and extracted a snapshot. 'This anything like her?'

Bruce took the photograph and stared. It was not only like her; it was life-like. He nodded.

'Hrrumph!' said Holt. 'Debonnet's nineteen thirty-eight lady-love, that was. Known in Paris as Mademoiselle Catherine de Bourcy. Yes, she's in this very deeply, Bruce. Von Romain, now—I wonder, I wonder! Well, it's not your angle: I'll have it covered.'

Murdoch was taken completely by surprise. For Fräulein Weissman to be Katrina Wellinkov *and* Catherine de Bourcy! That Debonnet, the French Minister for Defence, changed his mistresses annually was the cause of considerable ribaldry, in certain circles.

'Now,' Holt added: 'her relationship with von Romain. Who wears the trousers?'

'The Fräulein, I gather.'

'Hrrumph. She wouldn't have done, in Moscow, and she didn't in Paris. Interesting. Might be instructive. Now, the other thing . . .' He glared. 'If I'd been able to get you on the phone last night, my boy, the whole thing might have been off.'

'*What?*'

'Fact. I never did like this pesty country cottage idea. However, can't be undone! I had someone sent to Mere House to look round, this morning. He found . . .' Holt looked worried —'a body. We don't know whose, but we know he was killed by a knife in the back, in the drawing-room. Stains rubbed off, carpet flung over them—you wouldn't have noticed anything.

41

But in falling, he banged his hand on a table. Wore a wrist-watch. He died, if that's a reliable guide, at half past ten, near enough—practically to a moment, when you would have arrived, and even for von Romain, we wouldn't have let murder pass. However, can't be helped, and perhaps it's as well.' Murdoch looked as bleak as he felt. If he had arrived before the murder could have been covered up, it might have made a vast difference to Cardyce's journey.

'Well,' he said, 'how's Cardyce doing?'

'Nicely. Reached Luthia this morning—the first of five. Enkraine, Mavia, Dorshland and Brennia, in that order—any two against us will blow up the whole works. Now, you'll get over to Luthia. Say, twelve hours. Von Romain will fly from France, so he'll beat you by two or three hours, but he'll have to stay there long enough to find out that he's too late to beat Cardyce. You'll find Mary and the others—or one of the others—at the Lankessa Hotel. Go straight there.'

'Good.' Murdoch nodded. 'How much can the pilot know?'

'Nothing, in theory. Anything, in emergency. A useful lad, and you'll be able to rely on him. Named Graham.' Holt was speaking more jerkily than usual. 'Look here, Bruce. Play up the Clayton angle. If there's trouble, let it be inferred that you are working for him.'

'Can you fix it with him? He struck me as a man who would want to make his own decisions.'

'It's fixed. For once, we have the co-operation of anyone we want . . .' Holt chuckled, but the moment passed. 'Thing is this, Bruce. Berlin wants this Hawsman Bomber; so does Moscow. At the moment, only France, the U.S. and ourselves have the manufacturing rights, which means that we're well ahead of the others. So an agent from Clayton's will have more opportunities than a free-lance. Lead the double life, my boy. Clayton phoned me that you played Morely well—keep playing. Well—off with you, while the weather's good!'

Murdoch found Graham waiting, and expectant. He liked this sweep of that young man's jaw—and Sir Robert did not recommend a man unless he was reliable.

So the situation, now, was one up and four to play.

42

8 : Hotel in Luthia

As long as the progress of Nazification could be halted in
Central Europe, the State of Luthia was likely to remain one
of the few strongholds of democracy—with the limitations
of democratic countries the world over. The opposition to the
Karenki Government was vociferous but small, and Karenki,
the Premier, could do what he liked.

He liked England, chiefly because English money remained
sound currency. There was, of course, no direct payment from
the Hon. Gerald Cardyce to M'sieu Piotr Karenki, but by
some remarkable coincidence on the day of the signing of
the agreement between the two, which took place with some
ceremony but *in camera*, the Karenki account in a Paris bank
was swollen by some twenty-five thousand pounds.

Cardyce, smooth-voiced, precise, affable and formal in
turn, congratulated the representatives of the Luthian Government on their far-sightedness, and in the late afternoon his
return from the Government offices to the Hotel Libaplaz
was as circuitous as he could make it.

In the foyer of the hotel he saw a chunky, big-jawed man
reading a *Continental Daily Mail*; von Romain, whom he
appeared not to notice; and one of the most ravishing women
he had seen in his life. As though by accident, the lovely one
stood away from the desk as he passed. The encounter was of
the slightest, but the woman stumbled.

Cardyce caught her arm.

'A thousand apologies, Fräulein!' His German—the official
language of Luthia—was stilted.

'Oh, it was nothing.' She spoke quickly, almost breath-
lessly, and in perfect English. And within ten minutes, Cardyce had suggested she dine with him. Cocktails in his room
at seven-thirty? The Fräulein was delighted: a strange fact,
for Cardyce was middle-aged, austere of feature and possessed
of a thin and unprepossessing figure.

Up in his room, his *aide* was waiting in some anxiety.

'That,' said Cardyce, putting him out of his agony at once,
'is the first mission accomplished, Worthing.'

43

'You got it through, sir?'

'With very little trouble,' chuckled Cardyce, who could be surprisingly human. 'And von Romain is downstairs?'

'He arrived about an hour ago.'

'Indeed? Well, we'll be off in an hour. Can you be ready?'

'Yes, of course.'

'Good. A very charming lady,' added Cardyce, with a quirk of amusement, 'grew enamoured of my grey hair, Worthing. Don't you find that difficult to believe?'

'Well, sir, I . . .'

'Don't be an idiot,' Cardyce snapped. 'She is probably talking to von Romain now. I have a dinner engagement with her.'

Worthing stared.

'But I thought, sir . . .'

'My God,' said Cardyce, under his breath. Aloud: 'Never mind, Worthing—get that packing finished. I'm going to the Embassy, and I'll be back in half an hour.'

He left the Libaplaz openly enough. There was no sign of von Romain or the woman, but a square-chinned Prussian was lounging against a table, while the chunky Englishman was staring moodily out of the swing doors. Cardyce knew neither Mettink nor Fuller, but after five minutes' walking he was satisfied that he was not being followed.

Most of the 'unofficial' diplomacy of the British Cabinet had been carried out by Cardyce. He was vague about the number of 'under cover' missions he had carried out, but he was not vague as to the consequences of his success or failure. For that, he assumed full responsibility; as also for any danger there might be to himself. But in von Romain, with the full backing of Berlin, he had opposition of an entirely different nature from anything in the past. That the secret of his coming negotiations had leaked out was one of the major mysteries of the year—only five men, ostensibly, had known of it. The Inner Cabinet, taking yet more responsibility on its shoulders, and acting even more arbitrarily than it had done at Munich and other places, proposed to face both Great Britain and Germany with the *fait accompli*.

Yet von Romain had known . . .

Cardyce pondered on the possibility of a leakage from that sacrosanct inner circle, and his lips drooped when he contemplated the acid-voiced Paddon, the fussy Dalby, the supremely capable Glennister, and Tenterden, the Chief Lord. As well suspect the Premier, as one of those; but it remained a fact that the proposition had been discussed only by those five—that even Worthing knew simply that it was a race with von Romain: what the stake was, he had no clear idea.

Anyhow, Holt was looking into the leakage. Cardyce, the Treaty safe in a capacious, leather-lined pocket, was hurrying to the Embassy with it. The wires to London would soon be humming, and he had every reason to feel satisfied.

Yet he was conscious of his luck; he knew Holt hod been told to keep von Romain back, but he had not seriously expected the Pink 'Un would succeed.

Two minutes later, he came to the conclusion that he was, after all, being followed.

He had turned into the Hestrasse, a wide square lined with lofty buildings, home of the Embassies and Consulates. Immediately in front of him, with its two towers spiking towards the cloudless sky, was the Luthian House of Representatives. A hundred yards ahead, was the British Embassy, but . . .

The tall man was following him.

Big, fair-haired, Cardyce noted, and with the unmistakable look of the English toursist.

He made a detour, and the fair-haired man followed. Cardyce frowned as he approached the kerb. Traffic streamed past, more vividly reminiscent of Paris, although the colour of the cars was quieter: only Paris of all the Continental capitals went in for gaily-coloured taxis.

Cardyce saw the fair-haired man step in his wake—and at the same moment saw the high-powered car which swung suddenly towards the kerb. For a split second, Cardyce simply could not move—and the front of the car was gaping at him.

A hand fell on his shoulder, sent him staggering across the pavement.

He lost his balance and sprawled forward. He did not see the fair-haired man leap after him, nor the car mount the pavement and smash against the railings surrounding the Embassy. He did hear the shrieking of brakes and the screaming of women, and the low-pitched, urgent voice in his ear.

'Are you all right, sir?'

'Y—yes,' gasped Cardyce, and turned to look into the face of the fair-haired man.

'Murdoch,' said the fair one. 'The Pink 'Un. I'd get into the Embassy right away, sir, if I were you.'

'I—will,' gasped Cardyce, and saw the fair-haired man thrust his way through the crowd. As the driver of the car was pulled from the wreckage, someone helped a shaken and very thoughtful Cardyce into the Embassy.

. . . . . .

Paris is the home of the pavement café, Berlin of the beer garden, Luthia of the glorified coffee-shop. In the main streets, every fifth shop invites one to eat at the counter, with cocktail stools, or at the long, high-backed padded leather-type benches, and the average German has nothing on the average Luthian as the trencherman.

Faced with a very large sausage, smooth-skinned and dark red, was Bruce Murdoch. Opposite him, eyeing the dozen 'small' yellow-skinned sausages on his own plate, was Mick Fuller. Half an hour before, Cardyce had returned to the Libaplaz Hotel . . .

Fuller had been speaking in an undertone. Murdoch scowled as he carved a piece out of the monstrosity in front of him.

'I don't like the situation, Mick. You're sure the woman fixed an appointment with Cardyce?'

'Not a shadow of doubt.'

'He's too old a hand to fall for that, I'm not worried on that score,' Bruce mused. 'But if she expected to find him at dinner, she would know nothing of the Hestrasse incident. That suggests two different people anxious to prevent him getting through.'

'Oh, come!' The waiter approached with lidded tankards of the unbeatable Luthian lager; Fuller waited until they were deposited, then went on: 'More likely they tied to make sure.'

46

'H'mm. It's possible.'

'For the Lord's sake!' protested Mick. 'Don't make more difficulties—you've enough already. What time are you off, and where to?'

'Enkraine, in an hour—Holt's made sure there'll be no difficulties with the authorities. You say Mary's at the Lankessa?'

'Yes.'

'I wish I could spare half an hour—but we'd better not be seen together unless it's essential. She'll follow von Romain with Ted and Percy, and you'll go after the woman. That's the idea, isn't it?'

'If it's all right with you.'

Murdoch nodded. 'Right-ho, Mick; I'll get off first. If Katerina's waiting for that dinner appointment, von Romain will be on his way pretty soon, believing Cardyce won't start until midnight at the earliest; so don't eat too much!' He grinned, drank half the lager and left the rest regretfully, and in excruciating German wished his 'chance-met' acquaintance goodbye.

An hour later, von Romain and Mettink embarked on the Enkraine Express, which would take them to Malla, the Enkraine capital, in nine hours. Mary, Percy and Ted Angell were four carriages away from them, and Katerina was waiting with some impatience for seven o'clock.

In the hotel, Mick Fuller was waiting to trail her when she left and to try to judge her reactions after the realisation that Cardyce had stalled her, while Cardyce and the plump Worthing were already over the border, and flying towards a midnight meeting with President Sta, the white-bearded patriarch and virtual dictator of Enkraine.

Murdoch and young Graham were flying in his wake.

The border country between Luthia and Enkraine was high in the mountains—an off-shoot of the Carpathians—and strategically easy to defend, in war. But in peace-time, it was impossible to guard the frontiers properly. Five years before, there had been a Nazi putsch in Luthia, and hordes of refugees had braved the snows of winter and crossed to the Enkraine. Two years later, a Socialist rising in the Enkraine had sent them drifting back to Luthia. Whereupon Karenki had declared a political amnesty; and in Luthia, democracy reigned.

In the Enkraine, there was a 'benevolent dictatorship'; Sta's benevolence being generally attributed to his advancing years. In truth, the smaller European countries were all divided into two extremes—and the influence of Berlin was strong in them all. Only the desperate efforts of Great Britain, France and—morally—the U.S.A. prevented Berlin from achieving the stranglehold so badly needed for an offensive drive into the East and West at the same time.

All of which considerations grew more apparent to Murdoch as they flew through the night, and he did not notice the twinkling yellow light beneath them. Young Graham did, and his face was grim.

'I say, Mr. Murdoch, there's a plane down there—on fire. I wonder if it could be our quarry?'

9 : Fire Below

Murdoch's body stiffened.

'Are you sure?'

'Afraid I've seen too many of those things to be in much doubt, sir. Someone's crashed, all right.'

'What kind of landing-ground is it?'

Graham frowned.

'I dare say we could get down—and that blaze should give us some help. Shall I try? I ought to warn you that we might crash, but . . .'

Murdoch grunted. 'Try it, will you?'

'Right-ho.' Graham did not turn a hair and Murdoch, who had some flying experience, silently thanked heaven for the man's cool courage as he calmly pushed the stick forward. Murdoch glanced at the altimeter. Seven thousand feet—not too high, when some of the peaks reached five thousand.

'We're in a valley,' said Graham, as the plane dropped

48

quickly. 'Just passed the Grantas, and it's most of five miles to the Kraine Range. Lots of trees; but there are some flat patches, and it's cultivated a bit.'

'We've passed the frontier, then?'

'Two or three miles behind us, yes.'

Murdoch nodded, a chill at the pit of his stomach. He did not seriously consider the possibility that the crashed plane was anyone's but Cardyce's.

Three thousand feet showed them the flames more clearly and gave them some idea of the countryside. Immediately below them were the crags and rocks of the Granta foothills, but the comparatively fertile valley beneath might offer some landing place.

Two thousand feet . . . One thousand . . . Graham straightened the stick and tickled the rudder bar, taking the small plane round slowly. Its searchlight cut through the red-tinged gloom, revealing occasional copses of trees and clearly marked fields. Their main hope was picking a field which had been lying fallow and would have a hard surface and short grass.

Graham made two wide circles. Murdoch felt his pulse hammering. The plane—if it was a plane—was burning fiercely. What chance was there of Cardyce or the other occupants being found alive?

'Mind having a squint down there?' said Graham. 'I fancy I can see cows, and they'll be in a meadow where landing's possible.'

Murdoch put the night-glasses to his eyes. He distinguished the dark dots with difficulty; a dozen or more, clustered in one corner of a field perhaps three removed from the fire.

'I think you're right.'

'Well, here goes!' Graham grinned. 'Say your prayers, sir.'

But Murdoch had complete confidence in him now, and his only real thought was for Cardyce.

'All I hope,' said Graham, 'is that one of those blasted cows doesn't upset us. "Plane turned over by cow" would be something new in headlines, eh?'

A wheel bumped, the plane soared twenty feet into the air,

49

bumped and bounced again. For what seemed an age, the bumping continued, with Graham playing the searchlight right and left to make sure there were no obstacles. Murdoch gritted his teeth as it picked out a thick hedge no more than fifty yards ahead.

'Large, accommodating field,' murmured Graham, and turned the plane gently. He had its tail to the hedge, at last, and closed the throttle, then braked. 'Should have ample room to take off, sir. Would you mind grabbing that first-aid box?'

As he opened the cabin door, a keen, cold wind came through. Murdoch shivered and tightened his coat about him. Graham sniffed.

'Nippy, isn't it? They'll be having snow, before long. Lord, what a fire!'

The searchlight was shining straight at the blaze, three or four hundred yards away. They did not wait to find a gate or gap but scrambled through the hedge.

They crossed a field covered with corn stubble, and reached a second hedge. By now, they could feel the heat of the flames and hear the roar as they were fanned by the wind.

Murdoch's face was set as he scrambled through the second hedge and saw two dark patches against the flames; one a hundred yards from the mass of white-hot wreckage; the other no more than fifty. Graham overtook him.

'I'll get the second fellow, sir,' he called, and was half-way to the second huddled figure when Murdoch reached the first. Hunched up, one arm bent beneath him, the man lay prone and absolutely still.

The heat was terrific and his coat was scorching, his hair singed. Murdoch bent down and put an arm beneath the shoulders, another beneath the knees and, straining every muscle, lifted him. He could not see the face and did not try to, until he reached the hedge, well away from the fire, and laid the man down gently on his back.

The pale face of Cardyce showed in the shadows.

There was a cut on his right cheek. Anxious, but overwhelmingly thankful that he was alive, Murdoch opened the first-aid case, and took out the brandy flask. Graham came up

'My man's all right, sir. Knocked out, that's all, and burned a bit. Nothing to worry about. Look after them, will you?'

'Where are you . . .'

He was talking to Graham's back, and he jumped up and hurried after him. Fifty yards from the fire, the heat was unbearable; but Graham plunged straight on. Murdoch, breathing hard in his wake, saw why.

No more than twenty yards from the plane was a third man. The sight of the flames at his legs made Murdoch's stomach turn. As he reached them, Graham was struggling out of his coat.

'I'll wrap this round his legs—we'll carry him.'

It seemed an interminable time before they got their gruesome burden to the hedge. Before they had gone half-way, Murdoch was convinced that the man was dead. And, when Graham uncovered the legs, it seemed as well. He lifted his face, pale despite the lurid glow.

'All U.P., I'm afraid, sir. We'd better see to the others.'

They were startled by a low-pitched voice behind them.

'I'm—all right.'

Cardyce was trying to sit up. He had seen the third man, and his lips were thinly set. Murdoch unscrewed the brandy flask, and Cardyce swallowed enough to make him cough. As Graham dosed the second man, Cardyce said gruffly:

'I've certainly reason to be grateful, Murdoch. How . . .'

'We'd better talk later,' said Murdoch quietly. 'You'll excuse me a moment.' He turned to Graham. 'Is there any chance at all?'

'None at all, sir. Looks as though a piece of wreckage cut through his chest when the explosion came, and went out in one. Thank God!' His young face looked ghastly. 'If three of us can walk, we'll carry this one to the plane, and tidy up in there. Er—I take it you're in a hurry, sir?'

He was looking at Cardyce, and Cardyce nodded.

'Have to leave him, then.' For a moment, he stared down at the blackened, scorched face of the dead man; then he turned abruptly. 'Come on, let's move.'

Half an hour later they were in the air again.

Worthing had recovered consciousness, but he was too badly

burned to move, and the one hope was to get him to a hospital quickly. It was two hours' flight to the Enkraine capital, and Graham made straight for it. Murdoch and Cardyce—comparatively unhurt and with documents of vital importance intact in his pockets—made Worthing as comfortable as they could. Then as they saw the twinkling lights of Malla—the City of Hills—Cardyce said calmly:

'I've half an hour, Murdoch—I must get on. I'll leave you to look after Worthing. I'll be staying at the Growitz.'

'I'll look in,' Murdoch told him.

At the well-lighted airfield, Cardyce was expected, and a car was waiting for him. Murdoch struggled with the best Enkrainian he could manage, although the sight of Worthing made the officials understand more quickly what he wanted.

An hour behind Cardyce, Murdoch made for the Growitz Hotel, while Graham went with Worthing to the hospital.

The hotel clerk spoke English, and Murdoch was gratefully steaming in a bath within ten minutes of arriving. At half past one—when Malla's night-life was warming up—he went downstairs. But before he tried to locate Cardyce, or to find whether he had returned, he saw a tall, thin man, with lantern jaw and pendulous underlip, in earnest consultation with a porter.

And recognised the stranger who had tried to follow him at Folkestone.

10 : Flower Shop in Malla

Murdoch spotted the man a second before he turned away from the porter—and recognised him. A narrowing of the eyes, a sharp intake of breath was enough.

Bruce Murdoch had long schooled himself not to show recognition, but his heart was thumping. Here was a man who could report to von Romain that Mr. Morely of Clayton's was following him—or what seemed suspiciously like it. The

Clayton myth would be exploded and trouble might come in a flash. Not only to Murdoch—but between Berlin and London.

He of the pendulous lip had to be stopped.

Murdoch went to the desk, and in English asked for a good show where he could spend the next two or three hours. The tall man strained his head towards the desk, as the clerk recommended a casino where he doubtless received a substantial commission, and Murdoch said:

'Thanks. And I am expecting a Mr. Graham. Has he arrived, yet?'

'Not ten-twenty minutes ago; yes, *m'sieu.*'

'Telephone him that I am waiting down here, will you?'

'Yes, *m'sieu.* With pleasure.'

Murdoch crossed to a settee, lighting a cigarette. He banked on the probability that pendulous-lip would not let him out of his sight, and was satisfied when the man took a magazine and selected a chair near the door.

Away from a telephone, he could do no great damage.

Murdoch was thinking fast. Holt had three men in Malla, and countless lesser agents who reported to that trio. The nearest to the Growitz, which was in the Lubastrasse, Malla's Piccadilly, was the owner of a flower shop in a side turning. A man named Wright; big, burly, a naturalised Enkrainian who had met Murdoch once at Holt's office. The shop was no more than five minutes' walk from the hotel.

Graham had washed hurriedly, and changed from his soiled clothes. He looked puzzled as Murdoch made room for him.

'I've been spotted,' Murdoch said simply, and was satisfied when Graham showed neither surprise nor consternation. 'There's a man named Wright, with a flower shop in Ickstrasse. Telephone him, start off by bringing the words "Pink 'Un" in the conversation, and then tell him to expect two or three visitors in half an hour or less. If he says all right, we'll go out at once. Is that clear?'

Graham nodded.

'Should be easy.' He stood up, speaking in a louder voice. 'I must just slip upstairs first, Mr. Morely—I won't keep you a minute.'

Murdoch grinned to himself as, after a pause, he noted that the man with the pendulous lip was eyeing him narrowly.

Graham came back, smiling.

'That's fixed that!' he murmured. And aloud: 'Now where's this Palace of Delight you're talking about?'

'A taxi, sir?' asked a porter.

'I'll think we'll walk.'

'As you say, sir.'

Pendulous-lip was on their heels, too inexperienced a trailer. Murdoch was puzzled, wondering why von Romain used such a man. But he said:

'Get along to the shop, and ring. I'll bring our friend along, and he may be violent, although I hope not. Try to make sure you're not followed.'

Graham's eyes shone.

'I think we're all right, except for that customer. But I'll walk past the shop if anything seems wrong.'

He did not walk past.

The tall man was patently puzzled that they had separated —and startled, when Murdoch swung on his heel and began to walk back. He side-stepped, and appeared interested in a window.

Murdoch slipped his right hand into his pocket.

As he grew level with the man, he stopped and stepped sharply towards him. The other made a closer study of the window.

'Very interesting, I'm sure,' said Murdoch, softly.

The man swung round, startled, and Murdoch, his hand in his pocket, prodded him in the stomach. Not enough to hurt, but enough to scare him.

'You and I,' he added, grimly, 'need a chat, sonny. I've a gun in my pocket...'

'M'sieu, I am amazed! I...'

'By the time you have fallen,' Murdoch persisted, 'I shall be in a taxi, and there isn't much danger—for me. What is it? That, or a talk?'

The man gave in without a word.

Murdoch kept one pace behind him until they reached the flower shop. In the open doorway, Graham was talking with the burly Wright. As Murdoch nodded and urged his man through, he slipped his gun from his pocket: a Webley. And the moment the door closed, he cracked it on the back of the tall stranger's head.

A gasp, and the man's knees sagged. Murdoch stopped him from falling, and said quickly:

'Wright, you've got to look after this customer for a few days—maybe a week or more. Can you arrange it?'

Wright, comfortingly burlier than Murdoch remembered, nodded.

'Yes, that's all right. You want him questioned?'

'As much as you can. We'd better have a look in his pockets —we might get something.'

They turned out his pockets, and discovered enough to assume that his name was Heimer—and that he carried a German passport without an Enkraine visa. Murdoch took all the papers from his wallet, except the money—in Enkraine marks—and within a quarter of an hour he and Graham were off again.

'Good luck,' Wright said, as they shook hands. 'I don't know what game you're playing, old man, but it'll be hot. Let me have a look-see, if there's a chance.'

Murdoch smiled fleetingly.

'I hope there won't be, but if there is, you'll be in. Who's the best man in Mavia?'

'Oh, Clarkson, by a long way. He runs a restaurant; the Pelinka. Cabaret and all that.' Wright grinned, looking less like an Enkrainian shopkeeper than ever. 'So you're expecting to travel, are you?'

'I'm hoping to,' said Murdoch, drily.

'H'mm. Well, all the best!'

Outside, Murdoch looked carefully about him, but saw no one who might have been on their heels. Yet it was hard to believe that Heimer had been entirely on his own.

Still, he had to take the chance.

Graham was saying:

'My hat! You've got some organisation, Mr. Morely!'

'I'm only a part of it,' Bruce told him. 'And it's time you dropped the mistering and sirring, Graham. Get back to

55

the hotel and take what sleep you can—we might be off again in a few hours.'

'Dammit, I'm not tired!'

'You're at the controls, and I don't want you bleary-eyed,' said Bruce. 'Let the porter know that I've found a floozy, will you? It'll sound convincing, and explain why you've come back at such short notice.'

Graham nodded reluctantly.

'Right-ho. Where are you off to?'

Murdoch chuckled.

'I'm going to meet a dear friend of mine, but he doesn't know it. You carry on, young Graham, and be satisfied that you're getting a lot that you didn't expect.'

'Right-ho,' said Graham again. His face suddenly clouded, and there was something older than his years in his eyes. 'I say, Morely, that accident—the crash, I mean. Do you think it was engineered?'

'It wouldn't surprise me.'

'I see. Right—thanks!' Graham turned and walked away sharply and Murdoch was reminded of the way he had looked as they carried the dead pilot of Cardyce's plane from the wreckage.

. . . . . .

It was nearly half past two when a taxi deposited Murdoch outside the North Station, and the Enkraine Express was due at two-thirty-five. He had noted, not without misgivings, that there were more uniforms in Malla than he could remember seeing in any country but Italy and Germany; and he was not pleased. A Nazi *putsch* just then would be awkward and he knew their was a strong faction in Enkraine which considered the Patriarch too old and too lenient.

He positioned himself by a buffet from which he could see the ticket-barrier. Officials, in the navy-blue of the Enkraine Nationalists—Şta's party—were numerous, several carrying guns; the mark of a lieutenant or higher.

Porters, raggedly dressed, grouped along the platform as the train approached. It was running to time; almost a miracle. From behind a glass of lager, Murdoch watched the passengers disembark, and his lips curved when he saw Mettink and von Romain. They passed the barrier unquestioned, and Murdoch saw that all the officials were clustered about it, looking hard into the straggling crowd. Peasants formed the majority of the passengers, but it was the second- and first-class type who had the interests of the officials.

He saw Mary.

At the same moment he glanced to the right, and saw von Romain and Mettink standing and staring. Percy Briggs came up jauntily, laden with cases. Ted Angell's lanky figure was a step behind him.

And then four officials clustered about Mary, Briggs and Angell, while von Romain's face for once showed expression —a sardonic amusement matched by Mettink's grin.

While Bruce had to decide on the instant whether to follow the Germans or wait to see what happened to Mary.

11 : Effort For Mary

The decision was not long in the balance. There would be a way out for Mary and the others, Murdoch knew. But the casual public acceptance of that arrest at the station suggested that such affairs were commonplace—and that was a sign of the increasing autocracy of the Government.

But Sta was well-disposed towards Great Britain. Strings would be pulled, and they would all be released. His job was von Romain.

That was no sinecure.

From the moment of his descent on Mere House, he had known that in Europe he must keep out of von Romain's sight. He would have wanted to, in any case, but it was now vital. Heimer had been a threat, but Wright's help would be in vain if either Mettink or his master caught a glimpse of 'Morely' now.

Ted Angell was protesting in broken but vociferous German. Percy Briggs looked as if he was restraining himself only because of Mary's presence. Mary, huddled in her furs, for the early morning air was bitterly cold, stood silent. Her cheeks were glowing, her eyes shone, and in that moment Murdoch wondered what had made the Fräulein seem beautiful.

He heard a lieutenant order them to follow him. As there were four other armed men to see that his instructions were obeyed, even Angell was silenced as they were led off the station approach, their guards doing an imitation goose-step.

Two Mercedes cars were waiting outside.

Von Romain stayed where he was until he saw Briggs bring up the rear into one of the cars, then turned sharply to another exit. Murdoch was already sitting in a cab outside: the driver spoke French and had no difficulty in understanding his order.

As the chauffeur-driven car which met the Germans swung into the road, the cabby started after it. Murdoch sat back, tense yet confident, worried only about the reason for the trio's arrest. That von Romain had somehow contrived it was obvious, and it was disturbing to know that he had discovered the trio were on his heels. That, however, was of comparatively minor importance compared with the fact that the German had managed to effect what had all the appearances of a military arrest. How could von Romain contrive that, in the Enkraine?

Of course, he could have trumped up a charge against them: sent a message ahead from the train, or even from Malla. But despite the lowering of British prestige in the past few years, the arrest of three English people in a small state would not have been made without a firm basis. A casual charge lodged by an unknown Herr Lenster would have had a less arbitrary result.

So von Romain had 'pull'.

Murdoch stared bleakly out at the blazing lights from casinos, cabarets and nightclubs which made the street lighting unnecessary in the Breitweg and the major thoroughfares leading from it. The traffic was scarcely thinner than it had been in the early evening. Twice, his driver passed von

58

Romain's car, and twice slipped into a line of traffic where the other passed it.

After fifteen minutes' driving, von Romain stopped—outside the Garre Hotel, three minutes' walk from the station. The German had patently tried to make sure he had not been followed. Murdoch's cabby had been fifty yards behind the car. When he saw it stop he took a sharp right turn and pulled up with a screeching of brakes. He turned, his sallow face animated.

'What you would wish, *m'sieu*?'

'First-rate,' Bruce assured him, in French. 'May you stay here?'

'But of course.'

'Keep this as a retainer, and wait for me.'

He pushed a hundred-mark note into the cabby's hand, and hurried to the hotel. The car was driving off, and he could see von Romain and Mettink in the foyer. He waited to see them disappear into the lift, then went inside.

Inquiring for a Mr. Jackson, he was able to see the register. Von Romain was still travelling as Lenster: Mettink had not been entered.

A bearded clerk assured him that there was no Mr. Jackson.

'He will come,' said Bruce. And thoughtfully: 'The Fräulein Weissman, she is here?'

'*Non, m'sieu.*' Enkraine took its currency and official language from Germany, but a lot of French was spoken. 'It is strange, *m'sieu*, that you should ask. Only just now a room was booked for her.' Bright eyes peered at Murdoch. 'You would wish to be advised when she comes?'

'I'll enquire again.' Bruce slipped a ten-mark note over the counter. That might ensure that no word of his inquiry reached von Romain's ears. He was not sure whether to hope it would, or not. The more puzzled and worried the von Romain party was, the better it would probably be for Cardyce. He slipped into a call-box.

Thirty seconds later, Wright's loud voice announced that it was the *Ches des Fleurs* speaking.

'I'll take a dozen of the Pink 'Un's roses,' said Bruce, and

Wright snorted. 'Would you know von Romain if you saw him?'

'I would.'

'He's at the Garre Hotel. If you'll come and relieve me, it will be a help. How's our friend?'

'Nicely asleep,' Wright chuckled. 'I'll be right over, old man. Anything else?'

'Yes. What does the National Guard turn out a lieutenant and four or five troopers to make an arrest for?'

'Offence political, or suspicion thereof. Sta isn't having it all his own way; there's a lot of propaganda coming in from Berlin.'

'What are the Embassy people like, here?'

'Nervy. I wouldn't go to them unless in emergency.'

'It's an emergency, all right,' Murdoch told him. 'I'll wait here, old man.'

He waited in the foyer, where he could see the lift and the stairs without being seen by anyone who came from them. It was fifteen minutes before Wright, in evening-dress, arrived and came over, grinning.

'What's the idea?'

'If v. R. comes out,' said Bruce, 'trail him. I doubt whether he will, but be on the look-out. Then in an hour or so, Fuller should be here, on the heels of a beauty by the name of Weissman.'

He watched closely, but Wright showed no recognition of the name.

'Fuller will look after the woman,' he added, 'and I may be back in time to take over from you. If I have to get off quickly, I'll send a message. All right?'

'It sounds as though I'm to hang around, while you do the work,' Wright complained. 'All right, Murdoch—good luck.'

'You'll find me, under the name Morely, at the Growitz,' Bruce told him, as he left. 'But only in an emergency.'

The cabby seemed disappointed that there was not to be a further chase, but accepted another fee, and vowed eternal service.

It was nearly four o'clock. Cardyce had been with Sta for the best part of four hours, and the verdict had probably been reached by now. Murdoch wondered whether Sta was by chance playing a double game—Berlin against London, for the highest bid. The idea would not have occurred to him, but for Mary's arrest.

It was damnable not to know where she had gone, nor what had happened to her, but Wright's warning about the Embassy was enough to stop him from trying to get help there. He knew the difficulties of Embassy officials in states like the Enkraine; they had to make sure they gave no excuse for being accused of underground work.

The sight of Cardyce, self-possessed, clear-eyed, showing no signs of his ordeal, revived him considerably. Cardyce did not look like a man who had played a losing hand. He hurried into the hotel, and went straight up to his room—on the second floor, Bruce knew. He proposed to visit the Minister. But he waited for five minutes—and in that time, he saw two men come into the foyer one after the other, and sit down with magazines. The foyers of the larger hotels were meeting-places, day and night: but this brace, arriving so quickly on Cardyce's heels, suggested to Murdoch that they were tailing the envoy.

He registered the two faces in his mind's eye.

The distinguishing mark of one was a mole on the lobe of the right ear: of the other, exceptionally long eyelashes and vivid blue eyes. Satisfied he would recognise them again at any time, Murdoch went upstairs, wishing the porter a cordial good night to impress upon the others that he was a resident.

Pausing outside Cardyce's room, he tapped lightly.

Cardyce called:

'Who is that?'

'I've brought your Pink 'Un, sir,' he said quietly, and the door was promptly opened.

He slipped through quickly, and Cardyce shut and locked it.

'Well, Murdoch, what can I do for you?'

'It's more what you can do for yourself, sir.' Bruce was bursting to hear whether Cardyce had Sta's signature, but hesitated to ask. 'I'm one of five trying to keep you a jump ahead of v. R., and three of us . . .'

He explained, briefly.

'Well, and what can I do?'

'You can make contact either with the Embassy here, sir, or with the people at home, and make sure Miss Dell, Angell and Briggs are released quickly. They're all needed badly.'

Cardyce nodded.

'I'll see what I can do with the people here. Are you suspected yourself?'

'I don't think I'm known to be here, sir.'

'Good. You can take some papers to the Embassy for me —I must get some sleep. I'll write you a note for Lord Akeham; he'll see that everything possible is done for the prisoners. Now, Murdoch, I'm curious about the way you found me, in that field. Just what happened?'

'My pilot had good eyes.' Bruce told the story, without interruption. Finished, Cardyce smiled for the first time.

'Well, you've succeeded twice, Murdoch! I'm beginning to believe you'll see me through. Holt has probably given you an idea of the importance of all this?'

'I don't think he kept much from me or Miss Dell.'

'Right. Is there anything you want to know?'

'I'd like to know what happened with your plane, sir.'

Cardyce frowned.

'So would I. The pilot, poor fellow, told me that a mechanical fault had developed, but I have my doubts as to how it was caused. You will have the same, I imagine. Well, now, this note to Akeham . . .'

Murdoch left the room five minutes later with the papers that a King's Messenger would get to London with all speed. Two up and three to play made the situation a sight more satisfactory, but he was worried about Mary and the others.

Cardyce had told him he planned to start for Mavia at nine o'clock next morning. It meant little sleep for either of them, and he was glad he had made Graham get to bed early. He went to his own room and scribbled a note for him, intending to go in and leave it on his bedside table.

Then he changed his mind, and telephoned the night-clerk,

with instructions to call M'sieu Graham at seven o'clock. No word had come from Wright and he left a further message that he would be out until six o'clock, then hurried downstairs, keeping the brief-case under his coat.

The only occupants of the foyer were the two men who had entered after Cardyce, and one of them was about to leave. He wondered if he was suspected, and turned right from the hotel—in the wrong direction for the Embassy.

The man who came out immediately after him, turned left.

Murdoch made reasonably sure that he was not followed before taking one of the many empty taxis for the Embassy. Akeham was in bed, but his principal secretary, Sir Ralph Devenish, was still up. While Cardyce was in Enkraine, the Embassy was likely to stay alert.

Devenish was amiable, brushed away Murdoch's apologies for so late a call, but frowned when—as Mr. Morely, and without mentioning his errand from Cardyce—he explained the difficulty with his friends.

'Well, now.' Devenish was large, plump, immaculate. 'I'll certainly make inquiries, Mr. Morely, but—well, it isn't easy, these days. You won't get immediate results, and—well, I might be able to promise you something in two or three days, but an arrest like this must have some strong motive. Understand that I shall do everything . . .'

Murdoch pursed his lips.

'Things are like that, are they? I was told so, but I hoped it wasn't true.' He took the brief-case from under his coat, and Cardyce's letter from his pocket. Devenish glanced at the signature on the letter, and his plump face paled.

'Has he . . . ?'

The tension in his voice startled Murdoch.

'Yes, I've brought this from him.' He touched the case.

'My God!' said Devenish. 'We were jittery over here—the Sta regime looks like tottering, but the old devil's clever. He'll have this on the headlines in the morning. I—I say, Morely, do you know what it's about?'

'Yes, but I'm surprised you do.'

'I didn't, until we had a message from London last night. Look here, you'll have to excuse me. I must see . . .'

63

'I've no time to spare,' said Bruce. 'Check on the case, will you, and make sure that it's got what it should have in it, and then . . .' he spoke as Devenish obeyed, quickly— 'this letter is about Miss Dell and the others. Mr. Cardyce wants them out as fast as you can manage it. If you work it quickly, tell Miss Dell I'm following Cardyce to Mavia. Will you?'

'Yes, of course.' Devenish looked curious, but asked no questions, and Murdoch left the Embassy for the Growitz and, at the most, two hours' sleep.

But it was a seven hours' flight to Mavia, and he hoped to get more than a nap during that. He left word to be called at half past seven, and went upstairs.

Graham's room was next to his, and its partly-open door made him pause.

He listened, but could hear nothing save the steady rise and fall of the sleeper's breath. He stepped silently to the door, and widened it perhaps two inches. As he did so, he saw the man approaching the bed. And he saw, too, the knife in the man's hand.

As he snapped a word, the man swung round, startled— and he recognised the mole at the lobe of his right ear.

12 : Von Romain Takes a Trick

Murdoch had a gun in his hand, but he did not want to use it. A disturbed hotel would do him more harm than good. The man with the mole must have sensed it, for he ignored the gun and flung the knife.

Murdoch dodged.

The steel flashed over his head and he heard the '*ping!*' as it burried itself in the door. At the same moment, the man leapt forward, fists clenched. Murdoch straightened up, swerved, forcing him to miss with his right, and swung a vicious left to the stomach, hitting low. As the man gasped in pain and doubled up, he smashed a right to his jaw—sent

64

him sprawling across the foot of Graham's bed.

Graham was struggling to a sitting position, amazed and alarmed.

'Quiet a minute!' snapped Murdoch. He strode across to the man who had been prepared to use a knife, and hit him again. He wanted to hurt, and he succeeded. Within him, there was a fierce anger: he knew the man had meant to kill, and across his mind there flashed a picture of the legs and face of the dead pilot. Blood came from the man's lacerated lips, and Murdoch drew back.

Graham was out of bed, now, and wide awake.

Murdoch glanced round in time to see him pulling the knife, a stiletto, from the door. It had gone half an inch into the wood and would have gone a lot farther into Murdoch's neck.

'What the devil happened?' asked Graham.

'Our friend,' said Murdoch, heavily, 'paid you a visit, and it was lucky I was passing. Otherwise, a quick death, and no obituary. Lock the door, will you?' He looked at his prisoner, and he had never seen fear more naked on a man's face. 'You speak English?'

'*Ja—ja.*'

'Then speak it.' From his pocket, Murdoch took what looked like a three-inch tube of rubber. He fitted it to his automatic slowly, his eyes on the man all the time. 'In case you don't know what this is, it's a silencer.'

'*Ja, ja,* I 'ave seen, I know . . .'

'Good. Who sent you?'

Murdoch's voice was quiet enough, but there was an edge to it which suggested that he would kill quite readily. Graham had come near to hero-worshipping Murdoch in the past twenty-four hours. He came even nearer, now.

'I—I was come for der money . . .'

Murdoch doubled his left fist and struck, not hard, against the lacerated lips. Blood welled.

'Who sent you?'

'*Nein, nein,* I do not say!' He went into a spatter of German and Graham, catching every other word, gathered that he was in as much fear of his employers as he was of Murdoch.

65

The hotel room was a poor place for an interrogation, but Murdoch had to do the best he could. He raised his fists again, and Graham looked away . . .

There was a gasp—and the man broke down. As he began to babble, Murdoch knew that he was little more than a hired thug: no man of importance in the German Intelligence would have cracked so easily.

What he did say, helped little.

He was under orders from Berlin, and those orders had been telephoned that day. He—his name was Neumann—was to follow a Herr Carter (Cardyce's *nom de guerre*) and he had done so, also reporting the arrival of Herr Graham. To disobey was as much as his life was worth. The orders had been telephoned to his hotel by someone unknown. There was no password: he knew that voice. A man's voice. He had telephoned his reports to a number which he knew was that of the headquarters of the German Fascisti organisation in Enkraine. A house in the Willstrasse: the number was Malla 82182.

Had he reported the arrival of Herr Morely?

'*Nein, nein,* I did not think . . .'

'Unfortunate for you, little man,' said Murdoch coldly. 'All right, Graham: we'll truss him up and leave him here—you can make shift in my room, for what's left of the night.'

'What are you going to do with him?'

'President Sta will be interested to hear from him, I fancy, but we'll leave him until we're safely out of the country. The sash of your dressing-gown should do nicely . . .'

In five minutes, Neumann was lying on the bed, trussed so securely that he would still be there later that morning, when the police arrived. Murdoch proposed to telephone them immediately he was ready to leave, giving a garbled but in the main accurate story of what Neumann had told him. He felt no regret. The man was a hired killer: he did not even kill for a cause.

'Hadn't we better keep watch here?' asked Graham.

No need. We'll phone the desk not to call you, after all, and the first to see Neumann will be the police.'

'Did you say something about another man downstairs?'

'He isn't downstairs any longer. Hurry, man!'

Graham hurried.

Murdoch reached his own room at last. If he was to be up at half past seven, he had just an hour for sleep. His eyes were red-rimmed, the lids heavy, but an hour would give him just the respite he needed. He took off his shoes, collar and tie, and was about to lie down when the telephone rang.

'Blast it,' he grunted, and staggered to his feet.

'You do lead a life,' murmured Graham.

'Don't get ideas that it's romantic,' Murdoch growled. 'It's a wonder I ever sleep. Hallo?'

Wright's voice came.

'Hallo, Pink 'Un?'

'Call it read.'

'Listen, old man, there's some odd stuff going on, here. The woman and Fuller arrived half an hour ago, and the woman's raising a hell of a stink. Something about v. R. being missing, and without leaving a message. I've an idea that she's doing it for Fuller's benefit. He's trying to hide himself behind the palms, but that woman's got eyes in a lot of places she shouldn't have.'

Murdoch said sharply:

'Get up to von R.'s room somehow, and see if it's a stall. If he's really gone, tell Fuller to get to the airfield and travel in my plane—I'll keep after the Fräulein. Is that clear?'

'Right-ho.'

'I'll be there in twenty minutes,' Murdoch told him.

He had not shaved since the previous morning, and felt dirty as well as tired. But if von Romain had stolen a march on them, there was no time to lose. He hurried to Cardyce's room. The Minister did not look pleased to be awakened.

'What is it this time, Murdoch?'

'Our man's reported to have left, some time in the past two hours,' said Bruce, sharply. 'I imagine he's well on the way to Mavia, sir. The arrest did the trick, all right—it split our forces and we couldn't tag him all the time. Will you make an early start?'

Cardyce was already out of bed.

'I shall get off at once, thank you. You delivered the case?'

'Yes, sir, here's a note from Sir Ralph Devenish, acknowledging it.' He put the note on the table. 'You'll be followed by an man named Fuller, and my own pilot, Graham.'

'And what will you be doing?'

'The woman has recognised Fuller, apparently. I'll have to keep at her. As far as I can see, she's likely to join von Romain at Mavia. They split their forces to split ours and now they've succeeded, they're likely to join up again.'

'Ah!' Cardyce's quick, unexpected smile robbed his face of its austerity. 'Be advised, Murdoch, and do not ask her to dine!'

Murdoch chuckled.

'I heard about that, sir, and fancied you were side-tracking her.'

'H'mm. You seem to know a lot.'

'I have to,' said Murdoch, drily. 'But there's far too much about the Fräulein that I don't know. Did you recognise her?'

'Vaguely. I can't place her.'

'She was with Debonnet a lot, last year, and in Moscow some years back. Now she appears to be von Romain's right-hand woman—not an *affaire*; she's playing an active part. However, that's my job after this trip's over, sir. I suppose Mavia is the best place for you to go next?'

Cardyce hesitated, as he ran hot water for shaving.

'Have you any suggestions?'

'Purely from the practical side, sir, not the political. If von Romain has left, and I think it's probable, he will reach Mavia first. As far as I can see, this business is a matter of getting in the first offer, and von Romain is likely to have the Mavian ear. If you went instead to Dorshland, you'd be three up with one to play. In short, you couldn't lose—and you would quite likely get to Brennia in time to pull if off there. In any case, it couldn't be worse than a three-two win, so to speak.'

Cardyce looked very thoughtful indeed.

'Yes . . . But I want to get them all, Murdoch. If by getting to Dorshland I could also be sure of reaching Brennia first, I would take four-to-one, gladly. But three-to-two isn't good enough. I don't like the situation in this country. I wouldn't

68

be surprised at an overthrow of the Government, and that would mean a repudiation of this treaty. Indeed, the rebellion might come because of it. Sta will let the news get out, of course, in the hope of strengthening his hand. Cardyce hesitated. 'I'd best make it Mavia, Murdoch.'

'Right, sir. I'll have definite word for you about von Romain, very soon. Can I order breakfast for you?'

'Coffee and rolls.' Cardyce began to lather his face; a sign of dismissal. Bruce hesitated.

'I'd like to make a suggestion, sir.'

'Make it.'

'If you shaved your moustache, it might help.'

'Dammit!' exclaimed Cardyce. momentarily losing his poise. 'This isn't a stage show, Murdoch—don't talk nonsense! Are *you* going to dress up?'

'My face is,' said Murdoch, quickly. 'But it's entirely up to you, sir.'

When he reached his room, Graham handed him the telephone. This time, he heard Mick Fuller, who sounded doleful.

'Bird's flown, old boy.'

'Any idea where?'

'Nothing definite. He slipped out through the servants' exit, little more than half an hour after he arrived here, so he's got a five-hour start. What's all this about changing places?'

'If the Fräulein's on to you, you'd better get away from her. Go to the central airfield. You'll find a Hawker dual-control fighter, with a pilot named Graham. He's reliable.'

'But the woman knows you.'

Murdoch grinned. 'She thinks's she does. Be there in less than an hour, old man—and good hunting!'

He wished that he could relax for a few hours: he was beginning to feel dead-beat. Matching wits with the lovely Katerina was going to be no child's play. And there were so many different things crying out for quick attention.

He telephoned Cardyce's room, and confirmed von Romain's start. Cardyce said shortly that he had arranged for a plane and would be starting in an hour, taking with him a man named Elder, from the Embassy. Next Bruce phoned Devenish. He was not yet in bed, and so far had failed to locate the prison where Mary, Angell and Briggs had been taken.

'They admit there was an arrest,' he reported, obviously stifling a yawn, 'but they're blocking us all they can, Mr. Morely. We won't leave a stone unturned, believe me, but . . .'

'But what?' snapped Bruce.

'Well . . .' Devenish lowered his voice. 'There are some ugly rumours coming in. A *putsch* would not surprise me. Sta's house is being strongly guarded, but if I were you I'd get out of the country just as soon as I could.'

'I will. But look here, Devenish—that party must be freed.'

'I'll do all I can,' Devenish repeated. 'But three political prisoners are not going to get precedence today, I'm afraid. Everyone is going to be too busy making sure . . .'

'There's positively nothing—*nothing*—to prove that my people aren't tourists. Run that as hard as you can, for God's sake. I'll call you later.'

He rang off, and his forehead was beaded with perspiration. If a *putsch* was coming, it augered ill for Mary. The rising could only be Berlin-inspired, and anyone von Romain had informed against was going to have a difficult job to get out of gaol.

Dammit, the *putsch* had not started yet!

From the window he could see a narrow stretch of the Breitweg. The excitement in the streets was apparent. Now and again, he heard the heavy rumble of tanks or army lorries, and as he busied himself at the dressing-table, he saw three tenders of Sta's regular troops passing beneath him. Faintly into the room came the cries of a news boy and as he grew nearer, Murdoch heard the words:

'*Traite Angleterre—Traite Grande Bretagne!*'

So Cardyce had been right: Sta was using the previous night's agreement in his fight against a rising. He glanced out of the window, and saw the streams of people rushing to the paper-boy; saw them snatching papers and hurrying off, saw little groups reading quickly, could sense the tension. He tightened his lips as he took a small make-up set from his case and selected a packet of powder. It was a hair dye, water-mixed but soluable only in spirit.

Graham came in from the bathroom, ten minutes afterwards, and stopped on the threshold.

'Great Scott, what ... !'

'Shut the door,' grunted Murdoch. But he was pleased with the other's spontaneous tribute to his changed appearance. He had dyed his hair, eyebrows and lashes, and in another three minutes he had affixed a thin, dark moustache. When he turned round, Graham said warmly:

'It's damned good, Murdoch! The only things that might give you away are your eyes and that cleft chin.'

Murdoch shrugged. 'I can't do much about them. Ring for something to eat, will you?'

Another five minutes at the mirror, and he turned to show Graham the small imperial he had affected; hiding the cleft in his square chin, making his face seem longer. He had, too, darkened the skin beneath his eyes, making them look slightly puffy and pouched.

'Is that better?'

'Better!' goggled Graham. 'It's a miracle.'

'It'll serve, at a distance,' Murdoch conceded.

When the waiter brought breakfast, he stayed out of sight. As he ate, he gave instructions to Graham, mostly concerning the reliability of Fuller and the need for complete obedience. Then he hurried out of the hotel, carrying one small case. A cab took him quickly to the Garre Hotel.

Wright was there, and stared at him and past him.

Murdoch selected a small table near the door of the restaurant, which led from the foyer, and sent a boy with a message for the florist. Wright came in, his heavy features puzzled.

'Bon jour, M'sieu ...'

'It's all right,' Murdoch growled. 'Don't look like that, idiot! Is the woman still here?'

Wright stared.

'Yes, but ...'

'Will this serve?'

'Serve!' exclaimed Wright. 'It'll get you anywhere! Have you got the necessary papers?'

'Don't be all of a fool—of course I have. What do you think of things outside?'

'Not much. There's a rising in Enkra, on the other side of the river. It's isolated, so far, but I'm afraid something big is coming. You'd better get out while you can.'

'I'm waiting for the Fräulein,' said Murdoch, grimly. 'And I hope she won't be long. Has Fuller gone?'

'Yes.'

'Good. As soon as you get back, telephone Clarkson in Mavia, and ask him to have as many good men ready as he can, for quick work. Are things settled over there?'

'Nothing's been reported, anyhow.'

'Good again. And get a message to the police—Sta's police —to go to Room 81 at the Growitz. There's a man there, named Neumann, who might be able to give them some help. Tell them he knows the Nazi headquarters here. Right, old man, and thanks. I'll take over now.'

Wright shook hands.

Left to himself, Murdoch tried to keep his mind off Mary. All the time, the rumble of traffic came more loudly, the excited voices of the citizens of Malla reached the restaurant. Only a dozen people were eating there, and Murdoch watched the stairs and lift anxiously. Katerina, of course, would be more likely to eat in her room, and she would lose no time in getting away from Malla, if she proposed to go.

Supposing she intended to stay?

It would be a sound move, Murdoch knew. With the three prisoners already out of service, she might work on the basis that von Romain would have a better chance if she held the attention of another of the English party. He was almost at the point of telephoning for Wright to take over, when she came down the stairs.

She walked slowly, with the peculiar feline grace which suited her so well. Her head was high: and as three footmen bowed as though before royalty, Murdoch had an unpleasant feeling that it was not entirely due to her beauty. She was wearing a simple, polo-necked jersey dress in dark red. It was easy to understand that she had appealed to Moscow: there was a hint of the Slav in her wide, long eyes and high cheekbones; it was equally easy to understand how the impressionable Debonnet had fallen, for hers was a beauty which could hold a subtle, even fatal, fascination.

Two footmen preceded her to the restaurant, the manager bowing at her side. Another servant opened the doors with a flourish and stood bowing: it was fantastically like a royal progress.

She swept past Murdoch's small table and sat with her back to him, yet facing a mirror. Murdoch avoided looking at her, except casually.

Despite the fact that she seemed prepared to stay for some hours, he gave up the idea of sending for Wright. Against this woman's sublety, he would be useless: Katerina would spot him in minutes.

She had already spotted Fuller, and more than likely Mary and the others owed their arrest to her.

Would he, Murdoch, fool her?

He felt at ease in the disguise. He had adopted it a dozen times before, he could speak French like a native and he looked the part of a French dilettante. And yet . . .

He could only try.

Katerina stayed in the restaurant for an hour, then made a leisurely way upstairs. Within twenty minutes, she was down again, dressed for a journey—and Murdoch was already in a taxi, opposite the hotel.

A chauffer-driven Mercedes had pulled up outside the Garre, and the proximity of the manager and lesser officials had prepared him for Katerina's coming.

But where was she going?

There were fewer taxis about than usual, and he was surprised, as his own moved off after the Mercedes, to find soldiers with fixed bayonets standing at street corners. Malla gave the impression of being under martial law. As they swept round a corner into the Linkstrasse, he heard the unmistakable bark of a revolver-shot.

Confound, where *was* the woman going?

Twenty minutes later she was at the airport, preparing to

73

enter the Entente airliner which would call only at Mavia, Dorshland and Brennia before going on to Berlin. And in something under ten minutes Murdoch had to find a small plane, or take a seat in the liner and chance arousing her suspicion.

It was only when Katerina had stepped into the plane—receiving the same obsequiousness from the officials there, as she had at the hotel—that he saw the square-shouldered, vaguely familiar figure standing near the airport restaurant. Three minutes later, he had seen Mick Fuller and young Graham at their plane a hundred yards away, and realised that Cardyce had not yet left—but had, after all, shaved off his moustache.

What was keeping him back? Why was he not two hours' flying distance from Malla?

And was there any connection between this delay and the arrest of Mary and the others?

.   .   .   .   .

Their captors were courteous enough, even if they apologised for the inconvenience with sardonic, unrepentant grins. Mary was more concerned with the effect their helplessness would have on Bruce, and on Cardyce's journey, than for herself.

Which was as well.

Ted Angell did not allow his thoughts to take the form of words. He had spent some weeks as an inmate of a concentration camp, during a particularly delicate manœuvre conducted by the Department. He did not like concentration camps: particularly, he disliked the quarters apportioned to men—or women—arrested on suspicion of espionage, which suspicion could not be proved.

Of course, this was not Germany . . .

But Percy shattered his serenity.

'If you arsk me,' he offered, 'they're worse'n a lot o' blinkin' 'Uns.'

'Don't whisper!' Mary turned her head. 'I might just as well hear.'

'Percy,' said Ted, 'is forgetting himself. There are no

74

such things as Huns. We are all human beings, members of the commonwealth of nations, Jew and Gentile mixing with perfect accord.'

'Stow it,' growled Percy. Then: 'Sorry, sir—it slipped aht. Wot I means is, I think yer mistaken.'

'I was dreaming dreams,' murmured Ted, sorrowfully.

'Well,' said Percy, flatly, 'this ain't no dream. It's a perishing nightmare!'

He glared out of the window of the powerful Mercedes in which they were being taken from the station.

In front of them was another, filled with soldiers whose black leather trappings glistened beneath the glaring arc lamps as they passed along the street. Behind them was a second escort car, and there were two armed men with their driver: it was a military escort in the fullest sense of the word.

'I can't understand it,' Mary said softly. 'There's no reason for it, Ted. Are you worried?'

'What, me? I'm only glad of the chance to relax—and to cut Bruce out! I mean, I've a forgiving nature. The cottage and all that needn't come between us, sweetheart, and . . .'

'Idiot!'

His effort to amuse proved beyond doubt his anxiety, to Mary.

'Oh, well,' he said, and grinned lop-sidedly.

They had turned off the main road but were still running between high buildings, and appeared to be in the middle of the city. The streets were crowded, but there was at once an aimlessness and a tension about the people they passed. Cafés and coffee houses seemed to be doing a roaring business: picture-houses were ablaze with light.

'Seriously,' said Mary, so that Ted could just catch her words: 'what do you think?'

He stopped trying to joke.

'I'm not too happy, old girl. This military escort, the stunt at the station—it's all too showy for my liking. Of course, they like show—but if they were going to warn us to clear out pronto, they'd have done it more discreetly.'

'Meaning?'

Ted offered cigarettes.

75

'I'm not clairvoyant, but we've a few days here, I fancy. It's a pest—Bruce will need us.'

'He'll get through.'

'Yes.' He hesitated, then: 'My chief fear is that the beggars might try to starve us into submission, or somesuch.'

Mary sat back in her corner and said, very quietly:

'I see.'

Ted knew that she did.

He was afraid that the authorities wanted information from them, and would go to considerable lengths to get it. It might, as he had said, mean starvation. It could mean physical torture.

As the car swung into the courtyard through gates guarded by men with fixed bayonets, Mary said swiftly:

'But Enkraine's friendly to us, Ted.'

'So we think. Some of them may be. And it's possible that they think we're Germans—or working for Germany. It's the kind of trick von Romain could and would play, and laugh doing it. Or Katerina, who's probably the brain behind most of this business. If they managed to get word through that we were working to sabotage the Anglo-Enkrainian accord, for instance, they might feel it worth trying to find who we've come from and what we're about.'

'Well, we should soon know,' she said drily, and he grinned.

'That's my girl!'

The punctilious courtesy of the lieutenant in command was a little reassuring. But on a brass plate by the door through which they were ushered, Ted caught a glimpse of the word 'Poliss'.

'Looks as if it's a civil offence,' he whispered to Mary; then wished he hadn't. He was dragged back sharply, and sworn at in a fluent cascade of gutturals which actually earned Percy's grudging admiration.

They were taken to the second floor.

In a large, airy room with velvet hangings at doors and windows, gilt chairs and other impressive furnishings, sat a big, not unhandsome man. His name was Alsec, and Ted knew him for the Chief of Political Police.

Alsec's smile was not a pleasant smile.

76

'It is regretted that you need be so inconvenienced—
Mam'selle in especial. But we have word . . .'

'What possible reason can you have for this treatment?'
demanded Ted, as impressively as he could contrive. 'We are
assured that Enkraine welcomes tourists—we came here in
good faith.'

'Not for a moment do I disbelieve you,' Alsec broke in,
but the man was patently lying. 'It is a matter for inquiries
—a question only of a few hours. I *hope*.'

Ted altered his tactics.

'Then I wish to speak to the British Ambassador, immediately! Be advised, *M'sieu*—do not interfere with the
liberty of a British subject.'

The hands waved, as if in alarm.

'*M'sieu!* You have strange ideas! We place you under
guard for your own safety.' The wolfish grin came again, and
Ted began to worry even more than before. 'You are a personal friend of the Ambassador?'

'A friend of a friend.'

'I am honoured to meet a friend of a friend of Lord Akeham's,' said Alsec, ironically. 'But it is so late. *M'sieu* would
like, doubless, to be with *Mam'selle* for the short time you
will be detained. Lieutenant!'

The lieutenant sprang to attention. A hand gripped Ted's
arm; another Mary's. They were marched out of the big
room, down some stairs, and into a square, bare chamber
apparently on the ground floor. Percy was urged in after them,
and the key turned sharply in the lock.

13 : Difficulties

Sir Robert Holt banged down the receiver of his telephone
and glared at Gordon.

'The man's a fool!' he roared.

Gordon waited with unruffled calm.

'So are you!' snarled Sir Robert. 'Don't stand there like

77

a stuffed pigeon—go and make me some coffee. Strong. Understand? And quickly!'

'Very good, sir,' said Gordon, and reached the door.

The Pink 'Un grabbed a piece of paper from his desk and began to scribble furiously. Without looking up, he snapped:

'I don't want coffee. You know that as well as I do! Tea. *Indian*. Black as you can make it.'

'Very good, sir,' said Gordon, and disappeared.

Holt continued to scribble until Gordon returned, carrying a tray and China tea. The Pink 'Un poured a cup, and allowed himself to smile.

'You're very good, Gordon. Put up with a lot, I know. Reward you one day—when I retire.'

'I hope the day will never come, sir.'

'H'mm. So do I. But it will. I can't go on telling people what I think of them, and hold the job down. I used not to have a temper, when I was young.'

'No, sir,' said Gordon, discreetly.

'Don't say "no" as if you mean "yes"!' roared the Pink 'Un. 'I had the temper of Old Harry, and you know it! Still have.' A reminiscent smile crossed the Pink 'Un's lips. 'Thank God! Put some action into these old fogies before I'm dead —you mark my words, Gordon.'

'You succeed admirably, sir,' Gordon assured him.

'Don't blarney me,' snapped Holt. He sipped at his tea, glowering. 'Gordon, I'm worried. Asked Murdoch and Miss Dell to do more than is humanly possible. This Government —leave everything to the last minute, hedge and fidget till every man-jack in Europe believes they're gutless, and then make desperate efforts to prove they're not. They're not, of course! At least, some of them aren't. But they've played too many games to the wind, Gordon. No use using eighteenth-century diplomacy today. Honesty, that's what counts. Should have been on their knees to Russia, and what did they do? *What—did—they—do?*' The Pink 'Un's face went a deeper shade. He did not wait for an answer, and he was in the middle of reviling a politician, who shall be nameless, when the telephone rang sharply.

He answered it, and listened.

The anger died out of his eyes; but there was a strained, anxious expression on his round, pink face, and he said, 'I see, I see,' several times. There was a period of quiet while he listened, and then he exploded: 'You've got to—understand? Got to! Don't talk to me like that, Devenish—*you've got to get them out!*'

At the other end of the line, plump and amiable but perturbed, Sir Ralph Devenish protested:

'The situation here—you don't quite understand it, Sir Robert. It is tense—most tense!'

'*Dense!*' roared the Pink 'Un. 'I know you're dense! I said get those three out—and do it fast. Goddamit, what are you there for?'

'But ...' said Devenish, weakly.

'Don't but me! Where's Akeham?'

'He is engaged with the Enkraine Foreign Minister.'

'Disengage him! Prise him loose—tear him away! Break the bottle, if it's the only way you can do it. If you—hallo, hallo, hallo—what the devil—hallo ... ?'

'Have you finished?'

'*Finished?*' snarled the Pink 'Un. 'Finished—what in heaven's name d'you thing I'm here for? I haven't started! Who's that speaking ... ?'

'London operator, sir.'

'Well, you cut me off! Cut me off the most important call I've had this year! Understand? Get them back ...'

'Who were you calling, sir?'

'I wasn't. They called me.'

'They will doubtless call again, sir, if you'll replace ...'

'Don't teach me my own business!' howled Sir Robert. 'Get me the British Embassy in Enkraine, and get it fast. Hurry!'

'Very good, sir.'

Sir Robert replaced the receiver and wiped the sweat off his forehead, and grinned crookedly at Gordon.

'Those girls have the patience of Job. You see that they get their chocolates once a month, don't you?'

'It is arranged, sir.'

'Good. Well ...' the scowl came back. 'I knew something

like this would happen. Miss Dell and Mr. Angell under arrest! Thank God Murdoch's clear. Who's the policeman at Malla?'

Gordon waited.

'Alsec,' said the Pink 'Un, slowly. 'Yes . . . That might explain things. In fact, it probably does. How long will I have to wait for that damned call?' he demanded wrathfully 'All right, Gordon, get off. Go to bed. Good night.'

'Good night, sir,' said Gordon, and went out.

Holt lit a cigarette and stared at the telephone. His face had regained its normal baby-pink, and rose-bud of a mouth was puckered. After fifteen minutes, the bell rang again.

He snatched up the receiver.

'Hallo . . .? Yes, put them through—yes, hallo—speak up, can't you! Devenish? Why the devil did you cut me off? Don't argue, you cut me off! Is Akeman there?'

'He is about to come, sir.'

'Tell him to hurry. Godalmighty, is this a joke? British Ambassador drinking with some tuppenny ha'penny Foreign Secretary, and I'm—hallo . . . *What?* . . . Well, why didn't you say so? Listen, Akeham . . .'

Lord Akeham knew Sir Robert well enough not to be offended. On the other hand, he was not amused. He was a man singularly lacking in humour; a middle-aged, austere diplomat of the old school.

He listened. Then:

'Really, Holt, everything possible has been done. Devenish had reported your attitude. You don't understand the general situation here.'

'Blast the situation!' snapped Holt. 'They've picked on three English tourists and clapped them in gaol. Your job is to get them out. Fast!'

'I have spoken about it.' Akeham's voice was thin and precise. 'They are being held on a suspicion of espionage for a hostile power. Not England. Are you sure of the three people in question?'

Holt spluttered.

'Sure? *Sure?* Would I stay up half the night if I had any doubts? Never mind the situation—*get them out!* Before you know where you are they'll be murdered in their sleep.'

'Come, come!' protested Akeham. But he sounded uneasy, and Holt realised it. 'Your people have to take risks, Holt, and you must be patient. There's a virtual state of martial law here. Spies are liable to summary execution.'

'*What?*'

'Perhaps now you will take some notice of the general situation!' said Akeham, tartly. 'I will do all I can to help you, but they have been taken to Police Headquarters, and I can get no information about them at all. Of course, I am making the strongest representations.'

Holt said, suspiciously mildly:

'Of course. I know you are. Tell, me, Akeham, is Sta friendly towards us, or isn't he?'

'Oh, of course. But there has been an influx of—er—spies. Not English. There is considerable suspicion, I understand, about the three people in question. Considerable suspicion. It is difficult . . . Hallo? Hallo? Hallo!'

He tried for twenty seconds to make Holt hear, then turned to the plump Devenish, who was waiting at his side.

'He—he cut me off!' he said, incredulously. 'The—man's impossible!'

· · · · ·

'Yes, Sir Robert Holt,' Holt repeated quietly. 'I want to speak to Captain Meister—Meister, yes . . . Asleep? . . . Well, wake him up.'

Some two minutes later Meister, who knew Holt well, was speaking to him from the Enkraine. The call had come through quickly: a mile from Meister's house, Akeham was still shocked by Holt's manner.

'No,' said Meister, after listening for thirty seconds. 'I have not given the orders myself. Alsec . . .'

'Can you handle him?'

Meister, head of the Secret Intelligence in the Enkraine, was heard to laugh.

'I can try.'

'Do, there's a good fellow. It's most important. But for these three, Cardyce would never have pulled off that coup, that's a fact. Wonderful people. Wonderful! Like you.' He chuckled, and Meister laughed again. 'The thing is, Akeham can't get anything at all, and that's bad. I don't want any mistake made. Be most awkward . . . There's a good fellow —do everything you possibly can, and ring me back. Of course, it's not for me to talk about Alsec, but . . .'

'I think,' said Meister, 'that I understand, Sir Robert.'

'Excellent fellow! Well, good night. Call me back. Thanks.'

He replaced the receiver and stared at it, his hands crossed on his vast stomach. His pink face was set, as he said slowly:

'I don't like it, Gordon. I'm worried—Alsec could get rid of them quickly. If he does . . .'

The man known to his agents as the Pink 'Un looked up, saw the empty room, and confounded Gordon for going to bed without asking permission. He was more concerned than he could say about the likely fate of Mary, Ted and Percival Briggs.

. . . . . .

Of these things, Bruce Murdoch knew nothing.

The possibility that the airfield delay forced on Cardyce was connected with the arrest of Mary and Ted, if only indirectly, had to be faced.

'Just what's happening?' he asked Mick Fuller.

'The beggars won't let any private plane start till they've had permission from the Air Ministry, and the Ministry seems too busy to worry about it. Cardyce is going to take the liner, but he's not boarding till the last minute. I was going with him, but now . . .' He glared towards Katerina. 'She'll pick me out in a flash. Can you go?'

'Too risky,' said Bruce. 'Graham's the one and only chance, old man—have you got tickets?'

'Yes, but it wasn't easy.'

'That's the worst of revolutions,' jested Murdoch. He was not feeling humorous, but the events of the past few hours had brought him near to breaking-point, and he was damnably tired. He had to save himself from bad temper by flippancy. 'My God, this is a mess!'

He beckoned Graham over.

The mechanics were climbing down from the airliner, which had been tuned up with the quick efficiency of Enkranianian engineers. It was due to start in five minutes. Graham, playing up well, did not appear to hurry, but reached the others quickly enough. Cardyce was already walking towards the aircraft.

'You're flying on that,' said Murdoch, quickly. 'And I'm bringing the Hawker after you—I hope. You'll keep near the woman who got in a few minutes ago.'

'Phew!' whistled Graham, and his eyes gleamed. 'Is she . . . ?'

'For God's sake,' Murdoch warned him, 'don't lose your head over her—better men than you have! Be careful, and when she gets to Mavia, make sure where she puts up. Then telephone a man named Clarkson—here's his number. Tell him to meet you near her hotel, and when you start speaking, mention the "Pink 'Un". Is that clear?'

Graham's eyes were shining.

'Quite clear, sir!'

'Good. Tell Clarkson to watch the woman, then you go to the Noric Hotel—we'll see you there, all being well. Now, have you understood everything?'

Graham nodded. 'I'd better hurry.'

They watched him walking quickly towards the aircraft, and Fuller grinned.

'He'll be all right! But how are we going to get after him?'

'When the liner's out of sight, we're going up—whether they like it or not,' said Bruce, crisply. 'We mustn't stay here. They haven't touched the bus, have they?'

'No. But . . .'

'We can't afford any buts! It's a self-starting engine, thank God—we needn't swing the propeller—and it's got a good run, at the moment. We'll go over casually, get aboard, and then off.'

Fuller cocked an eybrow.

'They seemed pretty serious. And—have you noticed the stuff in that corner?'

Murdoch followed his gaze, and his eyes narrowed. Drawn

up across one corner of the field were two army lorries, and from one of them the ugly snout of an anti-aircraft gun was poking. A dozen uniformed men, three with fixed bayonets, were grouped about it.

'Yes. Well, we'll chance it. Sta's making damn sure he's got everything fixed, but he wouldn't go to these lengths if he wasn't worried.'

'Can't we get an O.K. from him?'

'Not a hope. Cardyce might have worked it, but the Embassy would take hours. Us for the high adventure, little man!' He grinned wryly. 'Now—how did Katerina get at you?'

Fuller chuckled.

'I don't think I gave myself away transparently, but I've been more or less in her line of vision for two days: she had to see me. What worries me is, how did she get on to Mary and the others?'

'Subject *verboten*,' said Bruce, more lightly than he felt. 'There she goes! Lord, they can build airliners, Mick—she's a beauty.'

The Junkers took off like a bird, without a quiver. In thirty seconds, it was flying high and fast towards the east.

'Odd thing,' murmured Murdoch. 'I mean, this embargo on private planes, when the liner can go and no questions asked, apparently. If Sta wasn't boasting about the treaty, I'd say he wanted to keep Cardyce back.'

'Maybe someone does.'

'Yes . . . But the someone has to be in authority. Trouble is, the Government's probably riddled with Berlin agents. Anyhow, we've got to beat the embargo, Michael—do or die, in the traditional spirit. Everything casual, mind you.'

He offered cigarettes and they lit up as they walked slowly towards the Hawker at the far end of the field. But casually through they went, they were observed. A man detached himself from the gun-battery and moved towards the plane. He would cut them off ten yards from it.

'Do we run?' asked Mick.

'Don't be a lunatic; we chat with him. Leave the talking to me and smile affably.'

Fuller grinned.

The man who approached them was even younger than Graham, Murdoch noted. He wore a Mauser pistol at his side, and a steel helmet like the polished examples of the Nazi S.S. Guard, but the down on his upper lip made a comic soldier of him.

There was nothing comic about the battery in the corner. Murdoch's heart began to beat fast.

'You go where?' The voice was unexpectedly deep.

'To my plane.' Murdoch's smile seemed easy enough. 'You won't let me use it, *mon Capitan*, but I must get my case from it.'

'It is forbidden.'

'I hope not!' said Murdoch, his voice hardening. 'I shall already complain to the British Embassy for this quite un-justifiable delay, and anything further ...'

'Your passport!' snapped the boy.

'As I am not travelling, is that necessary?'

The boy scowled, and touched his gun.

'Show it!'

Murdoch shrugged, and took out a passport which showed him in the disguise he had affected. It had been issued in London, announced that Jean Paul Murat was a British sub-ject, and super-imposed were the visas of a dozen European countries. Fuller offered his own passport.

The boy glowered. Probably, thought Murdoch, he was trying to conciliate M'sieu Murat's French appearance and name with his English passport. But it was in order, and Mur-doch said sharply:

'Need there be further delay, *mon Capitan?*'

'I shall accompany you,' announced the boy.

He turned abruptly. Behind his back, Murdoch and Fuller exchanged glances. Murdoch nodded slightly, and they follow-ed him to the Hawker.

'I shall enter first,' said the boy.

'As you please.' Murdoch shrugged and followed: Fuller brought up the rear. As they went further into the cabin, Murdoch slipped his hand into his pocket. He drew it out again, quickly, and the boy made a sharp movement towards his own gun.

But Murdoch's Webley was very steady.

'You will be silent, my friend, or else . . .'

The gun, and his expression, won a temporary victory. The boy's eyes widened, but he did not try to draw his Mauser. Fuller was already at the controls, and the engine roared to life.

Murdoch was watching the anti-aircraft gun.

It was just possible that, with the boy on board, they would get up unmolested. He snapped an order to him to take one of the passenger seats. Reluctantly, the boy obeyed. His lips were working and Murdoch was prepared any moment for him to defy the gun.

Out of the corner of his eye he saw three men, bayonets glistening, hurrying across the field.

'Snap into it, Mick! You keep quiet . . .'

But the boy had all the courage he needed.

As he leapt forward, Murdoch tried to hit him. He missed, but the lad lost his balance and lurched towards the door. In a flash, Murdoch opened it and pushed him out. The plane was moving very slowly; it was unlikely the boy had been seriously hurt. Tight-lipped, he watched the running men unslinging their rifles, while there was a burst of activity near the mobile gun.

The plane was bumping a little. Behind it, ten yards away at most, were the riflemen. A shot hummed, hitting the wing; others missed, but Murdoch could see the spurts of yellow flame as the trio fired.

Fuller pulled back on the joy-stick.

The little craft left the ground smoothly enough. Fuller took a chance and banked quickly, to gain height without loss of time. The plane quivered, but he righted it. In sixty seconds they had reached four thousand feet, and behind them was the city, with the high spires of two cathedrals spiking towards the sky, and the bronze dome of the House of Representatives gleaming gold in the sun. But Murdoch and Fuller were conscious only of the bursting shell a hundred yards to their right; the spreading flame and the billowing grey smoke.

They would have to fly through a barrage.

14 : Gun play

The one consolation, Murdoch had felt, was there had been only one gun at the airfield but he knew that meant little. By now telephone messages would be flashing to other stations —and in Enkraine that day they were likely to find anti-aircraft guns all along the main roads.

Fuller climbed as quickly as he dared.

Another shell exploded beneath them; and this time the Hawker quivered a little, but flew on. A third shot burst somewhere above their heads. A split-second later, they heard the rattle of shrapnel on the cabin roof. Murdoch saw a piece hit the wing, but the plane hardly quivered.

Fuller grimaced.

'They meant it, all right!'

'They're still meaning it. That one was short . . .' Another burst came, behind and below them. 'I suppose the chances of being hit are at least ten to one against. Where are we?'

Fuller glanced at the altimeter. 'Six thousand.'

'I wonder what their range is? Ten, probably, or a spot more. Are you full out?'

'Not quite, we're not high enough—hell, that was close!'

A small piece of shrapnel from another burst struck the windscreen to send a tracery of white lines shooting about it. Murdoch peered out. There were three guns in action, now. He could see them moving along the white ribbon of road, and needed no telling that a general warning had gone out.

'I wonder who they think we are?' said Fuller, drily.

'Nazi agents, probably. Mick, I think we'll make it.'

'H'mm?'

'The last three have burst well below us—we're at ten

thousand, are we? Give us another two and then get on the Mavia route—do you know it?'

'Graham has it marked out, here.' Fuller had not turned a hair, and he was looking at the route-map pinned to the board at his right. 'East-north-east, on a fairly straight flight, and the only danger spot the Carthias. But Graham said something about snow—if there's much, I'm not going to like it.'

'Join the club,' murmured Bruce, with a flippancy that was genuine. Beneath them the shells were still bursting, but unless something with a much higher range was brought to bear against them they would not be in danger from the ground.

High though they were, with the help of glasses he could make out the mobile batteries running along two wide main roads, and once a camp which looked large enough to house a division. Over a smaller town, he saw guns firing—but not at the Hawker. Here and there, tremendous bursts, flaring red and then smoky, told of direct hits. He could make out two lines with a constant speckle of fire from them, and he glanced at the map.

'We're over Enkra, are we?'

'If I'm flying right, yes.'

'Let me take over, and you look at the revolution.'

As far as they could see, there was little chance of the rebels in Enkra overcoming the heavy Government forces which had been flung against the town. In three places vast clouds of smoke, swept occasionally by the wind and revealing the fires beneath them, told of burning buildings and, to Murdoch, presenting with ghastly clarity a mental picture of the horrors that were taking place down there. Women and children, helpless in the grip of war. The rebellion would probably last a week at most, but there was always the possibility that it would last longer.

Two hundred miles to the west was the German frontier, strongly manned, probably with two or three divisions clustered near. The fifty-mile stretch of the Enkraine inside the frontier was peopled with a strong German minority. The Reich, rather than allow a long-drawn-out war, would probably interfere, to 'rescue the down-trodden, terrorised members of the Fatherland'.

He saw suddenly why Cardyce had not elected to take a safe three-two win.

He had the Enkraine only as long as Sta was the ruler.

If the *putsch* succeeded, the score between him and von Romain, now, would be level. An unpleasant thought. Nor did he dwell on Mary's plight; he dared not. It was all in the game, of course, but it was incredible to think that four short days before he and Mary had been at Cliff Cottage.

'They seem to have given us up,' Fuller commented.

Enkra was behind them, and the only evidence of the battle being fought there was in the drifting clouds of smoke. Small villages over which they passed seemed peaceful enough, although here and there military convoys trundled towards the frontier, like tiny caterpillars. The wooded country over which they were soon flying cut even that from view, but Murdoch knew, as they neared the frontier, that the Army was preparing against a surprise attack.

Odd, how remote they seemed from it all, in the air.

Below, there was something approaching the Czecho-slovak affair, without the same monstrous preamble and bargaining, and with one vital exception: there had been no serious warning of the coming rebellion. Did that mean a quick movement over the frontier by the Germans, a 'justified' interference on behalf of the minorities, and a *fait accompli* which England and France could only accept?

The fantastic journey, Cardyce's attempt against von Romain's, grew more understandable. A solid *bloc* of the small nations would stop the Reich marching too far, or too quickly: would call a halt, for a while at least, to the threat of war. But . . .

Had Cardyce started too late?

Was the flare-up down there the forerunner of a European conflagration?

He forced his mind back to more immediate concerns.

One thing puzzled him.

Why had no plane come after them?

In the present circumstances, the Enkrainian Air Force would be concentrated on the frontiers. He glanced at his watch. They had been flying for two hours, now: that meant they were thirty miles from the frontier—they could expect opposition at any moment. A damnable thought. He wondered whether the Pink 'Un had contrived to clear the Hawker in Mavia. If not, there was the added danger of detention when they landed. It was not likely to last for long, for the iron-ore mines of the Carthias had for a long time been British-controlled and worked by British engineers, and knowing the value of that small state, with its dangerous frontiers, the British Government had wooed it for a long time. Tariffs were comparatively low, and Mavia was the one state definitely friendly to Britain.

But there was the frontier to tackle first, and he spoke quietly:

'Climb, I think, Mick. What's our ceiling?'

'Twenty-five thousand—but we're not dressed for more than twenty.'

'We needn't stay long, but we've got to get over the border.'

Fuller turned a startled face.

'Good Lord, yes! I'd been kidding myself we were clear.' He had taken over again an hour back, and as there was comparatively little wind, had been able to lock the controls and fly direct on course. Already in the distance the snow-covered peaks of the Carthias were appearing: the frontier could be no more than twenty miles off. Say, eight minutes' flying.

He pulled back on the stick.

In thirty seconds, the air became appreciably colder and Murdoch's fingers were like ice. But he peered down, trying to see the frontier town of Ren, over which they were due to fly. He could make out little, for there was a slight mist marring visibility.

Then two fighters came literally, out of the blue.

One moment, he saw only a bluish blur. The next, the shapes of two small, waspish Enkrainian fighting planes.

Fuller had seen them, too.

'We can't be far from the frontier,' he muttered. 'What do I do? Cram on all we've got?'

'Better try and trick them,' Murdoch said. 'I'll take over.'

Fuller nodded and sat back as he took the other controls. The fighters were no more than a quarter of a mile away, and their machine-guns were already working: they could see the yellow specks of flame.

'Hold tight,' Bruce murmured, and throttled down until the plane stalled, keeping the stick well back.

He put the rudder well over to the right, and there was that moment of sickening suspense when the plane seemed to hover, as though it would fall headlong without any chance of regathering speed. Then it slipped to one side, so that they were flying at right-angles to the ground.

Murdoch pushed the rudder and ailerons over to the other extreme. The machine checked and went over in the opposite direction sharply, losing height all the time.

In front of them and flying high, the two fighter pilots were nonplussed. Murdoch's lips were set tight as he repeated the manœuvre four times and lost all of a thousand feet. The fighters went out of sight.

He pushed the stick forward and the plane dropped into a steep dive. Then he pulled back slowly and had the throttle out as wide as it would go. Keeping an eye on the route and the compass, he saw the speedometer touch two-twenty as he let the plane have its head.

Four minutes passed in tense silence, then Fuller broke it.

'Looks all right, Bruce—there's no sign of 'em.'

'Daren't chase us too far, thank the Lord,' said Murdoch.

He was sweating. He realised that Graham would have accomplished the manœuvre without the same tension, but Murdoch had not flown for several months, and he had never been an ace.

Another five minutes, and he knew that they were over Mavia. It was safe to drop, and he levelled out at ten thousand feet, with the snow-capped Carthias below them: ridge after ridge of mountain and valley. They were to fly over similar country for an hour before they reached the edge of the Great Mavian Plain. He would be happier there, and the weight of the possibility of trouble in Mavia lessened.

It was Fuller who sighted the plane ahead first. They watched closely as they went on, and it was obvious that they were gaining on it. Fuller was at the controls again, now, and Murdoch concentrated on the glasses. When he lifted them from his eyes, he was smiling.

'We'll be there before Cardyce or Katerina, anyhow: that's the liner. Get high again, Mick—I'd rather not be seen.'

．　　．　　．　　．　　．

Among the passengers aboard the airliner was a short, well-dressed Jew, with large, expressive eyes. A man who appeared to be pleased with life, despite the difficulties his race was encountering in Central Europe.

Several times he glanced across at Katerina, but she showed no inclination to respond. In fact, her lips curled when she looked his way, and she moved a little, as if to get as far as possible from a Jew.

The little man's bright eyes missed nothing, but he only smiled as though in amusement and turned back to his magazine.

Several times Katerina glanced behind her into the open sky. She saw nothing, but she could not be sure that Murdoch had been detained. She did not see the plane which Murdoch was piloting, for it went too far above them.

Both planes roared on towards Mavia.

．　　．　　．　　．　　．

The Enkrainian Chief of Political Police did not look with any pleasure at the small man opposite him. The meeting was a secret one, and Alsec would have been in considerable fear had it been generally observed. But he had taken the precaution of having the little man smuggled in, and only those in his confidence knew of the interview.

'It is difficult,' he was saying, sharply. 'Always, you ask the impossible!'

'You misjudge me.' The little man's face was pushed oddly on one side. 'My principals give me the instructions: I am only the messenger.'

'An unwelcome one,' retorted Alsec. 'Here am I, with the three English safely hidden where they can do no harm. And now word comes to have them killed!'

'You are unusually scrupulous,' murmured the other.

Alsec thumped the desk.

'Don't be impertinent! I—do I care for the lives of three English fools? But there is danger.'

'It is for the Cause!'

'It is for Berlin!' snapped Alsec. Then he shrugged. 'With trouble, it can be done.'

'It will certainly bring trouble, if it is not.'

Alsec regarded the little man for some seconds, then looked abruptly away.

'It shall be done,' he said. 'You may send word of that.'

15 : Counsels of the Great

To a house on the mountainside overlooking Vienna came three powerful cars, gleaming in the midday sun. The first was filled with men of the S.S. Guard; black uniforms immaculate, leather shining, guns ostentatiously on show. The third car might have been a replica of the first. But in the middle one sat a man gross of body and heavy of feature, clad in a uniform not unlike that of a general in the one-time Imperial Prussian Guard. Next him sat a slight figure in drab brown, with probably the most caricatured moustache in the world, and a lock of hair which fell loosely over his forehead.

A line of storm-troopers with drawn swords formed a guard of honour when the cars stopped at the entrance of the famous house on the mountainside, and the fat man and the lean man strode in, impervious to the worship about them. The name of the fat general was Mulke, and of the lean nondescript with the half-closed, peculiar eyes of a megalomaniac was Mitzer.

They entered a low-ceilinged room, pleasantly furnished and overlooking the spreading, hilly countryside beyond, a room where conferences which had shocked the world had taken place, where decisions on policy had been thrashed out —where the new technique of political blackmail had been perfected.

Outside the door, when it was closed, were three men with swords drawn. Inside, Mitzer pushed back his lock of hair with a tired gesture and asked:

'What is this of von Romain, Mulke?'

'Bad,' grunted Mulke. 'He has lost Luthia and the Enkraine. He advises he is first in Mavia, but he cannot work quickly there.'

'What does the woman say?'

'The Fräulein Weissman advises that the delays have been deliberate: that much can be blamed on the work of a man Morely—representing, she understands, the Clayton Company.'

'Ah, yes; what is this about Clayton?'

'He offers the machine for a quarter million English pounds, paid through New York.'

'*Gott in Himmel!*' The brooding eyes flashed. 'Money, money—it is always money! Where is the end to it? This machine, it is good?'

'We need it,' said Mulke, simply.

'All right, Mulke: you may proceed. Of von Romain—is it possible he has been bribed to fail?'

'It is unlikely.'

'Then why does he not succeed? *Mein Gott!* If it were not urgent, I should recall him. Mulke—there are places where he might learn the importance of success. To send others—is this possible?'

'It would be unwise.'

Mitzer drummed his fingers on the table beside him. He looked out of the window, over the scene that he had loved so well. He could remember vividly the days when it had been a 'foreign' country; recalled with a fierce exultation the ease of its conquest. The brooding expression disappeared from his eyes.

'He shall continue. The woman will report on what he does, and how he does it—she is clever, that one.' The nearest thing to a smile that Mitzer ever achieved, twitched his lips. 'The Fräulein, she is invaluable. She will be well rewarded, Mulke. Now . . .' He turned abruptly; fire in his eyes, tension in his body. 'What is happening in the Enkraine? How soon will that be over?'

'It will take time,' Mulke warned. 'Sta has subdued the revolt in Enkra.'

'It must not be allowed! We could overrun the province in a few days.'

'Until the final result of von Romain's mission, a movement would be ill-considered,' said Mulke, as if talking to a fractious child. 'This is precisely the importance of the mission, Excellency.'

'Why is this Cardyce allowed to go first?'

'It is being arranged, very carefully. The English . . .' something of the hatred of the military German for the English showed in Mulke's small eyes—'are clever, in that respect. It has been well achieved. Both in Dorshland and Brennia we have made preparations: Cardyce will be rebuffed. With these two, we can act. The *putsch* will succeed in the Enkraine, and Mavia will be cut off from communications with Luthia. Mavia, then, will bend to your will, Excellency. It was good that we should learn of what Cardyce was to do.'

'Yes, yes!' said Mitzer, impatiently. 'We learned, thanks to the Fräulein.'

'Word had already reached us,' Mulke corrected.

'But she confirmed it—she always confirms: she is invaluable. See that she is well rewarded.' Mitzer gestured impatiently, as though half-aware he had already said that. 'This Cardyce, why is he allowed to live?'

'He can die only by accident, Excellency—an accident which could not be proved otherwise. We are not prepared for a large-scale offensive, such as his murder would cause. Accidents have been arranged, but he has been fortunate. Now . . .' Mulke shrugged. 'He will find nothing in Brennia or Dorshland. He can try, and live; it will appear genuine. The world will believe what is true, that Brennia knows she is part of the Reich, and Josef of Dorshland wishes to have the comfort of the Reich's support.'

'You are sure of these things?'

'As sure as it is possible to be.'

'It must be made certain!' snapped Mitzer. 'See to it, Mulke!'

Again he gazed moodily from the window. Mulke took papers from his wallet, put them on the table, coughed, and said:

'Your speech concerning foreign affairs, Excellency—it is ready for approval. The necessary condemnation of the rising in the Enkraine is most convincing, as is the assurance to France that you are satisfied with our joint frontiers as they stand. They continue to believe,' he added, with a tight-lipped smile.

Mitzer's eyes were angry.

'They believe me because they know I speak the truth, Mulke—I do not lie! Today, I am satisfied. Only if I am angered shall there be alterations. Leave the speech: I will consider it.'

'It requires only the final touches of your genius,' said Mulke, suavely. 'Goodbye, Excellency.'

Mitzer did not appear to hear him. He was standing staring across that lovely countryside on which the touch of autumn was already apparent.

· · · · · · ·

Sir Robert Holt would have been the first to admit that he was a victim of prejudices. He disliked some people on sight, and many more on acquaintance, among them at least half the Cabinet. His idea of utter boredom was to attend a meeting at 10, Downing Street, and it was recorded that he had never attended such a meeting—unofficially, of course—without raising a storm of protest. He was blunt and uncompromising: when rebuked, he immediately threatened to resign. It was inevitably a successful bluff, for Holt loved his organisation and his work, while even Dalby and Paddon, who disliked the Pink 'Un intensely, admitted that under his control, the nation's Secret Service was unrivalled.

The Pink 'Un descended from a cab outside Number 10, was admitted, and found the Premier, Dalby, Paddon and Glennister waiting for him. Not the full team, then. He nodded bluffly, listened for ten minutes to what he considered an unnecessary preamble from Paddon—the Minister for the Co-ordination of Defence—and when Dalby looked as though he was prepared to give his version of the same preamble, broke in:

'All right, all right, Dalby! Hang it, man—we know what we've got to discuss. No need to review the European situation again this morning.'

As Dalby tightened his lips, Glennister broke in hastily: 'What news from Mavia, Bob?'

'Not much. Cardyce is there. So are my people—or some of them. I'm more worried about what's happening in the Enkraine.'

'We have Akeham's assurance that things have settled down and the regime has completely mastered the uprising,' said Dalby, sharply.

Holt rubbed his triple chins.

'Oh, yes, of course. Akeham knows everything. Let me tell you, Dalby—the rising in the Enkraine was a rehearsal; and an unofficial one, at that. Berlin is waiting for the Cardyce-von Romain result, that's all. They think they've got Brennia and Dorshland in the bag, and it wouldn't surprise me if they're right. However, we shall have to wait and see. If Cardyce can get there a jump ahead of von Romain, we might do it, yet.'

'I don't see,' said Paddon, 'any reason for this pessimism, Holt.'

Holt snapped: 'No, I know you don't! You didn't see any reason for alarm over Austria. You didn't think the Czech business would come to a head. You ...'

'Supposing,' said the Prime Minister mildly, 'you tell us just what you know of the Enkrainian situation, Sir Robert?'

Holt exuded a long breath.

'My reports are, Prime Minister, that there is a strong Nazi representation in Malla, as well as the larger towns, and that three of the higher Government officials are working for Berlin. Trouble is, we don't know who. Von Romain—or that blasted woman—was able to stage an arrest of three of my people, and it might just turn the scale against us. Akeham,' he added, with fine sarcasm, 'has been trying for forty-eight hours to get them out of gaol, but they're nearer concentration camps than ever. Which reminds me, Glennie— you must make strong representations, through Akeham, about them: Murdoch needs them badly.'

'It should be clearly understood,' said Paddon coldly, 'that your people have no protection . . .'

'Don't be a fool!' snarled Holt, reddening angrily. 'If any of my people get themselves caught with any suspicion of working under cover, they get themselves out or suffer for it. But there isn't any suspicion here; all they did was to follow von Romain, a German subject—which is no reason at all for the sympathetic pro-British Sta regime to hold them! Someone outside that regime is doing it, and the stronger the representations from here, the quicker the results. It might help Sta to find who's causing most of the trouble. *Protection, my eye!*'

Dalby stirred uneasily. The Prime Minister, worried by the continual quarrels among his Ministers and high permanent officials, firmly changed the subject. And two hours later, the placards and headlines of the Press announced a meeting of the Inner Cabinet, attended by Sir Robert Holt—while that gentleman and Glennister walked undisturbed through Sr. James's Park.

Holt was saying:

'I suppose they must do a good job somewhere, or the P.M. wouldn't stand for it. But when they try to understand—my God, Glennie, why don't you just represent me, at those meetings?'

'I like a peaceful life,' said Glennister, cheerfully. 'They'd miss you, Bob—you stir them up. But they forgot to ask whether you seriously believe that the freeing of Mary Dell and the others will help Cardyce now.'

Holt frowned.

'I have doubts, Glennie. They're so far behind. But I'm worried about them, if the blasted *putsch* comes off—anyhow, we ought to insist about it. We would, if they *were* private citizens. Don't say you're going to hedge!'

'No. I'll look after them.'

'Thanks. I can't do much more. Murdoch's still working,

98

with Fuller, and he tells me that Clarkson is co-operating well in Mavia. He seems to have developed a liking for his pilot, a youngster named Graham—useful boy; I always thought so. Positively no nerves. Well, I wish the next seventy-two hours were over. Mavia would have taken longer than the others, anyhow—it's nearly got a Government in practice, as well as in name! By the way, Glennie, there's another thing. Clayton.'

Glennister laughed.

'I mentioned your little impersonation to the Prime Minister. He was amused.'

'He's got the right stuff in him,' Holt said. 'I wish he were a little less inclined to listen to the easiest counsel. However: Clayton. I've heard that Berlin's deposited a quarter of a million, in New York. I trust we can rely on Clayton?'

Glennister frowned.

'So do I.'

'Like that, is it?' asked Holt, sharply. 'When, oh when, are we going to have national control of armaments? I'm having him watched, as well as young Hawsman—what's that Bomber like?'

'It does all that Clayton and Hawsman claim for it.'

'H'mm . . . So it's good, and it would be useful to Berlin. Is Clayton above supplying false designs and cashing in?'

'No.'

'Then he isn't above supplying the right designs. My God, what a patriotic race we are—if it doesn't touch our pockets! Are you coming to Sloane Square?'

'No, I'm lunching with Meg. We don't often get the chance.'

Holt chuckled.

'Long suffering, politician's wives, aren't they? Give her my regards—and look after yourself. I won't worry you at lunch, if I can help it.'

When he reached the house in Sloane Square, the telephone was ringing, and Gordon opened the door apologetically.

'There have been two calls from Mavia, sir, and one from the Enkraine. That may be . . .'

Holt hurried up the narrow stairs. A few seconds later,

he heard Murdoch's voice. Preliminaries over, Murdoch said:
'I think things are level, sir. C. has just left Government
House, and v. R. came out twenty minutes ago, looking fierce.
The woman's here. But I badly need Mary and Angell . . .'
'I'm doing all I can.'
'Of course,' said Murdoch. 'There's one other thing I don't
like. Clayton's here.'
'*What?*'
'He has a private room booked at the Noric, and v. R.
and the woman will be there. I could put Mary on to Clay-
ton, and look after the others, all right, if I had them.'
'I'll make some arrangements,' said Holt, shortly. 'Is that
all?'
'For now, yes. C. tells me that he's going on to Dorshland
at once, and sleeping on the way. I'm sending Fuller and
Graham after him, and looking after the others myself for the
time being. But when they break up, Clayton will have to be
on his own unless I put one of our local men on him.'
'Do that, if you haven't heard from me. All right, my boy.
I've another phone ringing—I'll keep in touch. Goodbye!'
Murdoch rang off. Holt lifted the other receiver, and re-
cognised the voice of Wright, from Malla. Only in exception-
ally urgent matters would resident agents telephone him, and
he pulled a pad and pencil nearer.
Wright gave the code; then:
'I'm worried, sir, about the trio.'
'What about them?'
'Alsec, the Chief of Political Police, is putting down the
rebellion pretty fiercely. Too fiercely to be genuine.'
'H'mm. Think he's playing double?'
'Reasonably sure of it,' said Wright, grimly. 'He's ordering executions, with the sketchiest of trials, and at least four
people have been shot "trying to escape". If our three are to
stay safe, you'll have to work very fast.'

16: Reprieve?

The Patriarch of the Enkraine had known that the announcement of the treaty with Great Britain would strengthen his position with the democratic elements in the country, but would also bring the extremists into greater prominence He was equally well aware that if the other states of the *bloc* chose Germany instead of Great Britain, the best that could happen to him would be exile; the most likely, assassination.

Sta did not believe the suzerainty of the Reich would be for the betterment of his country—and that betterment had been the driving power behind his work for fifty years. But he was worried. There were people in high positions whom he could not trust—and he did not know who they were. He was getting too old; too much was left to subordinates, too many orders were not obeyed or were 'translated' to suit the ideas of officials. Sta had ordered a degree of mobilisation: now, he was wondering if the troops would get out of hand. Word of the battle at Enkra, with the heavy losses among the hapless civil population, disturbed and horrified him. He was not alone in seeing the possibility that the Enkraine would be the battlefield of Europe.

The one hope was the newly-signed treaty.

But Sta was not foolish enough to believe that Britain could send help to his country in time to stop a German advance, unless the other countries in the *bloc* were prepared to fight. He knew that the overthrow of his regime would also mean the repudiation of the treaty, and that the situation for Britain would then be extremely delicate. He prayed that Dorshland and Brennia would do as he had done, but he was afraid that the Nazi influence in those countries was too strong.

Still, until the results of Cardyce's rushed journey were gathered, the pendelum was swinging evenly, and he was not afraid of a complete rising before that. If he could find the pivots of the *putsch* before the results came, he might even contrive to remain solid with the people, and with Mavia (whose signing of a treaty had been reported unofficially an hour before) and Luthia could present a united front against threatened German military action.

∴ A telephone rang on his desk. His secretary lifted it, waited, and looked at Sta, whose fine eyes and snowy but thick and well-groomed hair and beard made him still a strikingly handsome man.

'Yes?'

'Colonel Meister wishes an audience, sir.'

'Send him in,' said Sta.

Sir Robert Holt's opposite number in Malla came in. Short, broad-shouldered, mercurial, combining the facial characteristics of his Slovak parents with his Bohemian grandparents plus a touch of French blood, Meister was a man to be reckoned with—and the one whom Sta believed he could whole-heartedly trust. He was right.

Meister lost little time.

'I have heard from England,' he began; and proceeded to recount in essence his telephone conversation with Holt. Mary and the others were mentioned, but of greater importance was the mention of Alsec. 'And so, M'sieu President,' said Meister with vehemence, 'there is the trouble—that one makes the difficulty. Holt, he is never wrong.'

'But *Alsec* ... !'

'You forget, perhaps, that his mother was German.'

'No, no, I forget nothing! But *Alsec*! It is incredible.'

'I beg you,' cried Meister, 'to allow the Military Police to challenge Alsec. Catch one, just one, and we shall be safe—of that I am convinced!'

Sta smoothed his beard.

'Not quite so openly, Meister. I will send for Alsec—to discuss the situation at Enkra—and you will take some men yourself, and visit his office while he is here. These English people—have them removed to a place of safety: it is possible they are just tourists, but they must not go free yet. You will want a pass, for Alsec's office ...'

Ten minutes later, Meister left, satisfied and eager.

At that moment Alsec was saying to a subordinate:

'The woman Dell and the Englishman, Grull—there is too much bother about them, while they live. I am told they are

102

dangerous: they must go. Arrange it.'

Grull hesitated. He was one of two men in the Ministry who took their orders from Berlin, via Alsec, but his small eyes mirrored the crafty, cunning mind behind a slanting forehead.

'Yes, of course. But it is difficult: they are English ...'

'Allow them to escape. Deal with them then.'

Still Grull hesitated.

'In perhaps twenty-four hours, we shall do that with safety. Until then ...'

'Do it!' roared Alsec. 'Don't argue—do it!'

Grull shrugged. Alsec would not make a decision as clear-cut as this unless in receipt of orders he dared not disobey. For his part, Grull considered it unwise. Let a general rising begin, and it would be easy. But now ...

He went out, giving orders to a minor official.

In the House of Political Detention, Mary, Angell and Percy Briggs were playing a three-handed version of German whist. For some whimsical reason they had been allowed cards, but no books.

'Wot's trumps? 'Earts?' Percy sorted through a hand Ted had just dealt. 'Well, of all the lousy 'ands—beggin' yer pardon, Miss. Only a blinkin' five of 'earts in me 'and! 'Ow much do I owe now?'

'Nine-and-sevenpence,' said Mary, promptly.

She looked tired, for she had slept badly after the first night. From the barred windows of the room in which they had lived for the past three days, the sounds of the rebellion had come clearly, and she knew as well as the others what to expect if the Sta regime collapsed. But her hair was neat, and powder hid the shadows under her eyes. They had allowed her to have her handbag—after ripping out its lining.

Their detention might have been worse, indeed.

Despite awkward moments, she was glad that she had not been segregated with other women prisoners. Percy was constantly grumbling, but did not seem seriously alarmed. Angell was good-humoured, cheerful and careful of her comfort without being too solicitous. His pungent protests had brought three camp beds into the room, instead of the benches

103

on which the prisoners were supposed to sleep, and had roared loud enough to get cigarettes, of the thin, mild Enkrainian variety which Percy scorned each time he lit one. He had even bribed their guard for aspirins, which had helped her to doze, if not to sleep.

The food was good enough, if scanty, and again Angell had stormed and blustered until they were brought English tea twice a day. But none of it had eased her mind—or his— of the threatening shadow. If the Enkraine went Nazi . . .

Time and again, they pushed the thought away from them. Percy was invaluable to her, with his running comments, his naïve declaration of his weak suits, and his satisfaction with his good ones. Only Ted Angell knew that Percy was a poker-player of high standing, and that his antics were deliberately designed to lighten the atmosphere.

'Nine-an'-sevenpence, is it?' growled Percy. 'I'm goin' to claim it for expenses; it's barefaced robbery. Blimey, wot an 'and! Ace o' spades—beat that, if you can!' He beamed, as the four and the two fell. 'That's one you won't git, any-ways.'

Five minutes later, he had five tricks to Mary's two and Angell's one. When the key turned in the door, he looked round with a scowl.

' 'Op it, mate—I'm winnin', fer once.'

A walrus-moustached guard entered deliberately, closed the door behind him, and brought in a packet of cigarettes. Angell paid for them with an English half-crown. The guard went out without a word, and they heard the key turn in the lock.

Percy shrugged.

'Bet 'e's changed me luck!'

He stopped. Mary was watching Angell, who had torn the wrappings off the cigarettes and was staring at the slip of paper which took the place of a cigarette card. Tensely, they waited, seeing his face go pale.

'Wot . . .?' started Percy.

'I wonder,' said Angell, slowly. He showed them the note, which in pencilled English ran :

At exactly three o'clock the key will be turned. Wait three minutes. Turn left along the passage, and go through the first door. The room will be empty. Go through the opposite door, down the steps to the courtyard. A gate there will be opened, and a saloon Renault will be waiting. In it, you will find passports and visas. Get to the Mavian frontier and pick my trail up at the Noric. M.

'Gorblimey!' gasped Percy. ''E's done it! I knew 'e would ...'

Mary and Ted exchanged glances. Percy looked reproachfully from one to the other.

'*Now* what's the matter?'

'I wonder,' said Ted, 'if Bruce has been working here?'

'Of course he ...'

'Why "M" and not "B"?' Mary murmured.

Percy scowled.

'Well, of all the blinkin' ...! 'Ere, think it's a trick?'

'I don't know.' Angell glanced at his watch. 'We shall find out in twenty minutes, anyhow.'

'You're going?' asked Mary.

'I think we'd better. If we're careful, we might make something of it. If it's genuine, and we didn't take the chance, we'd never forgive ourselves.'

'I'll ruddy-well say we wouldn't!' Percy exploded. 'Beggin' yer pardon, but it's been gettin' me down.'

The twenty minutes dragged. None of them could force conversation and although they tried to play cards, it was only half-heartedly, to keep up appearance. At three o'clock exactly, Angell was looking at his watch.

And a moment later the key was turned, softly, in the lock.

The seconds ticked by. The three minutes of waiting seemed longer than the whole duration of their imprisonment, but it was time to move at last.

The passage was empty.

So was the room through which they had to pass.

From a window they could see a courtyard, and only Angell saw and understood what the three stakes close to a brick wall were for: only Angell recognised the bullet marks on the wall. Tight-lipped, he led the way downstairs, tensely he opened the door leading to the courtyard.

And then they heard the shouting from behind them; knew that their disappearance had been discovered . . .

17 : Two to Play

As Angell stopped dead, Mary halted uncertainly by the window. Movement in the courtyard, more than the shouting from behind them, worried Angell. The footsteps came nearer, and with them Percy's almost frantic:

' 'Urry, for Gawd's sake . . . !'

Angell had not realised till then just how much the three days' imprisonment and the uncertainty of their fate had weighed on the perky little Cockney's mind. He was startled when Percy pushed past him and rushed down the steps. The shouting from the passage grew louder, and Angell stepped swiftly to the door and turned the key. The handle rattled a moment later.

Percy reached the bottom of the steps.

Suddenly, there was a rattle of rifle-fire from the courtyard. They saw Percy fall forward, on his face, his right arm outflung, his left crushed beneath him. Mary gasped.

'The devils! So that was it.'

'I was afraid so. Better face the lesser of two evils.' Angell returned to the door and unlocked it, while Mary tried to keep her eyes from Percy. He was lying motionless and she would have rushed to him, but for the fear of drawing more bullets.

The door crashed open. Ted saw a stocky, blue-jowled man, in a light grey lounge suit at the head of the four guards who came into the room. He did not know Meister, who glanced round quickly, and snapped in good English:

'The other man, where?'

'Outside.'

'So, they did that!' Meister rushed past them and down the steps, calling a command which was effective, for there was no shooting and four gendarmes came forward at the double, their guns half-slung. Meister rattled off a stream of orders, and Mary saw the men who had shot Percy pick him up. She saw blood on the back of his hand and on his face, and her heart contracted. But:

'We seem to be among friends,' Ted murmured. 'Let me do the talking, and just hold tight.'

Meister came up, at the head of the quartette carrying Percy. He was a fierce little man, and he glared at Angell.

'Why you do this?'

'We...'

'Had the message? Yes, of course—always, it is like that! Never—never, my friend—try the escape from the prison political. The name is, what you say—suicide? Yes, suicide. Your friend, he is not hurt bad; he will be attended. You and Madame, you will please come with me to a place of safety. You need have no fears—unless you are in truth the spy for Berlin?'

Angell took a hold on himself.

He had judged Meister shrewdly at first glance and knew that this spate of words was for their encouragement; that he was in truth giving nothing away. The thing of importance was that he seemed friendly.

'We are English tourists, *M'sieu*, and...'

'Enough!' exclaimed Meister, and his eyes gleamed. 'I and Sair Robert, are we not good friends? To him, we owe the debt, *M'sieu*. Your further detention is a matter only of form —you understand? I regret the accident—the object was to have you dead, and that is not the object of Malla, or the President. It was from others. Names, they do not matter.'

'Oh,' said Ted, weakly.

'You are surprise,' grinned Meister. 'Madame, apologies innumerable for keep you prisoner—you shall be make comfortable. You also, *M'sieu*. At the Garre Hotel I leave two men to guard, but you will give assurance to not try again the escape without permission? In short hours, I hope I bring the passports. That is in order?' He beamed, rattled a stream of Enkrainian at a youthful lieutenant, bowed, and hurried off.

An hour after, Mary and Ted had rooms, with a communicating door, at the Garre Hotel. Percy was in hospital, conscious, and with only flesh wounds, while Ted had telephoned the Pink 'Un, and received orders to obey Meister, but get as quickly as possible to Dorshland.

And in the room recently occupied by the 'tourists', Alsec was in solitary confinement and trying to prevent himself from looking through the windows to the corner of the courtyard. He, too, knew what the stakes meant, and he was afraid.

He was executed, with Grull and two others, three hours after his arrest, and Meister was making frantic efforts to prevent word of that fact from reaching Berlin.

Before midnight, Angell and Mary were airborne. While in Dorshland, von Romain and Fräulein Weissman were eating in a room three removed from that of 'Jean Murat', who had received a message from Malla and was feeling confident enough to beard even Mitzer in his den. Beneath Bruce's good spirits, however, was disquiet. Cardyce was trying to get audience with the Archduke Josef of Dorshland, while Bruce knew from one of Holt's resident agents that little Clayton was already at the palace—and that Fräulein Weissman had been there, earlier in the evening.

.   .   .   .   .

'Then what,' demanded von Romain, pacing up and down and glaring at Katerina, 'is preventing it, Fräulein? We give the offer, we are close to Dorshland, and England is far away. The man must be a fool!'

Katerina said smoothly:

'Not such a fool, Kurt. It is always the same. We offer arms, we offer strength and supplies, but we cannot offer money. Josef needs a loan of five million pounds: forty million marks.'

'*Mein Gott!* I will talk to him!'

'You would be wiser to talk with Berlin.'

'Berlin, what will they say?' von Romain snarled. 'Get the results, get them, or . . . ! Katerina!' He tried to take her hands, but she withdrew quickly. 'Katerina—please! You can do what you will with Berlin. I—I am out of favour; I have failed. If this is true, if Josef wants the money, you must tell them.'

'I am with you to help and advise,' Katerina said coldly. 'Not to act for you.'

'Yes, yes, I know! But . . .'

'And the Archduke tells me,' she added, 'that he is to see Cardyce tomorrow, at ten o'clock. Cardyce will be able to make the loan, Kurt. I should hurry, if I were you.'

The German was glaring at her, keeping back his anger with an effort. He knew how much she was trusted in Berlin: he was afraid of her, and at the same time he hated her. Her suavity, her cold beauty, her contempt for failure, were all typical of present-day Berlin. Von Romain was used to giving orders and having them obeyed: he cursed the day she had been sent to work with him.

But without her, he would not have had this forewarning of what was in the tortuous mind of the Archduke. Josef was a supreme monarch in Dorshland; as supreme as Mitzer in the larger country. Ostensibly, he had been friendly with Berlin; but von Romain knew what was happening. The commencement of the journey had been secret, but the announcements in the Enkraine and in Luthia of the treaties with Great Britain had brought the searchlights of publicity. Secret agents were following him and Cardyce, swarming like bees.

They had one object.

To judge the way the balance would fall, and rush their own small countries to the winning side. It was a diplomatic war waged with a fury and a tension which had never been equalled. The death of Cardyce would no longer help von Romain: negotiations would be completed in Dorshland and started in Brennia through the Embassies: the 'secrecy' was now no more than a token gesture.

Von Romain's whole future was at stake.

And here was Katerina coolly ordering him to contact Berlin, knowing what the demand for money would mean. He was frightened, thoroughly, for the first time in his life. Rohm and Ernst and the others of the Nazi regime had been purged after basking in the sunshine of official approval: he had little doubt of his own fate.

'I shall see Josef,' he announced, coldly.

'There is no need.'

'I shall see him!' snapped von Romain. '*Mein Gott,* would that fool of a man deny the envoy of Berlin? I shall go to him.'

Katerina shrugged.

'It is for you to decide.'

'So. I do not need to be told.' He rang the bell sharply and when a waiter appeared, gave orders for Mettink to bring his car round to the entrance of the Dorsh Hotel. He went out five minutes later; inwardly fuming, outwardly cool enough. He knew that a door in the same passage opened; but he hid not see the dark-haired man who eyed him and, when he turned a corner, followed him.

Murdoch saw him get into the lift, and ran down the stairs. He reached the foyer before the German, and saw young Graham leaning against a cocktail bar—Dorshland's American-type bars were as numerous as the sausage shops of Malla—and looking bored. Murdoch nodded, and slipped out of sight as von Romain reached the foyer. Graham sauntered after the German, and Murdoch grinned to himself. Young Graham was a find.

The Mavian interlude had been restful, and he had been in Dorshland for nearly twenty-four hours, contriving eight hours' sleep. The news of Mary and Ted would have freshened him in any case, and he returned upstairs hoping that they would arrive in time to look after Clayton, whose mysterious arrival in Mavia and equally mysterious journey to Dorshland worried him.

He opened the door of his room and stepped inside—and had closed it before he saw Katerina standing there, beautiful beyond belief in silver brocade, a diamond circlet in her hair—and an automatic in her hand.

18: Face to Face

Murdoch had a fraction of a second to decide how to react. Acceptance would give him away at once, and it was just possible that she knew him only as Murat: that she did not recognise him as Morely. He stood staring, his eyes widened as though in alarm—and it was not all pretence.

Katerina said softly:

'You may come right in, M'sieu Murat.'

Was that a bluff, or did she see only the swarthy-skinned, dark-haired Murat? Murdoch prayed that she did as he slowly took a forward step. He looked at the gun and not at Katerina's face, but he had seen enough in her expression to know that she would not hesitate to kill him, if she thought it necessary. And at the end of the automatic's barrel was an ugly silencer.

'*Mademoiselle, I* . . .'

'I shall do the talking, M'sieu Murat.' She seemed to harp on the name, and he had an uncomfortable feeling that she would enjoy playing with a victim—man or woman. 'You will answer my questions, quickly. Why are you so interested in Herr Lenster?'

'Lenster?'

'I warn you, *M'sieu*—I can shoot quite straight. A little help from you, and I shall be only too happy to leave you alive, but—you understand, I hope?'

Murdoch licked his lips.

'I—I understand nothing, *Mam'selle*! I am appalled to see you with that gun . . .'

'Frightened, *M'sieu*?'

'I—confess I am not happy.' Murdoch forced a nervous little laugh, and blessed the fact that he had played the part of Murat so often that he could make it fit skin-tight, even to mannerisms. '*Mam'selle's* beauty is enhanced by the ugliness of her gun.'

He won a smile; slow, just showing those even, pearly teeth.

'*M'sieu* is gallant. But I am on business—and you have

not answered my question. Why are you so interested in Herr Lenster?'

Murdoch lifted his hands.

'*Mam'selle* insists, but . . .'

He saw her trigger-finger move and his lips tightened, but he kept quite still. There was a loud, sneezing sound—and he heard the bullet bite into the door behind him.

Her voice was incredibly hard.

'I am serious, Murat!'

He was beginning to believe that she knew him only as Murat, and had not seen through his disguise. He realised, suddenly, that he was in the shadows; that the light was not good enough for her to detect the lines of grease-paint which might have betrayed him.

'But, *Mam'selle*, I . . .'

'At Malla,' she told him coldly, 'you followed Herr Lenster . . .'

'It is not true!' Only as Murdoch had he followed the German at Malla. He was sweating—afraid, now, that she knew the whole truth.

'At Malla,' she said, 'you breakfasted at the Garre Hotel while I did, *M'sieu*. You were at the airfield soon after I entered the Entente Express. You were in Mavia, and now I find you here. It is no coincidence, *M'sieu*.'

Murdoch licked his lips. He had a card and he believed it might prove a useful one. The more hesitation he showed the better it would be.

'But—but, *Mam'selle*, my private business brings me . . .'

'On Herr Lenster's footsteps?'

'No, no! I—I will make an admission . . .'

'It is time. Keep 'back!' Her voice sharpened, for he had taken half a step forward. He stopped abruptly, his lips working.

'If you would put that gun away, I should feel happier, Mam'selle Weissman. It . . .'

'You know that, *M'sieu*?' Her lips twisted.

'*Nom de Dieu*, should I not! Did I not see you in Malla? Have I not suffered all manner of inconvenience to find you, to meet you . . .'

She said abruptly: 'To do *what*?'

He had jarred her.

'Is it a crime, *Mam'selle*, to follow beauty? I—I will admit that I have been as close to you as I could: I have been anxious to meet you. I did not dream that you . . .' he gulped— 'you would honour me, tonight.'

She laughed. It was a light, mirthless sound, yet she seemed amused. Whether by the game he was playing and the fact that she could see through it, or whether her sense of humour had been tickled, he did not know. Beautiful women, in his experience, rarely had a sense of humour; but they had vanity. It was his one card, that vanity.

'You almost make me believe you, *M'sieu.*'

'Is it so difficult?' he demanded, and she lowered her gun. He stepped forward again cursing the bright circle of light through which he would have to pass, to reach her. He hesitated, as though uncertain of his reception if he approached too near. 'Such beauty, *Mam'selle,* it—it overwhelmed me! Forgive me: I was constrained to follow. I—I could not help myself.'

Her blue eyes seemed puzzled.

'You were not following Herr Lenster?'

'I do not even know this man!'

'Then why did you follow him, a few minutes ago?'

'Follow him, *Mam'selle*? You mean when I go down-stairs to take my table? I remembered my cigarette-case was nearly empty, and I returned to . . .'

'*M'sieu,*' said Katerina, with a soft menace in her voice: 'I would like a cigarette.'

'*Certainement!*' Murdoch took out his case.

He was on stretch, for he could not recall whether he had two or a dozen in it. He opened it quickly, held it towards her, and as she extracted a cigarette he glanced down: there were three left. He felt the perspiration at his forehead and he took one himself, slipped a lighter from his pocket, and flicked it open.

Smoke from their cigarettes merged.

He had crossed that tell-tale light, but she did not appear to have noticed that the lines at his eyes and mouth were not genuine. Only a careful glance, by an expert, could have told that. He took a plunge.

'*Mam'selle,* our meeting has been most unusual, but none the less delightful. Can I hope that you will join me at supper? The orchestra here is superb—and I need no telling that *Mam'selle* will dance like an angel.'

Had he overplayed his hand?

The last thing he wanted was to dance with Katerina; he would never get away with it as Murat. He felt hot and cold in turn, as her blue eyes appraised him; and then she shrugged. In a flash the menace had gone from her. It was difficult to believe she had actually shot at him—would have shot to kill, as easily.

'*M'sieu* is too kind: I owe him apologies. I regret I am unable to accept . . .' Murdoch was overwhelmingly relieved —'and there is another thing I regret.'

'And that is, *Mam'selle*?'

'*M'sieu,* my work is delicate. You understand? It is important that I am not followed. It will be necessary for *M'sieu* to leave this hotel, and to undertake not to repeat his past efforts.'

Murdoch's mouth dropped open.

'But *Mam'selle!*'

'It is unfortunate.' The edge crept back to her voice: she was menacing again. 'Accidents, *M'sieu,* may happen—there are those who would consider you a—danger. I could not prevent—but I am sure I have only to request of you . . .?'

Murdoch looked hurt. 'If you insist . . .'

'So much, *M'sieu,* that I shall expect you to find other accommodation tonight.'

He stared.

'*Tonight?* But . . .'

'I can recommend several hotels where you will find the service and comfort equal to this—and I assure you, M'sieu Murat, that you will be very wise to go, quickly.'

Murdoch cleared his throat, and looked away.

'If you insist, *Mam'selle,*' he said stiffly, with every appearance of wounded pride.

'For your own good, M'sieu Murat.'

'Perhaps—in the future . . .?'

'You will forget the Fräulein Weissman.'

Murdoch lifted his hands again in a helpless gesture, bowed, and turned slowly. At the door, he paused.

'*Mam'selle,* I shall carry your image always.'

She was laughing again, the little bitch.

'M'sieu Murat, you appear to forget that this is your room—for another half hour, perhaps.' She took a silver mesh bag from a table, slipped the gun into it, and moved towards him. Murdoch could not resist murmuring:

'I had intended to open the door for you.'

Her eyes gleamed—and he was surprised when she held out her hand. He took it, bowed low and touched it with his lips.

She laughed.

'You are gallant, *M'sieu*—almost you make me regret! *Adieu,* M'sieu Murat.'

He waited until she had disappeared along the passage before he closed the door. Then leaned against it, wiping his forehead with his hand. He had broken out in a cold sweat: that had been a close thing, and he was more than ever aware of the very real danger she presented.

And it was not yet over.

She had played her hand superbly, but he did not believe she would take the chance that M'sieu Murat, even if genuinely dumbstruck by her beauty, would forget her, or fail to talk about her. In the next half hour, he was going to walk on very thin ice.

He lit a cigarette jerkily, locked the door, and went to the telephone. Mick Fuller was at the Bristol, nearly opposite the Dorsh. He telephoned him, giving quick instructions, then began to pack. He was ready in fifteen minutes, and spent ten more in a voluble effort to persuade a distressed assistant-manager he was moving to the Wistra Hotel because a friend was there, and not because he was dissatisfied with the ser-view. Part of that conversation, through an open door, was heard by Katerina as she passed along the passage.

The assistant-manager's protestations and his own account settled, Murdoch went downstairs to a waiting cab. Graham was not back yet: he hoped the youngster would do nothing which would lead to trouble. The fact that he had not previously worked for Holt was a help, but Katherina would probably be suspicious by now.

Still, after Dorshland, Brennia was the last lap. Murdoch believed he would be able to see it through—provided he slipped Katerina's envoys. He saw the taxi which started from the hotel immediately after his, and touched the gun in his pocket, but he was praying to the gods that he could escape without gun-play.

The two cabs swept through the brilliantly lighted streets. They passed the Palace, flood-lit and imposing, and caught a glimpse of Graham; walking up and down, one of a dozen other pedestrians.

So von Romain had called, even after midnight, to see the Archduke . . .

Momentarily, he forgot his own difficulties, and was startled when the cab stopped. He looked up, to see the name of the Wistra Hotel emblazoned in huge neon letters. Alert again, he watched the following cab pass on, to pull up fifty yards along the street. By the time he had paid off his own cab, two men from the other had sauntered close to the hotel entrance, and Murdoch's heart thumped when he recognised the vivid blue eyes and long lashes of the erstwhile companion of the man with a mole.

Had he come to make sure that M'sieu Murat obeyed orders? Or had he come to ensure that *M'sieu* could never relate his strange adventures at the Dorsh Hotel?

19 : Misfortune in Dorshland

It was not beyond the bounds of possibility that they would open fire on him then and there. The regime in Dorshland was capable of blinking an eye at little indiscretions of that nature, for the sake of general peace. Dorshland, particularly under Josef, was the most sublime mixture of contradictions conceivable. Its people were seventy per cent German blood, Prussian variety, and yet the man in the street had a hatred for his blood-brother over the border comparable only with that blood-brother's hatred for him. The people had the Prussian habit of refusing to be led, but raising little objection to being pushed, hard.

The Archdule Josef was an adept at pushing in the right direction. He knew exactly when to squeeze on taxes, would drain his people so nearly dry that the rumble of revolution sounded heavy in his ears, and then would relax the tithes so completely that there would be a sudden reversal of feeling. And while minor officials suffered—often with their lives —Josef remained high and dry, and the state-controlled newspapers rang with his praises.

Following the same two-way system, he allowed the extremists both to right and left a comparatively loose rein. The centre *bloc*, and far the most powerful, was solid for him most of the time, and by allowing the Nazi and Communist parties to shout, occasionally brawl, and once in a way perpetrate a shooting outrage, he presented them with a safety valve.

Murdoch knew all that.

He knew that if either of the two men who had followed him from the Dorsh opened fire, the chances were that they would get away and his death be hushed up. Dorshland was the home of secrets.

His scalp was tingling as the pair hesitated outside the hotel. His hands were stiff when he pushed against the panel which sent the door revolving, and he slipped aside, out of the line of a shot, so quickly that he stumbled.

No shot came.

Perspiring, he approached the desk. He had already booked two adjacent rooms, and he had chosen the Wistra instinctively, because it was there that Mary and Angell would go. But as the place might now be under observation, he was prepared to send one of the resident men to the station to warn them off. Before that, however, he wanted to be sure of Katerina's next step.

Is she had given instructions for murder, probably he would have been attacked by now, and he felt more satisfied that as Murat he had managed to deceive her. He spent ten minutes at the dressing-table of his new bedroom, taking off the imperial, removing the mascara from his eyes and lashes. That done, he slipped on a loose, raglan mackintosh and a Tyrol hat, complete with feather, changed his shoes to large, yellow monstrosities of the type affected by so many German tourists, and taking advantage of its three entrances, left the hotel—the automatic snug against his hip.

No one appeared to be watching the entrance he used. Nor was the man with the long eyelashes, or his companion, at the main entrance. The third, which was used only occasionally and led to a small car-park for residents, was murky and ill-lit. Murdoch reached one end of the alley leading to it, and in the gloom ahead, he saw a figure move.

He strained his eyes: two men were walking towards the entrance.

Above the doorway itself, a dim light shone. The men reached it and slipped through, but not before he had recognised the shorter of them.

He needed no telling what was happening. Orders had, after all, been given to have M'sieu Murat put in a place of safety—but to do it quietly. They would slip into his room, and when they found him missing, would wait for his return. He had never liked Katerina, even if he had at moments been awed by that breathless loveliness of hers. Now, he felt a resounding hatred. But his mind was working very fast.

He was worried by the possibility that a chambermaid would go to prepare his bed and meet the trouble intended for him. He hurried to the foyer, where he startled the reception clerk, for he used Murat's voice, while appearing a different man. Murdoch slipped a hundred-mark note across the counter, for in no country—except, perhaps, Italy—does money have such magical effect as in Dorshland.

'Can you arrange that no one goes into my room, M'sieu?'

'But yes, of course. But . . .'

'No one,' said Murdoch firmly. 'When I need service, I shall call for it. You will give those instructions?'

'Certainement—it is done, M'sieu!'

'Thanks,' said Murdoch.

He hurried from the Wistra to a typically Dorshland tele-phone-booth, with padded leather seat, ashtray, and leg room. He sat down quickly and called the number of the Hon. Fredrick Cunningham, known in Dorshland as the Baron von Lurath, a German who had quarrelled with the Nazi regime in Germany.

Cunningham, in Holt's opinion, was the best resident agent he had. In a measure, this was due to the fact that he was re-markably *au fait* with most of the Archduke's household arrangements, and was by way of being an acquaintance of Josef. Cunningham probably knew more about the tortuous mind of Dorshland's ruler than any man living, save Josef's own *aides*.

Murdoch mentioned a Pink 'Un, Cunningham replied in kind, but retained the guttural, hectoring voice of the Baron. Speaking in English, Murdoch said:

'I want a couple of phials of tear-gas, old man. Can do?'

'This,' said Cunningham, 'is not a shop. I can probably get them for you in the morning.'

'I want them in twenty minutes.'

'My dear man . . . !'

'Ten,' said Bruce, 'would be better.'

Cunningham hesitated.

'I might do it in half an hour . . .'

'Bring it to a Tyrol tourist near the telephone-booth op-posite the Wistra, will you? We can talk then.'

'Well,' said Cunningham, 'I can't promise, mind you, but I'll try.'

In twenty-five minutes, a taxi pulled up near the kiosk and the stocky, bullet-headed Cunningham, in evening dress, walked sharply towards the gentleman with the Tyrolean hat who was coming from the opposite direction. Murdoch turned a convenient corner, and Cunningham followed. In the shadows of the side-street, he smiled.

'What's this for, Murdoch? That get-up's good, by the way—I'd never have recognised you.'

'I hope you won't be the only one,' said Bruce, grimly. 'Have you managed the miracle?'

'Yes—we've got a man in the Military Laboratory here,

and he does some work at his flat. Thanks be. But what's it for?'

'The discomfiture of a lovely lady.' Briefly, Bruce explained. 'There's another job I want you to do, Freddie. Mary and Ted may arrive any time—if a car or cab deposits them at the Wistra before I show up again, head them off, will you? They'd better go to the Bristol, for safety's sake—tell 'em to keep right away from the Dorsh. All right?'

'I'll see to it. But look here, Bruce, you ought to leave this job to me—you mustn't take chances. The Pink 'Un gave me an idea of what you're after, and . . .'

'This isn't a risk.' Murdoch was by no means sure that he was right. 'Have you seen Joey, lately?'

'Not for a week. He's busy with affairs of state and has no time for the tables—or the lovelies. One of his periodic fits of energy, and I don't need telling what it's about.'

'H'mm. Has he any weak link for Cardyce to work on?'

'The usual one. He's short of money.'

'So?' said Murdoch, thoughtfully. 'That might be a help. Damn all these tin-pot states with their tuppenny Princes— this trip's the nearest thing to farce I've met.' They were walking back to the main street. 'Is there any news from the Enkraine?'

'The last I heard—about midday—things were quiet. I was talking to Wright: he thinks they'll go whichever way we go here.'

'I like that "we"!' remarked Bruce. They were near the brightly-lit main street, now. 'I'll go ahead, old man. Don't alarm Mary: tell her I'll be at the Bristol some time in the morning. And if . . .' few people would have suspected that he was preparing the ground in case he failed to return—'I'm delayed, here are two other jobs for you. A youngster named Graham, at the Dorsh, is following v. R. Replace him with a resident, and tell him to contact with Fuller, who's at the Bristol. And tell Mick to tag Clayton . . .'

'Clayton?'

'Mick'll know. Tell Angell to put on some side-whiskers and transfer his attentions to the Fräulein Weissman. That's the lot, I think.'

'No, it isn't,' said Cunningham, dryly. 'You've forgotten to say where you'd like to be buried.'

Murdoch grinned.

'Better ask the Pink 'Un! So long, Freddie—and thanks. Look me up next time you're in London.'

He slipped through the shadows, wondering if his precautions were necessary—whether Katerina's men would, after all, be in his room. He went up by the stairs, and his heart was beating fast when he reached the door.

He hesitated for a moment, then tapped the door.

In his left hand were the two small phials of what would be tear-gas when the glass was broken. He knocked again, and this time heard a slight movement.

Deliberately, he stamped away.

He reached the lift, an automatic one, and pressed the bell. When it came up, he sent it down again empty, to satisfy the waiting men that whoever had wanted to see Murat had gone away. Softly, he approached his room again and slipped the key into the lock.

Again, he heard a slight movement inside.

Opening the door three or four inches, he tossed the first phial into the room. As he snapped the door shut, he heard the glass smash—and this time, the movement was as audible as the guttural exclamations. He had locked the door in a flash and darted along to the second room. From the door, he heard the sound of hurried footsteps. Opening it, he saw the short man, over by the communicating doorway.

In one movement, he leapt across the room and sent his man flying into the next. The second phial followed him, and Murdoch pulled the door to. Already, the gas was biting at his nose and eyes, and holding his breath, he hurried to the window and flung it up. The commotion in the next room lasted only a few seconds.

From his case he took a respirator—blessing Mary, who had first suggested that all agents be equipped with one—and slipped it on, together with a pair of rubber gloves. Then, automatic in hand, he opened the communicating door.

He did not need the gun.

Both men were on the floor, gasping and rolling in pain.

Murdoch had twice before passed through tear-gas, and he knew the shattering effect of a severe dose; neither of the men would be serviceable for several hours. He flung open the windows, went back for cord from his case, and trussed the pair effectively. Finished, he grinned down. Tears were streaming from their eyes already red-rimmed and puffy.

'Most satisfactory!' he asserted, with justifiable pride.

He had originally taken the two rooms in the hope that Mary or Ted would arrive, and he could talk with them easily; but he found another use for the spare. Dragging the helpless pair into the smaller room, he put them on the two single beds, tied them to the mattresses, then bolted the passage door. A few minutes later, in the larger room, he took off the respirator. His own eyes were red-rimmed, now, and his nose was tickling. A boric-acid solution helped, and he set to work to clean the black dye from his hair, eyebrows and lashes.

As he finished, he beamed at the mirror.

'Mr. Murdoch, I believe!'

Mr. Murdoch beamed back—then proceeded to disappear again.

In his repertoire—as in all of Holt's agents—were three disguises, for it was the opinion of Samuel Augustine Webber, the Department's make-up expert, that every face fitted into one of the five prevalent types, and that every type had its normal variation and three alternatives. Webber had concentrated on training Holt's agents to adopt those disguises which would alter the whole bone-construction appearance while using it as a satisfactory background. Murdoch had been plunged head-first into the game with his first job for Holt, but since then he had spent three months with Webber and learned not only the most effective disguises, but the quickest way of adopting them.

It was Webber's dictum that no man could sit beneath a powerful light, face-to-face with anyone who knew him well, and get away with a disguise. But he could get away with it from anyone who was little more than an acquaintance. Von Romain, Katerina and the others came into the latter category, and Murdoch felt cheered by the success of his effort with Katerina.

He dismissed the possibility that she had recognised him. Her plan to 'look after' the lovesick M'sieu Murat was an indication of her complete heartlessness. Murdoch hoped that a reckoning would come, one day. Not for him: when this business was over, with luck, he would never see Katerina again.

Working quickly but thoroughly, bleaching his skin with a strong peroxide solution and lightening his hair from its natural corn-colour to the flaxen fairness of the typical Swede, he pondered over Roland Clayton.

He had practically forgotten the armament king, since reporting to Holt at Croydon. He had been so surprised to see him dining with Katerina at Mavia that he had almost given himself away.

Just what was the man up to?

The admiration he had felt for him was now swallowed up in a suspicion that concentrated his earlier, instinctive dislike. He would as soon trust Clayton as he would Katerina.

And now Clayton was in Dorshland—and had a meeting with the Archduke arranged for the next day.

Could he be helping von Romain? Or was his trip independent of the German's? Was it concerned with the Hawsman Bomber? Had von Romain arranged for the credit in New York—and was Clayton taking advantage of the meeting thrust upon him to make more capital out of the new plane?

It was an added complication, and he had already had more than enough on his hands with Katerina. Von Romain was no longer the central figure: he was concentrating on his negotiations. Katerina's job, clearly, was to see that he was protected—and that Cardyce was, where possible, delayed.

Cardyce was at the Dorsh with Anderson, who had replaced Worthing at Malle, and Murdoch had talked with him earlier in the evening. He knew that for Cardyce, zero hour was ten o'clock next day. Negotiations with Josef were likely to be difficult, but Cardyce had a mind at least as tortuous as the Archduke's.

His thoughts raced on as he worked. Gradually the mirror

reflected the harsh, clean-shaven face of a true Nordic type. With electric clippers, he cropped the hair at the sides and back of his head—the latter a task to tax a contortionist—leaving the top hair long and swept back from his forehead. And now Gustav Morenson, of Copenhagen—he had the necessary passport—peered at him from the glass.

Satisfied, he telephoned the desk, announced that he expected a visitor, Herr Morenson, who would take the spare room next his own. The clerk, remembering the hundred marks, assured Herr Morenson's proxy of the best possible service.

From the moment that he had tossed the first phial into the room, just an hour had passed. He had not dared to go out earlier to see Cunningham, for Murat's disappearance had been of vital urgency. As he packed away the paraphernalia of make-up, he saw that the two prisoners were conscious, bleary-eyed, and coughing.

They stared up at him; one in fear, the other with a defiance Murdoch admired.

He did not waste time talking, but dosed them both with chloroform, ensuring that they would be out for at least an hour. Then he hurried downstairs, chose the third exit, and found Cunningham propping up the bar of a small restaurant across the road. It was turned one o'clock, but the traffic was thicker than ever: many of the shows, Murdoch knew, would only have been started half an hour. A party of youngsters at one end of the bar were already half-drunk, and their gaiety appeared infectious, for Murdoch approached Baron von Lurath and nearly fell on his neck.

His stilted German, with just the right accent, went over well. Cunningham accepted a drink, but clearly believed that the newcomer was drunk. The bar-keeper's preoccupation with a girl who had climbed to the counter and, skirts up to her waist, was entertaining her companions with an impromptu belly-dance, gave Murdoch his chance. When he used his normal voice, Cunningham started.

'Good God, man, it's a miracle!'

Bruce grinned. 'We'd better go for a walk.'

'It worked?'

'Hundred per cent, thanks to your laboratory friend.' They went out, chattering in German, and strolling up and down so as to keep the entrance of the Wistra in sight, ran through the preparations.

'So you,' said Cunningham, finally, 'are going to meet the Weissman woman again. God, but it's dangerous, old man; are you sure sending someone else wouldn't be wiser?'

'I daren't risk it. The connection between her, Clayton and von Romain is too damned queer. I'll be all right—and we're so near the end of the run, now, that I can afford to think of something other than Cardyce's job. I wish I could be sure how he'll get on with Joey, but we'll have to wait. Meantime, if you'll go over to the Dorsh and get word from Graham, I'll wait here for Mary and the others.'

'Take things easy,' warned Cunningham.

'That's how they come!' retorted Bruce.

He felt tired, and wished Mary would arrive quickly; five hours' rest now would make a lot of difference. He ran through his arrangements. Everything was covered, as well as it could be—Katerina, for the moment, was without a good tail. One of Cunningham's assistants would be reporting on her, but Murdoch knew that no one not of the top flight could hope to match wits with her.

Mick was doing his best to watch Clayton, but dared not get within sight of Katerina. Nor was he an adept at following Samuel Augustine Webber's teachings, and that was a drawback. Angell and Mary would be able to get busy in different guises, and he was depending on their arrival before the move from Dorshland.

In just half an hour, Cunningham returned to report.

Graham was back at the Dorsh. Von Romain had left the Palace an hour and a half after going there, and appeared to be in a foul temper. Murdoch's eyes gleamed.

'A flea in his ear, perhaps?'

'Probably Joey's asked for cash,' said Cunningham, 'and that's never popular with Berlin. Von Romain is going to be dispensed with, after this. I can see it coming—so, I suspect, can he. Well, now. Cardyce is still in his room: he's all right. And Clayton seems to have gone to bed—your people are the only ones missing their beauty sleep! Let me stay for Mary and you get up to your room. You'll need what sleep you can get.'

'Yes . . . Room 57, then, and they're to come up as soon as they arrive. The only other thing is young Graham; can you arrange for a man to relieve him now?'

'Yes, I'll do that.'

'Good,' said Bruce. And five minutes later he was being shown up to M'sieu Murat's room by an attentive footman.

His prisoners were still unconscious. He found their pulses strong enough and supplemented the first dose of chloroform with a second, then gagged them securely. There must be no disturbance from them before he left. He smiled as he pictured Katerina, waiting impatiently for assurance of Murat's demise—then became savagely angry at his abtuseness. Katerina would not only expect word from the prisoners, but when she failed to get it, would certainly send to investigate!

How many more men could she call on?

Berlin would have its resident agents as well as London, and in all likelihood she would be as well-supplied as he was. He cursed his carelessness and was about to go out again to Cunningham, when he saw the handle of his door turning.

For a moment, he felt a rush of fear, and his hand shot to his pocket. Then the door opened—and Mary peered in, intent on making no noise.

Not until Ted Angell made a melancholy remark on the perils of young love, did they separate. Mary's cheeks were flushed, her eyes shining; and as Murdoch took his hand, Angell's grip was unusually strong. As he gazed at them both, Murdoch felt a deep satisfaction with their efforts, a confidence temporarily undismayed by the difficulties of dealing with the Archduke.

At which moment Josef and Roland Clayton were deep in conversation.

.   .   .   .

Among the few people who had seen Mary and Ted arrive at the Dorsh was a short, well-dressed Jew, with large, expressive eyes. A man who appeared to find humour in everything. Whether reading a magazine, or examining the empty chairs, or looking at the sleepy-eyed night commissionaire, he seemed amused. Certainly there was nothing about him to suggest a member of an oppressed race.

The only time he stopped smiling was when Katerina walked through the foyer.

He looked hard at her.

If she saw him, she gave no sign of it.

He shrugged lightly, as if resigned to rebuffs from that beauty, and sat on. He avoided the eyes of Ted and Mary, and it was doubtful whether they saw him.

They had been in the hotel for perhaps an hour when the swing-doors were pushed open and a little man came in. His face, curiously lop-sided, was expressionless; yet his rigid features looked sour. While if one peered carefully into his eyes, it was possible to imagine fear . . .

He went to the bar, visible from the foyer, and ordered a Pilsener. After a pause of perhaps five minutes the smiling Jew stood up, went to the bar, and also ordered a Pilsener.

The little man glanced up, then looked away.

The Jew took his drink and drank in it one.

As he ordered a second, the other's eyes fastened on his, and it seemed as if some message passed between them. The Jew, reaching for his second glass, slipped from his tall bar-stool.

The Pilsener shot over the other's shoulder.

It was skilfully managed, for scarcely a spot touched the other's immaculate grey suit. But the Jew was full of apologies, and insisted on fraternising. They went to a small corner-table and conversed, loudly at first and then more sedately. There was no one present to overhear them.

'Well,' said the man with the lop-sided face, 'what is your news, Kelorin?'

'I fear, very little.'

'So. It is bad.' And now there was no doubt that the small man who had once talked with Alsec was afraid. 'I have tried—how I have tried! No man could have done more. Yet someone learned of Alsec's part—he was prevented from carrying out the orders I gave him. But why should I be punished for another's failure?'

'There are strange times. But your own good work will surely be reported. Why are you here?'

'To watch—there will perhaps be an opportunity of acting, and thus averting the risk of further danger.'

'You have my very best wishes. But I am reluctant to leave you so dismayed, my friemd. Is there nothing I can do?'

'Nothing. Unless . . .' The little man eyed him slyly, then looked away abruptly and repeated: 'Nothing! We shall not talk of it. Tell me—you are a Jew?'

There was a humorous quirk at the other's lips.

'I am.'

'Why should they employ you?'

Kelorin shrugged.

'Perhaps because I am less likely to be suspected.'

'Yes . . . It is false, all of this—false from beginning to end! They ill-treat your race, yet they employ you. And you take their money—money stolen from your own people.'

'You exaggerate,' said Kelorin, softly, and for once the humour had gone from his eyes. 'These things must be done, and we have the opportunity. And the pay—well, it is good.'

The lop-sided face was a dusky red.

'Pay! What use is money, in prison?'

'You are pessimistic, my friend. Dachau is not for you or me. At least, I shall be surprised if it should prove so.' Again, there was that amused gleam in his eyes.

'We shall see. Well—I must go.'

'With all my good wishes,' said Kelorin. And as the other man disappeared, the Jew's eyes were set very hard, and there was no hint of amusement in his expression.

Meanwhile, the Archduke Josef and Clayton talked, and Murdoch made plans with greater confidence than he had felt for some time.

20 : Negotiations With Josef

Solving the problem of Katerina's reactions to the non-appearance of her man was simple, with Ted Angell's arrival. He and Mary had rooms on the third floor. Bruce shared Angell's, and if anyone visited the suite of M'sieu Murat, all they would discover would be the two unhappy gas victims, and a garbled story from the clerk of 'Herr Morenson', who proposed to keep out of sight as much as possible. Katerina's suspicions of Murat might be increased, but she would merely believe that he had tricked her assassins and made himself scarce.

With one of Cunningham's men stationed outside, to warn him of her arrival—in the unlikely event of her coming—Bruce felt satisfied. He heard Mary's story, and was appalled. But Percy was likely to be out of hospital in a week, and Mary had given him instructions to get back to England.

'Good work,' Bruce approved, when she had finished. 'Well, my story can wait. How have you folk done for sleep?'

'Just about made up,' said Mary, and her clear eyes were confirmation of that.

'Good. I'm going to get to bed—properly, in pyjamas for the first time in a week! You two can adopt Alternative Character Number One before turning in—we'll all be busy in the morning. Do you think you were followed?'

'I'm sure we weren't,' said Angell.

'Fine,' Bruce yawned, and as the other two tried not to and failed, he went into Ted's room and in five minutes was asleep.

They did not call him until nine o'clock, and their report was negative. Their appearances were not, for Mary looked the Parisienne to perfection, and Ted Angell looked and sounded like the American tourist prepared to scoff at everything which had not come out of God's Own Country.

It was ten o'clock as Bruce finished breakfast—at which moment Cardyce was taken, with some ceremony, into the Audience Chamber at the Archduke's Palace . . .

. . . . . .

Josef was all smiles, all affability, and Cardyce knew he must be planning a particularly astute trick. Against him, he wondered, or against von Romain? Josef derived great pleasure from his cunning manœuvres. Cardyce prepared for a difficult interview.

The Archduke, at fifty-seven, looked nearer seventy. His face was lined and pock-marked, and the pouched eyes, thin lips over too-perfect dentures, balding head and ultra-Roman nose made him a living caricature. He spoke excellent English, thanks to an Eton and Balliol education, and he assured Cardyce that the two armed guards at the door could not understand what they were saying. He offered whisky, claret and sherry, and Cardyce, knowing the man's habits, settled for a weak whisky-and-soda. Josef's was not so weak.

Cardyce talked; quickly, precisely, and to the point. The Archduke listened courteously, his smile rarely missing, and with every moment Cardyce was more convinced that the man had something up his sleeve. Was Josèf going to tell him that he had already accepted Berlin's offer?

He finished at last, and Joseph slumped back in his chair. 'Well,' he conceded, thoughtfully. 'It is attractive, Mr. Cardyce. And of course, I have always desired to be at one with Great Britain. Believe me, I take no heed of the rumours. The products of Balliol—could they be unfit to govern the Empire?' He laughed, and Cardyce stirred uncomfortably. But he had received word from Murdoch that von Romain had, so far, received no satisfaction.

'We have never been stronger,' he pointed out. It was at least a relief not to have to mince words.

'Prepared, do you think, for a struggle, Mr. Cardyce?'

'Assuredly. And confident of its outcome.'

'Supposing . . .' Josef leaned forward, jabbing a long Russian cigarette towards Cardyce—'I found that my advisers could not recommend the acceptance of this very generous offer, Mr. Cardyce. Would you still be confident?'

'It would—make a difference.'

'Ah!' Josef's smile widened.

'To you,' Cardyce added, suavely. 'With Dorshland's help, Berlin *might* resort to invasion. It would be unfortunate, for much of the early fighting would take place here. Without your help, they will certainly take the wiser course, and be satisfied with what they can get through negotiation.'

'So.' Josef relaxed a little. 'Not much, I assume?'

'Very little,' Cardyce agreed. 'And then again, Your Excellency—you would be on the losing side . . .'

'Yes, yes—naturally, you think this.'

'I know it,' said Cardyce. 'Tell me, Excellency—how much do you believe of the stories of the English lag in armaments?'

'I know the English habit of understatement, Mr. Cardyce.'

'I am gratified to hear it.' Cardyce quoted some figures. Josef's relaxation was complete; he slipped in an occasional question, sometimes made a pungent comment, but seemed impressed. Cardyce warmed to his subject. British armaments for Dorshland, British credits, a British loan. He saw Josef's eyes narrow at the 'loan'; was prepared for his objection.

'Our internal finances, Mr. Cardyce, are not strong. You do not need telling that. To add five million pounds to the National Debt . . .!' The Archduke shrugged eloquently. 'You know that I am virtually sitting on a live bomb. On the right, I have the Nazi element just waiting to touch it off; on the left, the small but very strong Social-Communist party. At a time such as this, an additional call on the slender pockets of my people . . .' he shook his head. 'I will be frank with you, Mr. Cardyce. I have been offered a contribution from—er—friends of ours, of exactly the sum you mention. A nominal payment for goods, but—you understand?'

Cardyce said that he did. He also knew that there was no such offer, or Josef would have doubled the figure—without mentioning why. He said firmly:

'It could only be negotiated on a long-term loan, Your Excellency. But the repayments could be made extremely suitable—let us say spread over twenty years, to commence in ten years' time.'

Josef's eyes narrowed.

'That is an inducement, certainly. But against the other arrangement . . .'

Cardyce came into the open.

'There could also l᠊᠊᠊ an additional accommodation, Your Excellency. You will forgive me if I speak plainly?'

'I shall appreciate it, Mr. Cardyce.'

'On the signing of this agreement, then, within two hours —a draft for one million pounds on a London Bank, in whatever name you choose.' Cardyce waited, inwardly tense, wondering if what little was left of Josef's pride would rise in his gorge. The Archduke played with a cigarette-box, and there was silence for some moments. Then he murmured:

'A loan, Mr. Cardyce?'

'A payment for services,' said Cardyce, bluntly.

'But my dear sir—that is virtually bribery!'

'I am speaking plainly, Excellency.'

'You understand that I shall have to submit your second offer to my Ministers, together with the other?'

'I believe Your Excellency can persuade them to take the wiser course without that.'

'Yes, perhaps. . . . The welfare of our country is vastly important to us all, small though it is in size.'

'It is,' said Cardyce, pointedly, 'nearly as large as Great Britain, and its natural resources have not yet been exploited. Concessions to my Government will ensure the greatest value—and this agreement will virtually exclude the possibility of war, for some years to come.'

'Yes, yes . . .' Josef seemed lost in thought. Then: 'Where are you staying, Mr. Cardyce?'

'At the Dorsh.'

'In two hours, I shall send word to you.' The Archduke began to smile again. 'Another drink, Mr. Cardyce? No? Perhaps you are wise. But I am too old to change my habits.' He nodded, the two men at the door opened it, and Cardyce backed out of the royal presence. And as he travelled the stately corridors, he reflected bitterly that diplomacy had gone back to the Middle Ages. Then derived a brief, ironic amusement at the thought of what Cabinet reaction would be, to a verbatim report of that conversation.

Not that they would ever hear it.

Downing Street would be satisfied with Josef's signature,

for the Archduke retained one unexpected trait. When he made an agreement, he kept it.

But could von Romain offer more?

.   .   .   .   .

'It is unfortunate, my dear von Romain,' Josef was saying in excellent German, 'but circumstances drive me too speak plainly. The terms are not, surely, difficult?'

'But Excellency! Only yesterday, you advised me . . .'

'The speed of developments today,' said Josef, with a touch of hauteur, 'are inspired by the quickly changing policies of the greater Powers. That, you must surely understand.'

Von Romain choked.

'Of course, Excellency. And I am sure that, in twenty-four hours . . .'

'In one,' said Josef, smiling very widely.

'But Excellency, it is impossible! With the greatest difficulty, I have persuaded my principals to agree to a long-term loan of three million pounds, and . . .'

Josef pushed back his chair and rose.

His figure, imposing at any time, was set off to real advantage now by the full uniform of Field-Marshal of the Dorshland Army decorated with an impressive array of medals; and in this moment, there was regality in his mien.

Von Romain, the 'reward' for failure staring him in the face, had failed to see the glitter in the Archduke's eyes at that begrudged assent.

'Is that,' he roared, 'the value that your principals set on my country, Herr von Romain? You may go—it is finished!'

'But Excellency . . .!'

'It is finished!' bellowed the Archduke Josef.

.   .   .   .   .

'My dear, you are the loveliest woman of my acquaintance—but then, I have told you that so often that you must surely

believe me.' The Archduke Josef looked positively debon-
air as he smiled into Katerina's icy eyes. 'I have watched with
amusement your *affaires* in Moscow, Berlin, Paris and even
London. You have my warmest admiration, but—international politics are not woman's work.'

Katerina said:

'You promised me!'

'And it grieves me to break a promise to you, my dear.
But Dorshland is always on the winning side. If your friends
in Berlin had concerned themselves only with internal
affairs and the improvement of their trade, it is possible that
in another ten years they might be prepared to enter armed
conflict with some chance of winning. At the moment, I would
not give them one chance in a hundred. But what do we two
want with such talk? Stay in Dorshland, my dear, and . . .'

Katerina's eyes blazed.

'To think I let you . . .'

'To think,' Josef forestalled her, 'that you believed I could
be so easily misguided. You may take back what message you
like to your friends, my dear. But remind them that the
assassination of so close a friend of Great Britain would be
an unforunate thing. I am sure you appreciate that.'

Katerina's breast was heaving.

'I think you will regret this decision!'

'You are so much more delightful when you forget Berlin,
my dear. The boudoir is so much more fitting—you are leaving, Katerina?'

She swept from the room and as the doors closed behind
her, the Archduke Josef thoughtfully resumed his seat. He did
not underestimate the danger from Katerina's principals,
even now. But he was fully satisfied with the terms of the
British offer. He believed the frontiers of his State would be
inviolate for years to come and was already wondering if it
would be possible to persuade Whitehall to send men as well
as armaments.

He lifted the telephone and gave instructions to his Chief
Secretary. Ten minutes later, three cars—the first and third
carrying ostentatiously armed guards and the other Dorshland's ageing Chancellor—drew up outside the Dorsh Hotel.

Into the middle car stepped the Hon. Gerald Cardyce. Along the pavements, people lined up as if by magic; rumour of the coming treaty was already spreading. Flags were being run up or flown from windows, and the shouting grew to a roar of approval, as the royal car passed along the streets on its way to the Palace.

Von Romain and Katerina saw it: von Romain's face haggard, the woman's expressionless. Graham and Fuller were in the crowd, and Cuuningham and several of his men were helping to swell the roar. Mary saw it, with Murdoch and Angell, from the Wistra. Bruce smiled down at her:

' "Secret mission", they called it.'

Mary grimaced.

'Dangerous journey, would be more like it. You really think it's all over?'

'Bar the shouting, I hope. Brennia can't keep out, now. And even if they do, it doesn't matter much—it will simply give Mitzer an excuse to brag a bit more. I'd like to know what Katerina's thinking.'

Mary nodded slowly.

'I've never met that woman face to face—but she frightens me, Bruce.'

'You're not alone,' he told her, with forced lightness. 'But I can't see what she can do now, even with Clayton. I'm going to phone London—Holt may take us off Cardyce and let me get at friend Roland. He warrants some attention, I feel.'

'Aren't you satisfied?'

'For Cardyce, yes. Otherwise, I'm uneasy. But I shan't keep it up any longer than I can help, *Mam'selle*. Morenson is beginning to bore Murdoch.' Grinning at his own joke, he went in from the balcony.

'He's worried,' Mary said, after a pause.

'M'mm . . .' Ted Angell scowled. 'I'd like to know why.'

'We will, in time.'

On one telephone line, the Pink 'Un, in London, was agreeing fully with Murdoch that a rising in the Enkraine, at this moment, might split the new *Entente* dangerously.

And on another, Katerina, as von Romain's proxy, was agreeing fully with someone in Berlin.

21 : Desperation

General Mulke was speaking quickly.

About him, the dozen men who virtually directed the movements of Mitzer were listening: some with sympathy, several with enthusiasm, others with annoyance.

'There is,' said Mulke, 'one thing, and one thing only, to do. Brennia *must* be with us, and when that has been settled, we can begin in the Enkraine. Alsec has gone, but there are others. Dorshland, between the two states, will collapse—*Gott in Himmel*! What is the signature of that drunken fool to us? It is our one chance—if we fail now . . .'

He paused, significantly. Then as five men started to speak at once, he thumped his fat hand on his desk and roared:

'*We—must—not—fail!* Understand, all of you—the Fräulein can control Clayton. That is of importance. With Clayton, **B**rennia and the Enkraine, we can still contrive . . .'

'This talk of Clayton!' Hiddenthrop growled.

'The map!' Ignoring him, Mulke pushed through the group to a table where a vast map was spread. His thick forefinger began to move, tracing the borders of the five small countries: Dorshland and Mavia each possessed short German frontiers. Brennia and the Enkraine stretched, pincer-fashion, about them. 'A squeeze, a few days, and it is over! But if we let Brennia tie herself with Britain—*ach*! do I have to keep talking?'

'Could it,' asked one man, 'be as bloodless as Austria?'

'*Mein Gott*! What does the blood matter, if it is quick? Here is what I say. The revolution in the Enkraine—swiftly, with the help of the first and second divisions. Then the establishment of our Reich. First, before that, the dismissal of all newspapermen.'

'There are the Embassies.'

'Am I dealing with children?' Mulke bellowed. 'Here is the one chance—the last chance—for the establishment of the Reich over what is otherwise to become a pro-British *bloc*. Take it now, and we win. Neglect it, and for ten, twenty, thirty years we are stifled—the Fatherland ringed around with enemies, the way to the West, East and South blocked!'

His voice had risen to a near shout, his face was flushed, there were specks of froth at the corners of his mouth, and his porcine eyes were glittering. For ten minutes he ranted on with the Cabinet no more than half with him. Then little white-haired Blaka said mildly:

'If we allow this *bloc* against the Reich, gentlemen, we shall have to beg for help from Great Britain, the United States, and France. We shall be compelled to disarm, and . . .'

In five minutes, only two still stood out. In ten, Mulke and two others were preparing Mitzer's next speech, while the wires were humming to the Enkraine and to Brennia. And soon, von Romain was listening like a man who could not believe his ears. Win Brennia, and the other failures would be forgotten! He must win Brennia. . . .

.   .   .   .   .

The Archduke had qualities which Cardyce had not suspected, and which he liked. As the signatures were blotted, those tired eyes beamed at the Minister, and Josef murmured:

'You have, I believe, another urgent mission, Mr. Cardyce. You will return from there and we shall arrange a banquet to celebrate this. Out of my private pocket, yes?' Josef chuckled, and Cardyce's face relaxed in a smile. Dammit, the man had a sense of humour.

The streets were thick with people, British and Dorshland flags were everywhere, military and police had been rushed to clear the route. The triumphal procession was swelled this time by five other cars: Josef was, as ever, prepared for would-be assassins—his own or Cardyce's. Murdoch, his telephoning done, was watching from the balcony again with no enthusiasm.

The demonstration was not one of friendship to Great Britain—nor hostility to Germany. It was born of belief that the treaty would bring peace, and keep peace. And as the cars passed, with Cardyce sitting there unbane and unruffled as ever, he was still uneasy. Mary sensed it, but said nothing.

137

'We'd better get sorted out,' he decided, aloud, suddenly. 'I shall stick to Katerina, Mick will keep after Clayton, you and Ted will nurse v. R. and his bodyguard. We're all packed, and . . .' He paused. 'There are the brace downstairs, of course.'

'Cunny will look after them,' Ted pointed out.

'Yes, he'll be down there. Right, then. Different cabs—and strangers till we meet again. You going, Ted?'

Angell grinned.

'Get your foot off my neck. I can take a hint.'

'There isn't much time,' Bruce said, as he went. His hands tightened on Mary's arms. 'Keep yourself clear of trouble, darling—and if the spirits get low, think of Cliff Cottage.'

'I do, all the time. I . . .'

But her next words were stifled as his lips crushed hers. And then they parted; went into the milling streets outside, found cabs with difficulty, and started out.

By arrangement, Graham and Fuller met Herr Gustav Morenson some hundred yards from the Dorsh Hotel. Graham had been busy. He had learned that Katerina was going to Brennia by train, von Romain was off by air, and according to the hotel servants, Clayton appeared to be staying indefinitely at the Dorsh.

'Which means you can stay and celebrate,' said Bruce. 'Both of you. Ted will look after your Hawker, young Graham, as if it were his own. At any slightest move from Clayton, tell London as well as me—I'll be at the Brenn, barring accident. If you can't get me there, you'll find directions with the local man, Sanderson. 'Bye!'

The Brennian Express did not start until midday, and it was not yet half past eleven. He decided to walk to the station. The sight of a man carrying two heavy cases was not so remarkable as it would have been at normal times: Dorshland, having started slowly, was waking up to the fact that there was really something to celebrate. Cabs were filled with yelling people, blowing horns and whistles, bursting into noisy song. Flags and balloons were everywhere, and even, here and there, fireworks. There was hysteria in the crowd: an hysteria of relief.

Was it justified?

Bruce began to wonder whether he would make the station in time: he was sometimes able to move at a snail's pace. Then he reached a narrow turning, and saw three taxis, well down the road. He hurried to the first, and snapped at the resigned driver:

'Can you get me to the Nor Station, in ten minutes?'

'I think so, *M'sieu.*'

'A hundred marks, if you succeed.'

'I will, *M'sieu!* '

He did. But it was a nightmare journey—and even then, rumour had spread that Cardyce was leaving by train. A dense crowd was milling, shouting, roaring throughout the vast entrance-halls and spilling on to the platforms, and ambulance men were already stolidly attending dozens of casualties.

But with the cabby grimly forging a way with the aid of the two bags, Bruce reached the platform with three minutes to spare.

A white-haired inspector wanted to see his ticket.

'Can you supply one?'

'Yes, *M'sieu*—there is no hurry. The train will start late. Further along the line, the crowd has caused obstructions— they are being cleared. It is a great day, this, sir. A great day for Europe.'

'A great day,' Murdoch echoed, his own throat tight: for there were tears in the eyes of the old man. A great day for Europe, not merely for Dorshland. The habit of thinking internationally was the biggest factor for peace: it was universal and overwhelmingly strong in many quarters, these days, but. . . .

Had it awakened too late?

Walking along the train, peering into carriages nearly all well-filled, he saw Katerina. She was seated alone in an empty carriage, her cold eyes appraising the crowd. Behind Murdoch, a man shouted:

'See it is empty!'

Katerina's lips twisted. 'The carriage is engaged, *M'sieu.*'

'There is no other room!' snapped the man, and leaning past Bruce, he pulled open the door. The cabby, apparently inspired by the hundred-mark note in his pocket, jumped in, banged the cases into the rack, and half-pulled Bruce after him into the compartment.

The train jolted into motion.

Murdoch collapsed into a seat, the insistent passenger jumped in, the cabby jumped out. As he slammed the door to, Murdoch was still breathing hard from his exertions—and shattered to find himself face to face with Katerina, whom he had not wanted to meet for the next twenty-four hours, at the very least.

22 : Travelling Companions

In icily disapproving silence, Katerina opened a magazine and began to study its pages. Murdoch picked up the newspaper the cabby had thoughtfully provided, and caught a sidelong glance from the other man, a stocky little Jew with a humorous mouth. There was a note almost of appeal in the large, dark eyes, as though he wondered if the male passenger was also German and contemptuous of his race. Murdoch returned his grimace; the humorous lips curved, and the Jew applied himself to his own paper.

The first half hour passed slowly. The train dragged along a line bordered with shouting, waving people. It was unnatural, Bruce decided, for them all to make no comment on the events of the day. He lowered his paper, thanked the gods—and Samuel Augustine Webber—that with every 'variation' of character, he had a voice to fit. In uncertain French, he addressed the Jew.

'They are pleased, these Dorshlanders.'

The other jumped at the chance of conversation.

'And with good reason, M'sieu.' His French had a guttural note, but was better than Murdoch's. 'They have seen freedom, the freedom for which they have worked so many years. Ah, my friend, you do not know what it is to live under the fear of the Reich! You are from Denmark, no?'

'*M'sieu* is a good judge. I am from Copenhagen.'

'So. In your country, *M'sieu*, this lust for power is not a threat; the voice of greed and fear is not raised. In Dorshland, other countries—ah, my friend, there is fear! And this . . .' he nodded at the waving, cheering crowds—'is the relief from it. Picture the heavy feet of the Reich over these fair countries! Picture the horrors that have so narrowly been averted. I could tell . . .'

He broke off, and his droll lips tightened: there was horror in his eyes—horror, Murdoch felt, of personal memories. Katerina, her elegant legs crossed, her lovely head bent over the magazine, did not stir, but he wondered how she was enjoying this.

'*M'sieu* was saying . . . ?' he prompted politely.

'It is not a day for gloom,' said the other, cheerful again. 'But for rejoicing. There is hope, of lasting peace in this troubled world. I am a Jew—I lived in Berlin, although I was a Dorsh subject. It was eighteen months before I came out, *M'sieu*, and what I saw, what I experienced . . . But . . .' his eyes gleamed—'it is impossible to kill Jewry, *M'sieu*! When Mitzer is away from Berlin, in three short years the Jews will be there: the greatest traders, the greatest powers —powers for good, *M'sieu*. I ask you to believe that. Evil is not with the Jew, it is . . .' He glanced at Katerina. 'But enough . . .'

Out of the corner of his eye, Murdoch saw that she had lowered her magazine. Her face was expressionless, but her right foot was moving, as though with impatience. That humorous quirk curved the Jew's lips again.

'Yes, my friend—enough. You have only one paper, I see. You are welcome to anything of mine . . .' he indicated a selection of magazines by his side. 'You travel far?'

'To Brennia.'

'Then we have a long journey, *M'sieu*—there will be other time for talk.'

Again, that elegant foot moved agitatedly. Katerina, thought Bruce Murdoch, was not going to enjoy this journey; and perversely he hoped the other man would talk a lot, and mostly about Germany. But all the time his misgivings about the importance of that day persisted—and so did the fear that in his blond Morenson, Katerina might recognise either Murdoch or the dark Murat.

And there was an eight-hour journey ahead. . . .

An hour and a half after leaving the Nor Station, heavy clouds let fall the first snows of autumn. They were some five thousand feet above sea-level, and the carriage was in semi-darkness. The reading lights shed only a dull glow. Katerina put down her magazine at last and leaned back, with eyes closed. The friendly little man in the corner put his feet up on the opposite seat, switched off his light, and apparently slept.

Murdoch did not feel tired. But the ordeal of sitting opposite Katerina was getting on his nerves. The only relief was in the gloom, provided by the leaden skies, and he could not be sure that it would last.

But the train was crowded, and to leave the compartment for one already full would be to invite suspicion: his only choice was to brave it out. He was waiting for lunch to be announced: it was already overdue, and he was impatient to get where he could relax for an hour or more away from Katerina.

She appeared to be asleep, and but for the tightness of her lips, she had, in this light, an ethereal, almost an angelic, beauty. And there, of course, was Katerina's strongest weapon. Forewarned as he himself was, even he had found it hard to believe, at first sight of her, that she could truly be as black as legend painted. What chance did a stranger stand? Supposing she had tried to work on young Graham, for instance? And at the other end of the stick, Clayton. . . .

That business was getting more worrying.

Clayton had warned him against Katerina. But if the reports from Cunningham's men had been reliable, Clayton, von Romain and Katerina had dined together in von Romain's rooms, and the armaments manufacturer had spent considerable time alone with the beautiful Fräulein.

Why?

He did not believe Clayton had been overwhelmed by her beauty: he was not an impressionable man, and his one interest was money. Was he—could he be—driving a bargain with Berlin, through Katerina?

It would be too ironic if, in trying to stop the German, he had helped to start an intrigue that would do inestimable harm to the *bloc* which Cardyce was creating. But then, Clayton had interviewed Josef twice—and Josef had come out strongly for the *bloc*.

Murdoch stirred uneasily. A single false step, now, might lead him into real trouble; could easily make it impossible for him to watch Katerina closely.

He tried to read one of the Jew's magazines, but it was heavy going in German, which he could speak fluently but read with difficulty. He frowned suddenly. Why did the Jew, with his confessed hatred of the German regime, choose German magazines for his journey?

He glanced at the other periodicals.

There were seven altogether, one in French, two in Dorsh, four in German. Of course, the man had lived for years in Berlin. It was natural that he should have the magazines to which he had, in all likelihood, subscribed for years. Moreover, the Dorsh bookstall market was flooded with German and French periodicals: native products were few and far between, and catered mostly for the cheaper markets. He discarded the German for the French, and was in the middle of a satirical political sketch when the attendant at last came bustling along the corridor, thrust open the compartment door, and barked:

'Lonch—first lonch, ready now!'

The Jew continued to sleep. Katerina opened her eyes, and from her momentary confusion Murdoch knew that she really had been sleeping.

'Will *Madame* need a ticket?'

Unexpectedly, she flashed a smile, and he felt his heart thumping, in his fear that she might actually accept what was no more than a normal courtesy—the omission of which could have been dangerous.

'Thank you, no—I shall take the second lunch.'

Murdoch inclined his head stiffly, and smiled. Among the finishing touches to the appearance of Herr Morenson were two teeth which appeared to be gold-capped, and he could safely smile.

143

The lunch was good, and he was cheered by the fact that Katerina would be following him to the dining-car. That cut at least two hours out of his ordeal. They were more than a third of the way, now, and after the second lunch there would be no more than three hours on the train.

When he returned to the carriage both Katerina and the man were missing, but before he finished lighting a cigarette the Jew looked in.

'How is the food, *M'sieu*—edible?'

'Excellent.'

'Good. Make yourself free, please, with anything of mine you might find of interest.' He smiled, turned, then looked back. '*Mademoiselle*—she does not appear to appreciate me, *M'sieu*.'

Murdoch looked embarrassed.

'She was, I think, annoyed at our intrusion.'

'Yes, yes—she was annoyed!' The hazel eyes sparkled. 'I see from the labels of her cases that she is Fräulein Weissman, of Berlin, and that would explain much. A pity that one of such beauty should be possessed by the hatred of her race. *M'sieu* finds her pleasant company?'

'I have hardly exchanged a word with her.'

'I shall make a point of delaying my return—you will find that she unfreezes, until I come again!' He laughed. 'That is life, *M'sieu*. But I am praying that today will have made a big change. Until later, then.'

Murdoch scowled when he had gone.

In the dining-car, much of the conversation had been along the same lines—a conviction that things had altered for the better. He was aghast to discover that the race between Cardyce and von Romain appeared general knowledge. The actual announcements of the treaties, Murdoch knew, had not carried Cardyce's name.

Was the new confidence justified, or was Europe going to wake up to a new wave of horror? Would Berlin take these diplomatic defeats lying down, or. . . .

He heard sharp footsteps along the corridor. A moment later Katerina appeared. He opened the door for her, wondering uncomfortably whether the Jew had been right and she

144

would unthaw. Knowing Katerina he doubted it, and the last thing he wanted was conversation with her.

She had hardly settled when the train began to slow down, and through the now heavily-falling snow Murdoch saw the dim outlines of small buildings. There were no platforms at the stations *en route*, and he knew that they had reached the frontier; that the buildings were the Customs huts. It meant delay, and any kind of delay was generally the signal for passengers to complain—and in complaining, break the ice and begin a talking acquaintance for the remainder of the journey.

He glanced at Katerina, a half-smile on his lips. She was taking her passport from her bag, and returned his smile brilliantly.

'They are always quick on this frontier.'

'That is good.'

'*M'sieu* will forgive me for my ungraciousness.'

Murdoch stopped himself from a flowery rejoinder that would have come easily from Murat's lips, and said with awkward tact:

'It was understandable, *Mam'selle*.'

'You are too kind.' She smiled again, naturally, but their conversation was interrupted when the uniformed frontier guard pushed back the door. He examined Murdoch's passport first, beamed as though he too was obsessed with the new feeling of freedom, stamped it after a perfunctory question or two, and then applied himself with considerable obsequiousness to Katerina. The compliments over, he glanced at her passport—and his eyes widened.

'Fräulein Weissman, yes?'

'That is right.'

'There is a message for you, Fräulein. By telephone. I am requested to advise you that Herr Lenster has returned home, and you are to proceed as arranged. This is understood, Fräulein?'

Katerina's eyes had narrowed. Murdoch, forcing himself to look out of the window and to show no reaction, saw out of the corner of his eye that she was breathing more quickly. But she answered promptly enough:

'Thank you, yes—I understand.'

145

She took a five-mark note from her bag and the guard expressed his eternal gratitude. And thereafter, as she sat staring blankly ahead of her, Murdoch did not know whether to be elated or otherwise that von Romain was off the map and he had only Katerina to worry about.

But one unquestionable fact had emerged: Katerina was definitely high in the favours of Berlin.

23 : Brennia

Other factors impressed themselves on Murdoch's mind. The message was an urgent one, or it would not have been sent by word of mouth or over the telephone. The use of a Customs station for the transmission of that message from Berlin was a daring step which only extreme necessity would have justified. Katerina, too, who so rarely showed her real feelings, was tight-lipped; quite heedless of the travelling companion to whom she appeared willing to talk. Everything pointed to the fact that whatever 'arrangements' she had to proceed with were of vital importance. If only he could read her mind. . . .

His thoughts wandered.

Von Romain had been recalled, which was unfortunate for the Prussian. But the death of the pilot, the attempt to kill Graham, the attacks on himself and Cardyce, made sympathy for the man impossible, despite his likely fate.

He could not rid himself of a feeling that Katerina's orders were in the nature of an ultimatum—that it was essential he learn what they were. The task was no longer simply a matter of ensuring that Cardyce would arrive first. There was something bigger than a treaty at issue, now: he felt it in his bones. And he must make no mistakes. . . .

The train started off, at last.

The Jew returned, and the comic expression in his eyes at the sight of Katerina's expressionless face was a signal of admission—he had been wrong. Murdoch found himself liking the man and wondered whether it would be possible to use him to convey a message to Mary and the others when they reached Brennia. He was convinced of one thing: he must not let Katerina out of his sight. There would be no open negotiation with the Brennian Minister of State—the equivalent of Prime Minister—except through Embassy officials. Katerina's work would be under the surface.

Unless there was someone in Brennia whom she knew as well as she did Debonnet. . . .

It was quite dark when they left the frontier, and the snow was still falling heavily. When at last, twenty minutes late, the train steamed into the Central Station at Brennia, it was six inches deep on the ground. A line of brown-clad porters stood shouting and shivering as the doors opened and Murdoch, against his inclination, said formally:

'Can I be of assistance to *Mam'selle*?'

'If you will send a porter to me . . .'

'A pleasure.'

She treated him to one of her ravishing smiles, which brought a grimace from the little Jew. Murdoch snapped instructions to a lanky, hungry-looking porter, and a few minutes later saw the man struggling with her heavy luggage. His own porter made easy work of his two cases. The friendly little man had given two others his orders, in fluent Brennian, and was now at Murdoch's side: it was one of the unavoidable things of travelling. But he cursed the man, for he wanted either to overhear where Katerina sent her luggage, or to follow the taxi which her porter was hailing.

There was one relief: the bustle was greater than usual because of the crowded train, and there seemed trouble in finding taxis. Brennia lacked the cab-consciousness of other European capitals, and most drivers were trying to prevent porters depositing separate loads of luggage. The main exit was like Bedlam, and the Jew said thoughtfully:

'There are, *M'sieu*, advantages even in Berlin. Their organisation is masterly—there would be nothing like this, there. Nor of course . . .' he darted a mischievous glance at Bruce—'in Copenhagen. Yes, the German have their good points; even the rulers. Can we share a taxi, *M'sieu*, in view of the difficulties? I am going to the Brenn . . .'

Bruce lied: 'I am meeting a friend here, *M'sieu*, and he will be some time: he is travelling from Bucharest. Otherwise, I should have been delighted.'

'So! At all events, it has been a pleasure to meet you, *M'sieu*. I would that our companion had been so affable! If you find you have an hour to spend, I shall be at the Brenn for three or four days—my card.'

He handed one quickly. Looking at him and trying to watch Katerina, Murdoch blessed her lanky porter, for the man stood a head above the others. He was beckoning a cab, while Katerina waited some ten yards away.

Murdoch took out his own card-case, presented Herr Morenson's card, and shook hands warmly. By the magic which seems to affect Jews everywhere, the little man found a cab quickly, and the last Murdoch saw of him was a puckish grin as he leaned out of the window and lifted his hat to Katerina.

Murdoch was still chuckling when his own man found a cab, a moment later.

Katerina's porter was still waving and shouting, without success. He took a chance: the journey had been nerve-racking, but another ten minutes would not make much difference. He told his man to wait, and approached her.

'*Mam'selle* . . .'

She turned quickly, frowning a little.

'I have seen your difficulty,' he explained, with the awkwardness which might be expected of him. 'My own luggage is light—most of it is following. If you would care . . .'

'Thank you; it is most kind.' She spoke sharply to her porter, who seemed thankful that his quest was over, and shouldered his heavy burden in their wake. Murdoch handed her in, paid the two porters, and turned expectantly to Katerina.

'Your hotel, *Madame*?' Deliberately he called her '*Madame*' and '*Mam'selle*' alternatively; deliberately he kept his face rigid, his manner one of slight embarrassment.

'The Brenn.'

'That is convenient—my own hotel is near the Brennstrassa: the Lasburg.' He gave orders to the cabby in halting German, and settled back beside her.

The streets were comparatively empty. Brennia, like Dorsh, Mavia and Malla, could expect an interval between business traffic and night traffic, between seven and nine o'clock. He sat in his corner, trying to keep up a conversation, but getting little help from Katerina. She was preoccupied with her plans for the next forty-eight hours, Murdoch fancied, and his belief that she was preparing a vital coup strengthened.

As the cab pulled up, Murdoch opened the door.

'Do not get out, *M'sieu*. I am extremely grateful.'

'*Mam'selle* is most kind.'

Katerina smiled, momentarily radiant, and offered her hand. Murdoch gripped it, not too firmly, and watched her walk quickly and gracefully into the Brenn. Porters unloaded her luggage, and within five minutes Murdoch was on his way to the Lasburg.

He knew Brennia reasonably well. The Lasburg was in a side-street, and it had one advantage for his present purpose: its back rooms had a view of the rear of the magnificent Brenn—a modern hotel built of white stone. He smiled as he thought of the possibility of Katerina and the Jew meeting in the hotel, then remembered the man's card. He took it out, and read:

Joachim Kelorin,
8, the Dorstrasse,
Dorsh.

It might be useful, he reflected, to call on Kelorin if he wanted to go ostentatiously to the Brenn. It was possible that his chance-met acquaintance would provide him with good cover even in the next few hours. But for the moment, he had to get quickly to work in other directions.

He pondered on what he knew of the Brennian Government. It was politically moderate and had been in power for several years; but its real strength was in the backing of the Army Council—a Committee of Five who controlled the military forces outwardly, and the political decisions under a veneer of advice. The President was the old but capable Field Marshal von Eff, and it was known that von Eff's rigid opposition to Nazi influences had prevented a *putsch*.

The titular head of the country was Prince Viktor, a boy of eleven. The Regent, Prince Riol, had few powers; but he was suspected of violent pro-Nazi sentiments. Konrad Besra, the Premier, was a capable administrator, but only too glad of the support of the Army Council.

There was a strong Nazi group, under the leadership of Bernhard Rakken, and the lieutenancy of a man named Nortch—Murdoch did not remember hearing or seeing Nortch's Christian name. It was suspected that the Police Department was with Rakken; but the Army had always proved a deterrent, and once the treaty was signed, Murdoch did not think Rakken would remain long in the country.

With three frontiers common with Germany, the Berlin influence was necessarily strong, and Brennia's chief strategical advantage for the Reich was its fourth frontier—with Dorshland—across the Middle European plain, and therefore one which could not be easily fortified. The Dorshland-German frontier was in the foothills: a difficult military objective, even for the mighty Reich.

. . . . . .

The resident agent in Brennia whom Cunningham had recommended was a jewel-merchant named Sanderson. Sanderson had a genuine business, with important connections in most European countries, and he mixed with the wealthy—which, in Brennia, meant the favoured of the Government. Murdoch had never met him, but Holt had occasionally waxed enthusiastic over his success, and enthusiasm from the Pink 'Un was rare. Cunningham would by now have telephoned, to prepare for Murdoch's arrival: Sanderson confirmed the fact when he called him up. A sharp, precise and rather disagreeable voice mellowed a little when Murdoch introduced himself.

'Oh, yes, Baron von Lurath advised me that I might expect a call from you.'

'Will it be possible for me to meet you in the foyer of the Lasburg?'

'I would advise the Café d'Amon, which is nearly opposite.' It was obvious that Sanderson could not speak too plainly, which suggested that he was being overheard. 'Ten o'clock is the best time, you will find—perhaps you will ask Georges for my table.'

'Right,' said Bruce. 'Goodbye.'

'Goodbye, goodbye!' said Sanderson, in that high-pitched and disagreeable voice.

Murdoch grimaced as he replaced the receiver. It was half past nine: Sanderson at least was losing no time. He washed and shaved, and went out at five minutes to ten.

The Brennstrassa was the murkiest of the main streets of Europe's capitals: there was none of the brilliant lighting found in most of the others. It was a comparatively silent city: the motor-traffic a mere trickle. But Murdoch felt uneasy. That quietness was a characteristic of Brennia, but his sense of foreboding increased. Things were too silent: he wondered if anything had happened, in the past eight hours. Hours, these days, could work miracles. He was not reassured when he saw that the gaily-uniformed police were patrolling the street in threes. All of them were armed.

The foyer of the Café d'Amon was ill-lit and gloomy; the attendants were silent, almost sullen. He sensed the same atmosphere of brooding, of waiting, here, and wondered whether the café itself would be as discomfiting.

He was reassured.

Behind the heavy doors, music and dancing merged in a scene of colour and gaiety that would not have disgraced Paris. He had arrived in the middle of the cabaret, and he waited on the dais, looking down on the café proper, his lips curved and eyes glistening—as Herr Morenson would likely do. It was a good show. The girls, wearing only diamanté bangles and the briefest of diamanté shorts, could dance, and as they threaded between the tables, a clear soprano sang words and music unfamiliar to Murdoch. The lights changed, slowly. The music was soft. That sweet, clear voice was divine. . . .

In London, it would have been indecent; in Paris, mildly exciting. In Brennia, it was as lovely and as seriously-admired as the ballet. He waited for ten minutes, and one dark-haired little minx came half-way up the stairs towards him, legs and arms and torso moving in the subtle rhythm of the dance, teeth gleaming, eyes bright and challenging. Murdoch smiled and bowed, cursing the spotlight, which shone on himself as well as the girl, and was heartily relieved when she laughed and turned back.

As the dancers finally disappeared at the far end of the café to loud applause, a tall, dignified man who had been standing at the foot of the stairs throughout the turn approached him with a bow.

'*M'sieu* wishes a table?'

'I am looking for Georges.'

'*M'sieu* has not looked astray. You are the guest of M'sieu Sanderson?'

'Yes.' Murdoch was relieved at the ease of it. He was conscious of a dozen curious glances as he followed Georges —and also of the small tables, here and there occupied only by one woman. They could be very lovely, the Brennian women. These certainly were—and very accommodating. At every table, there was a telephone, and the soft ringing of the bells was intriguing. He had seen it before, in Berlin, and the system had its advantages. Had he been foot-loose and fancy-free. . . .

Outwardly expressionless, he followed Georges to a small table in a far corner of the room. Dancing had started, now, and a Hungarian orchestra was playing from a dais opposite that where he had waited.

But he hardly heard them. For it had suddenly struck him that fully half the tables were empty, or only partly-filled. And in the same moment, he realised with a sickening sensation of alarm. . . .

Not a single Jew was present. . . .

The next moment, he was being greeted by a tubby little man with a ruddy face, sparkling blue eyes, thick lips, a button of a nose—and long, white hands which did not fit with his general appearance.

He had risen as they approached and Georges bowed, announced Herr Morenson, and went off. As Murdoch shook hands, the other's bright eyes reminded him vividly of Joachim Kelorin.

'I'm glad to see you, Morenson—very glad. You can talk quite safely here; we shan't be overheard.'

Murdoch had seen that the table was well-removed from any other, and noted that the tables in every corner of the room were similarly placed. Sanderson had set the stage well. But would he be able to do or say anything which would relieve him of that sickening sense of impending trouble?'

'That's good.' He dropped into English, as Sanderson had done. 'You heard from Dorsh, of course?'

'Yes, I have the Brenn covered. The woman has a suite on the second floor, and has booked it for one week.'

'Nice work.'

'Miss Dell and Angell telephoned London for instructions when they learned that v. R. was returning to Berlin, and they followed his plane to the frontier and then came here. They are at the Brenn, sharing two rooms, as Mr. and Mrs. Newman. On the third floor, and immediately above the other woman's.'

'Even better!' said Bruce.

'Yes. . . . Fuller has telephoned that Clayton is going by train to Berlin: he and Graham have the Pink 'Un's orders to follow him.'

Murdoch stiffened.

'Has he, by Jove! That's not so good, Sanderson—I don't like his travels.'

'No one does,' said Sanderson, grimly. 'Well, we'll see what we shall see. Now—what do you think of things here?' He poured out a thin white wine: he had already ordered dinner, for which Murdoch was grateful. A waiter brought a clear, appetising soup, and when he had gone, Murdoch said:

'I haven't been here more than two hours!'

'Noticed nothing strange?'

'It's always strange when the Jews are missing.'

'Ah, you got that, did you? Anything else?'

Murdoch repressed his irritation.

153

'The police are patrolling in threes, and the traffic's not as thick as usual. But you ought to be able to explain it—I can't.' He was hungry, and the soup was excellent.

'Nor can I,' said Sanderson, surprising him. 'But I can think of several answers, and the obvious one will be as obvious to you. There was nothing unusual at midday, just excitement when the papers brought the news of the Anglo-Dorshland Treaty, and then—atmospherics. I've never known anything like it, and I can't say I'm happy. There's been a general exodus of Jews, over the Dorshland frontier, and down into Yugo-Slavia, and the Government offices are busy even now.'

The soup suddenly lost its savour.

'You're sure?'

'I've had reports in by the dozen: there isn't any question of it. There isn't a rumour of any kind in the papers, but at least twenty people have asked me whether I've heard that the Government has resigned, and that Rakken has been offered the Chancellorship.'

Murdoch's eyes were very hard.

'Rakken, is it? If it's true . . . !'

'We'll be Nazi overnight,' supplied Sanderson. 'And the surest guide to a real upheaval is the Jews. This migration proves not only that they know of a change in the Government, but that they're prepared for the worst. There was a slump on the Bourse, this afternoon—everything's down. It's being cleverly handled, Murdoch, but it's happening. Rumour has it that there's to be a special news broadcast at midnight, but I can't guarantee it's true.'

'Does the Embassy know anything?'

'No. I was talking to Neville half an hour ago—he was at my flat when you called, with his wife. He's worried, but he can't do anything because he knows nothing. If this thing is coming off, Murdoch, it's the most completely successful manœuvre in Nazi history—and the beggars are such perfect organisers that it may *be* happening. The police reinforcements make it quite certain that trouble of some kind is expected—and of course if Rakken has the Government behind him, the police will be used to quell anti-Nazi disturbances.'

The waiter whisked away half-finished soup, and replaced it with grilled sole. Murdoch tried to eat.

'It's far worse than I expected,' he said, slowly. 'I had a feeling the Dorshland business would make Berlin jump, and if they're jumping here—but confound it, Sanderson! They can't gag all the permanent officials, they can't blind the Press, and . . .'

'I learned from Neville,' the blue eyes were no longer sparkling, 'that the long-distance lines are all out of order—due, they say, to the snow. The official explanation of the thin traffic is the snow—and that's at least half-justified : it always makes a difference. There's another thing. Neville tells me he can't get short-wave stations on his radio, and I've heard the same thing from the French and Dutch people. Neville's tried to transmit three messages to England, but there's serious interference, and he gets no reply. He can't even be sure whether London can hear him.'

'He's complained?'

Sanderson lifted his hands expressively :

'The weather gets the blame.'

'In effect, then, Brennia's isolated?'

'More thoroughly than I would have believed possible,' said Sanderson, gruffly. 'There are other things, Murdoch—sorry to load all this on you, but you've got to know the worst. Trains coming over the frontier are running, all right—but "snow" has caused serious delays on all the outgoing trains. No train has gone out of Brennia since two o'clock this afternoon. Private airline services have been cancelled, and—well, I've seen it snowing twice as hard and for twice as long, and we haven't had all these troubles. It all points to a complete Government control—to the fact that it's been brewing for a long time. The Dorshland Treaty, coupled with the storm, has made them strike now.'

Murdoch listened, bleak-faced and sick at heart. He felt helpless, bitter at his abortive journey. He understood something of Katerina's mission now, he would not be surprised if she was to be liaison officer between Brennia and Berlin. His premonition of impending calamity was more than justified.

Yet beneath his helplessness, he felt impatient—as though

he held somewhere at the back of his mind the key to the problem. He said slowly, now:

'Cardyce is here, of course?'

'He's at the Brenn.'

'He hasn't gone out?'

'I checked before I came here—he was still in his room.'

'I'd better see him,' Bruce decided. 'And . . .'

He broke off, for Georges approached them: suave, unsmiling, courteous. He had his back to the huge room, and to Murdoch's surprise he said quietly and in English:

'The Fräulein has left her hotel, *M'sieu*, after she was visited by Nortch—Rakken's chief lieutenant. The direction they took was the Chamstrassa.'

Murdoch kept his face expressionless: Sanderson nodded as if agreeing they had everything they desired, and:

'M'sieu Cardyce, has he left?'

'There is no report.'

Georges bowed, smiled, and turned away. Murdoch felt Sanderson's eyes on his, and said quietly:

'I expected that, but it gives me a chance of seeing Cardyce without the possibility of her looking in. That woman is damnably dangerous! I wish to God I'd . . .' he shrugged. 'I'm feeling homicidal! Will it create a sensation if I go out now?'

'Wait five minutes—there's another cabaret turn, and you won't be observed. There's a side entrance: Georges will show you.'

Impatiently, Murdoch waited until a troupe of dancers, clad this time in feathers, streamed from the higher dais. He left quietly, and outside the rear exit, found a cab waiting. Georges said:

'Good luck, *M'sieu*!' Adding, as Murdoch thanked him: 'The driver knows where you are going, and can be trusted.'

'Thanks again!'

As he sat back in the cab, he reflected on the thoroughness of the ramifications of Holt's organisation. His own job was comparatively easy. But men like Cunningham, Wright and Sanderson controlled a widespread system of espionage year after year, without being suspected—and they had their business at their fingertips. The complete reliability of all who had helped him was amazing, and yet. . . .

Despite it, this cloud of official silence could fall on Brennia in a few, short hours. As he drove through the almost deserted streets, he was appalled. The snow was falling, thick and steady, but that could not explain the empty thoroughfares and street cafés.

The foyer of the Brenn Hotel was a blaze of light, but there were few people about. He asked for Mary's room and was conducted by a page to the third floor. The boy tapped and Murdoch opened the door. Then stopped on the threshold, fear surging through him.

In one glance, he took in the hopeless disorder of the room: the opened drawers, the clothes and oddments strewn about, the overturned table, the vase of flowers on the soaking carpet. The telephone was on the floor, too—but its receiver was in position; someone had noticed, had not wanted to alert the hotel operator. The door leading to the next room was open. He sprang towards it.

The same disorder, perhaps worse. One of the beds had been stripped and the mattress ripped open. Across a sheet was a stain, already turning brown, and his heart seemed to freeze.

Mary's blood or Ted's?

He turned abruptly to the goggle-eyed boy and sent him for the police; but he felt a sickening conviction that the police would get no results. He had not dreamed that Mary and Ted would be spotted so quickly, and he hated to think of what might happen to them—or had already happened.

His own danger was acute.

Katerina had arranged this—and Katerina's agents would get a good description of the man who had come to visit, and had caused the alarm. He turned abruptly from the room: there was nothing he could do, and he had to see Cardyce quickly.

Cardyce's room was on the second floor, but in the west wing: Katerina's was in the east. He knew the layout well enough, and reached the door in less than two minutes.

Relief came when Cardyce's sharp voice answered his knock.

He opened the door and slipped inside, and Cardyce—

sitting by an electric fire, a book in his hand—stared up in blank bewilderment. Murdoch had forgotten that Cardyce did not know him as Morenson. He pushed the door to, behind him.

'It's Murdoch, sir. Have you had any trouble?'

The voice identified him and Cardyce said crisply:

'What kind of trouble?'

'You'd know, sir,' Bruce assured him, grim-faced. 'For God's sake get out of here—to the Embassy. They're liable to do any crazy thing, tonight . . .'

'Murdoch, what . . .'

Bruce drew a deep breath.

'Sorry, sir.' He knew that the disappearance of Mary and Ted had destroyed his balance, but there was a deep-rooted conviction in his mind that Cardyce was in danger here. 'I don't know whether you've seen Neville.'

'I did, this afternoon.'

'You've heard nothing since?'

'No. Murdoch, what is this all about?'

'As far as I can find,' said Bruce, grimly, 'there's a complete switch from the moderate regime to Rakken's people—Brennia's virtually smothered. You've heard no rumours?'

'None. I was asleep until an hour ago, and—how serious is this, Murdoch?'

'So serious that I wouldn't like to guarantee your life if you don't get to the Embassy, sir. Have you made any appointments?'

'I arranged with Besra to meet him tomorrow morning . . .'

'I don't think Besra's Government counts, at this moment—and it will certainly be wiser to check that with Neville. I'm not losing my head, I assure you, sir. It looks like a *coup de grâce*—a desperate effort to prevent the *bloc* operating. If the Reich gets Brennia, it can laugh at Dorshland . . .'

'All right, Murdoch—I'll be ready in half an hour . . .'

'Five minutes is going to be risky.'

Cardyce stared; then with a shrug, picked up a portfolio, glanced inside it, and locked it. Taking a hat and coat from a chair, he said with a glimmer of a smile:

'I hope you're not stampeding me, Murdoch! But you've

been justified so far—I'd better ring for a cab.'

'Mine's waiting downstairs—and we can trust the driver.'

Cardyce's lips twitched, but he made no comment. They hurried towards the staircase—and as they reached it, heard a jumble of voices, from somewhere near. The police and the boy, probably, puzzled by his disappearance. Murdoch turned his collar well up, and they hurried down the stairs.

As they reached the foyer, Murdoch saw four policemen in their absurd fancy-dress uniform standing idly around. But even then he did not dream that they were interested in Cardyce, until he saw two of them exchange glances and move towards the stairs. As Cardyce went forward, the two men blocked his path—and Murdoch knew in a flash that the Minister was to be prevented from leaving the hotel.

24: Last Resort

In all, there were ten people in the foyer. And outside, through the falling snow, Murdoch could see the taxi; already covered with snow, greyish-white in the dim lights of the main street.

He was thinking very fast, as Cardyce paused, looking in surprise at the policeman in front of him: a middle-aged lieutenant.

'What is it?' he asked, calmly and in fluent Brennian.

'It is regretted,' said the lieutenant, heavily, 'that no one is to leave: there has been trouble upstairs, and all are to wait. It will be for only a little time.'

'But that is nonsense.'

'Will you leave this to me,' Bruce suggested—and to the lieutenant's astonishment, he fired a question in English. The man stared blankly: the expressions of his companions were equally blank.

'They don't understand English,' Bruce said. 'We're all right. I suggest we make a dash for it.'

'But . . .'

'This is a stall to make sure you don't get out,' Bruce explained, with a flash of impatience. To the lieutenant he said, in Brennian clear enough to be understood: 'Herr Carter has most urgent business. If he is detained...'

'He must not go from here,' said the lieutenant.

'By whose orders?'

'*Ach,* the orders are clear!'

Murdoch opened his mouth to reply—and then a man and woman in evening dress hurried down the stairs and passed the police without any attempt being made to stop them. It was all he needed to convince him that Cardyce was the only one to be detained, and he had no time to marvel at the chance Rakken was taking.

The four men were clustered in front of them, now, as thought to prevent a rush. All were armed, but none had taken a gun out, and Murdoch slipped his right hand in his pocket.

'So,' he said, slowly. 'I—back, you!'

The gun flashed out with the words, and he snapped in English:

'The taxi, quick!'

Cardyce ran. The four policemen stood petrified as Murdoch shouted at them, herding them round in a half-circle until he could back towards the exit. He saw one man go for his gun, and touched his trigger. He missed intentionally, but the movement stopped and the report of the shot was still echoing when he reached the cab.

Cardyce was inside, the door was open, and the engine ticking over. Murdoch snapped:

'The British Embassy, fast!'

As he jumped in, a volley of shots came from the hotel. The car skidded in the snow as the driver accelerated too quickly, half-turned, and then straightened out. Bullets struck against the back of the car, but missed the tyres. Murdoch looked back: in that few seconds, they had travelled far enough for the Brenn to be cut off entirely by the snow.

Cardyce was breathing very hard.

'That was well done, Murdoch.'

'It's only started,' said Bruce. 'They may be watching the Embassy, but I doubt if they'll do anything flagrant there.

One disadvantage of you travelling as Carter is that you can't claim diplomatic privilege—not that Rakken is likely to worry about that. However, it's not more than half a mile, and the snow will slow down anyone following us.'

No one appeared to be, and in ten minutes they pulled up outside the British Embassy. The gates were closed, and two men were walking up and down outside them, but they made no attempt to interfere. Murdoch breathed more easily as he pushed open the cab door.

'I'll telephone you from a kiosk very soon, sir. If you'll find out all you can, it might be useful.'

'But aren't you . . .'

Murdoch smiled. 'I'm not a British citizen at the moment. We mustn't break the international laws! I'll be all right.'

Cardyce nodded and hurried across the snow-covered pavement. Murdoch saw a man open the gates and watched the Minister go through, before he asked to be taken to the Lasburg. There were no messages and he was driven across the road to the Café d'Amon.

Georges was in the foyer and came over at once:

'M'sieu Sanderson has left: you will find him at his flat. He wishes to see you urgently.'

'Thanks,' said Murdoch.

'The driver,' Georges added, 'will know the address.'

Georges, reflected Murdoch, was a tower of strength in this mad world that was Brennia. But he was on tenterhooks until he reached the block where Sanderson lived. His flat opened on to the street and obviously Murdoch's arrival had been seen, for the door was opened before he could ring, by Sanderson himself.

As Murdoch shook the snow off his coat and hat, the icy wind cut into the hall. But Sanderson ignored it, and his voice was sharp, anxious.

'Was Cardyce all right?'

'They tried to keep him there, but I made him run for it. Thank God he was officially Carter and doesn't become Cardyce till he wants to! But why?'

'I've had word that he was to be detained.' Sanderson's eyes were sparkling again. 'Thank the Lord you managed to get him out, Murdoch—it would have been disastrous!'

'The damn fools can't have meant to harm him, surely?'

'I think they meant to cause trouble.'

'How?'

'Well, an offence against Cardyce, even as Carter, would fetch a sharp protest from London, and I fancy Rakken's trying to get one. He'll probably make an insolent reply and —up goes the balloon.'

Murdoch stared.

'You're not serious!'

'Never been more so. I've a man in the Home Office here and he managed to get out. All Government officials of any importance are being kept in their offices until the *putsch* is over—yes, it's coming all right! Rakken has already taken over unofficially, and will do so officially at midday tomorrow. Every man-jack of the moderates has been detained —the police department is riddled with Nazis. Trains are being commandeered, and there are Storm Troops massed on both the Brennia–Dorshland frontier and the German–Dorshland border. They're going to take the chance of marching in.'

'Lead me,' said Bruce, 'to a strong whisky. Sanderson, I can't believe it's so far gone.'

'It's practically finished. My man tells me that the Government offices have been taken over today. I'd no idea the Nazi element was so strong: it's all been done under cover and we can't stop it now. They'll probably shoot Josef and hold a pistol at the Dorshland Government's head— "take us, or we'll break you". If the same thing happens in the Enkraine—and I know they're ripe for it there, if Berlin pushes hard—the *bloc*'s about as much use as a cream puff. It's their last resort.'

'But Mitzer *can't* want to fight.'

'He's had to do one thing or the other—he's got to climb down and be a good boy and put the German revolution years nearer, or else he's got to pull off a triumph like this to hold the country. He's taking the chance that we won't fight . . .'

'He's wrong, we will.'

'You're sure?' Sanderson snapped.

'Holt said so, in so many words.'

'Holt's usually right,' Sanderson conceded. 'But you know, Murdoch. the thing might be finished before London knows anything about it. I've had word from the Press Association that all the Foreign Correspondents were called to Government House and are kicking their heels there. Every means of communication is either Government-controlled or blocked.'

Murdoch felt he really needed the whisky Sanderson poured: his hands were shaking as he lit a cigarette. He dared not let himself even start to think about Mary, yet.

'But damn it—oh, I suppose the one thing I can't swallow, is the Army. They'll need the Army, to take full control—and I always understood it was strong behind the moderate Government?'

'It's puzzled me, too; but there it is. My information's reliable, and the North Command is massing on the Dorshland border: I'm told there'll be a general mobilisation order tomorrow. So you're stuck, and so am I. I wish I could think of a way to get you out of the country, but you'll have to wait till the snow's finished, before you try.'

'Something's got to be done inside!' snapped Bruce.

Sanderson shrugged.

'My dear Murdoch, we can't perform miracles. If the whole moderate regime can be kicked out at a moment's notice, you and I can thank our stars if we ever see England again. That's a fact. I . . .'

He broke off as a shrill ringing echoed in the room. Frowning, he moved towards the door.

'I'm not expecting callers—it might be wiser if you're not in evidence.'

Murdoch's eyes narrowed.

'A raid?'

'It's just possible. Hurry!'

Murdoch slipped into the bedroom as a white-faced Sanderson went out to the hall. If Holt's resident chief had been unmasked, their chances of getting out of Brennia were negligible. His pulse was racing as he waited, with the door ajar—and when he heard what sounded like a man falling, he drew his gun. Then Sanderson called:

'It's all right, Murdoch! Give me a hand.'

Almost weak with relief, Bruce strode out of the bedroom —and through the sitting-room doorway, saw Sanderson down on his knees by the huddled body of a woman. And as he drew near, he recognised Mary's disguise.

25 : Hope

She was wearing a tailored costume and thin court shoes, all of which were soaked through, and the melting snow formed little pools all round her. Her face was deathly white, her lips and hands blue, and her dark hair clung wetly about her face.

Murdoch's heart seemed to stop beating.

But he forced himself to help carry her to a settee near the electric fire. And then as Sanderson fetched brandy and moistened her lips, he said hoarsely:

'It's no use—we'll have to get those clothes off her. Can you fix a hot bath in a hurry?'

'Yes, of course. But I've sent my servants away.'

'Damn servants! Run the bath, will you? And get me some blankets.'

She was breathing, but very uncertainly, and her pulse was weak. Her flesh was tinged with blue—mocking the memory of its radiance, in the days at Cliff Cottage, when Bruce had been compelled to remind himself that their agreements with Holt precluded marriage for nearly three years.

Almost sick with anxiety he undressed her and carried her into the bathroom. The water was not too hot, and he let her lie there for five minutes, supporting her head all the time. Sanderson had produced several bath-towels. He had the nervousness of the middle-aged bachelor in the odd situation, but when Murdoch carried Mary back to the sitting-room at last, he had rifled the maid's wardrobe for clothes.

The blue tinge had gone from her skin, and she was breathing more naturally, now. Bruce wrapped her in a dressing-gown and blankets, to Sanderson's relief: the tubby little man had not looked forward to helping dress her.

Murdoch could speak more easily now.

'She'll be all right, thank God. Light me a cigarette, will you? And pass me that brandy!'

His cigarette was half-finished before Mary's eyes opened; and another five minutes passed before she was able to realise just what had happened and where she was. Another peg of brandy gave the necessary stimulant, and she sat up, with Bruce's arm about her. Sanderson had turned pink, and the happiest sound Bruce had heard for weeks was Mary's laugh when she understood why.

'The Pink 'Un didn't sign you up for this, did he?'

'Well—er . . .'

'Purely a business relationship, sad though it is!' said Bruce with forced lightness. 'What the blazes have you been doing, sweetheart? I'll acquit you of trying to seduce Sanderson, but . . .'

'Don't shock him any more,' chided Mary, but the lightness had gone out of her voice. 'It was all so silly. Ted got into the room next to Katerina's, to listen-in on what she was saying. Then she went off with Nortch, and Ted came back—and on his heels were three of Katerina's brigade. We didn't have a chance. It was all over in five minutes, and Ted had a nasty crack on the head.'

'And then?' prompted Bruce.

'Then they carted us off in an open tourer—brr! I was frozen stiff, in ten minutes. But the snow was a help; they had a skid and I managed to slip away. I suppose it was five or six miles out—I didn't think I'd get here.'

'My dear girl!' exclaimed Sanderson. 'It's incredible! Five miles through this . . .'

'Incredible,' Mary grinned wanly, 'is mild. Anyhow, I'm here. But heaven knows what's happened to Ted.' Her eyes were filled with shadows, but she went on quickly. 'I gathered that the idea was to dump us in the car—make it look like an accident. That Katerina . . .'

165

'Her orders?'

'Who else could have given them?'

'Did Ted overhear anything worthwhile?'

'He hadn't time to say much, but he seemed cock-a-hoop. Apparently Katerina and Nortch had run over the arrangements for the *putsch*. All Ted managed to tell me was that the first job had been to get the Army Council at the Palace and keep them under guard. Nortch was confident that without the Council, Rakken could keep the Army in hand—what's the matter?'

'Matter!' breathed Murdoch.

Sanderson was almost bursting with excitement.

'*The Army Council is under guard at the Palace?* Is that certain?'

'Yes, but . . .'

'The Army's the whole key to it,' Bruce told her crisply. 'The Council is with the moderates: Rakken wants to keep them on ice—face them with the new regime when it's a *fait accompli*. He knows they can cause trouble afterwards, but if they were murdered, and word spread through the Army, it would scotch his plans right now. He's got to have the Army solid behind him.'

Mary's eyes were glowing.

'Then if you could get them out . . . !'

'If,' exclaimed Sanderson. 'The Palace will be crowded with Rakken's men—it's absolutely impossible!'

'Let's get this straight,' said Bruce, almost casually. 'The Palace is occupied by Prince Viktor and his Regent.'

'The Regent is pro-Nazi,' Sanderson reminded him.

'Yes. . . . Presumably that's how they got the Council there. They'd naturally obey a summons—and once in, it would be difficult to get out.'

'It would be impossible, with Rakken controlling it.'

'How big a place is it?'

'Comparatively small. It's just outside the city—you know? It's walled, and very well guarded. The Regency under the moderates was little more than a puppet-show, which is why Riol would go strong for Rakken—with the idea that he'd get a better deal from Berlin.'

'Which shows,' said Bruce, 'how much he knows about Berlin! Where are the barracks?'

'Why, not twenty minutes' walk from here. But . . . ?'

'Is there a strong garrison?'

'Usually five or six thousand—but they won't move without the Council's orders.'

'They might, if they learned what's keeping the Council.'

'Oh, this is fantastic!' snapped Sanderson. 'Do you think Rakken's such a damned fool as to take the precautions he has then let any Tom, Dick or Harry get through and spread the alarm? It'll be impossible to get at any officer of importance —and probably impossible to get inside the barracks.'

'For whom?'

'You or anyone else who doesn't belong there.'

'Exactly. But there'll be officers and men outside, on leave.'

'They'll all be watched. I tell you, Murdoch, you've no idea of the thoroughness of this business—they won't take a chance of any kind.'

'Do you know of any officer on leave?'

'I know several.'

'Give me a chit for them, will you?'

'But . . .'

'My dear man!' Bruce was impatient. 'It's the one chance we have. If I can get inside those barracks—or even get word to the officers that the Army Council is being held prisoner in the Palace, it will just stem the tide. Free the Council, and you'll swing the whole balance of power over.'

Sanderson looked doubtful:

'You might, in Brennia itself. But outside the capital, you couldn't get word—and you're forgetting the German troops ready to come and "restore order".'

'You're forgetting that Mitzer doesn't want to fight—and he'll know damned well that if the Brennian Army is operating against him, the fight's started. With the Council free to act, we can get Rakken and Nortch kicked out, get control of the Police Department, and—well, it might not work, but it's worth a try! Where are these friends of yours?'

Sanderson shrugged wryly and took three cards from his pocket. He signed all three and scrawled on each:

This introduces a worthy friend of mine.

On the reverse side, he wrote the names and addresses of three officers then on leave from the Brennian Garrison. But as he pushed them across the table, he said slowly:

'Each man will be watched, and there's probably a look-out for you, after the Cardyce business. But if I go, it might mean the collapse of Holt's line-up over here. I daren't risk that—once you fall into Rakken's hands, you're finished.'

'I'll chance it.'

'Isn't it possible,' Mary offered, 'that if we both went, Bruce, we'd arouse less suspicion in anyone watching?'

'Sorry, old girl. This one's my job. Sanderson will look after you. He might even,' Bruce could laugh now, 'persuade you into the lingerie his maids seem to like. How reliable is the driver of the taxi, Sanderson?'

'A hundred per cent, if he can get his engine to go.'

'You may be damned effective,' said Bruce. 'But you're not an optimist, old chap. No, don't growl—just hold Mary's hand until I get back.'

'*If* you get back,' said Sanderson.

26: Bold Effort

Sitting in a snow-covered car outside the small house in the suburbs which, the driver assured him, was the nearest of the three addresses supplied by Sanderson, were five policemen. Murdoch tapped on the glass and told him to drive past.

A block of flats which housed, among two hundred others, the second man on the list, was covered by policemen at all five entrances. Sanderson might have been pessimistic, but he was apparently justified. Rakken did not propose that any officer on leave should carry a rumour of what was happening back to the garrison.

The third house was four miles from the city centre and could almost have been styled a villa. The country was hilly and in places they had been forced to drag the car out of drifts; but there was enough military and private traffic along the main roads to make it fairly easy going. The house was approached by a long drive: at the gates, a car-load of police looked with interest as the taxi swung past, but made no attempt to interfere. All the police had to to do, then thought Bruce, was ensure that Kommandor Sigismund Greichin did not leave his house.

Not that it was likely, that night; for the storm had increased in fury, and as they churned their way up the drive, they were slowed to a crawl. Eight inches of snow had fallen, and against the walls of the house, there were drifts two and three feet high.

A bright light shone from the windows, two of which were uncurtained, and the strains of radio music were audible. When a uniformed servant opened the door, the music came more clearly, as did the laughter of women and the deeper voices of the men.

Herr Kommandor was throwing a party.

Bruce handed the card from Sanderson with his own.

'If Herr Kommandor can spare me just a few minutes in private,' he said, 'it will be much appreciated.'

'If you will please wait . . .' The man led him into a small room, furnished entirely with Louis Seize models, where a cheerful log fire blazed in the wide grate. Murdoch warmed his hands, thankfully—and wondered whether by mischance Greichin would be a Nazi sympathiser. Sanderson would hardly have recommended him if he was, but Murdoch was on a stretch of uncertainty: the release of the Army Council was of such vital importance.

The door opened and Greichin came in.

He was as tall as Murdoch, with much the same build, and Murdoch liked the rugged face and direct blue eyes— also uncannily like his own.

'A friend of Sanderson, Herr Morenson, is a friend of

mine! What can have brought you out tonight?'

Murdoch smiled as he shook hands.

'Something of importance, as you can guess. Can we be overheard, Kommandor?'

'No, you can talk quite safely.' Greichin looked puzzled.

'I must warn you to be surprised.' Bruce hesitated. 'Have any rumours reached you from the capital?'

'Rumours of what?'

'Rakken's control of the Government.'

'*What*?' Greichin roared the word, and Bruce needed no more telling that his sympathies were anywhere but with Rakken. 'It is impossible! That blackguard...'

'It is the truth,' said Bruce, simply. He spent the next few minutes explaining: cramming every detail he could into his report: talking without a stop. Greichin's brow was thunderous.

'It is incredible, Herr Morenson! I cannot believe that in so short a time this could have happened. Only ten days ago there was talk of Rakken leading a revolt—but the Army Council would never join him—the attempt failed before it was born. The Council is a firm friend of democracy—but you know this.'

'The Army Council was summoned to the Palace this morning, to confer with the Regent. It is still there. Until its members are released, the Army is under the nominal control of Rakken and Nortch.'

'*Lieber Gott*—they are being detained!'

'At a guess, the only reason they are alive is that when it is over, Rakken will look for their support to prevent a revolt.'

Greichin drew a sharp breath.

'Herr Morenson, it is a convincing story and one difficult to fabricate, but—I must have confirmation.'

'At your drive gates, you will find a car-load of police. If there is another gateway, there will doubtless be a car-load there. To my knowledge, two other generals are watched in the same way—to make sure they do not reach the barracks with reports of what is happening.'

'I have only your word for this.'

'And Herr Sanderson's.'

170

'A merchant can know nothing of . . .'

'Kommandor, Herr Sanderson has for many years been the Director of British Intelligence in Brennia.' Bruce disliked making the statement, but he imagined that it would shake the other, and he was right. Greichin's eyes widened: for a moment, he was speechless.

'*Sanderson*. Director of Intelligence?'

'It is true. Less than three hours ago, Kommandor, I was fortunate enough to be able to assist Herr Cardyce to the British Embassy, despite desperate attempts to prevent him leaving his hotel—is that a thing I would imagine?'

Greichin looked grim.

'No, no. I will take your word. A moment . . .'

He turned abruptly, and Bruce said:

'What do you propose, Kommandor?'

Greichin laughed, without humour.

'It is fortunate that to celebrate the engagement of my younger brother, I have a number of his fellow-officers from the Southern Garrison here, Herr Morenson. I do not think the car-load of police will prove a deterrent! I shall be able to fill three cars—you have another?'

'A taxi.'

'I shall need two more, then. In a moment, I shall ask you to join me in the ballroom.'

Bruce heard him giving orders to a servant, saw him walk swiftly back from the foot of the stairs. In three minutes, a startled dance-band was listening, with twenty couples, to a rehash of what Murdoch had told the Kommandor. In ten minutes, twelve armed men were crowded into three cars, and they swept down the drive. A policeman jumped out at them, then disappeared. From the second car, there was a volley of rifle-fire: then a louder explosion. The three cars were all running steadily, which meant the police-car had a punctured tyre.

And as they sped along the road to the capital, Murdoch felt that the miracle was finally coming to pass.

●　　　●　　　●　　　●　　　●

171

Greichin had given clear orders.

One car was to proceed to the barracks, force its way through and break the news to the Commanding Officer. Two, with Greichin and Murdoch, would make for the Palace.

'The guard will probably be strong,' Murdoch had warned.

'There are nine of us, Herr Morenson.'

It was a good enough answer.

Murdoch sat next to Greichin and saw the second car swing off the main road towards the capital, while the others kept on towards the Palace. The street lighting was poorer, here; and few people were about. But at all the important corners, clusters of police were to be seen, stamping in the whirling snow in an effort to keep warm.

'We are near,' Greichin said.

'Shall I drive straight through the gates, if they are open, Herr Kommandor?' asked his chauffeur.

'Straight through.'

The gates were open and a dozen policemen, huddled near a sentry-box, watched the cars swing towards them. Two of them rushed out to intercept the first car, and Murdoch saw one man thrown aside and heard his scream. But the car was through.

The snow-covered Palace-yard was almost deserted, but the police had started shooting from the gates. Others at the main doors of the Palace came into sight, and flashes of yellow flame sparked through the gloom. Murdoch heard one man gasp, and knew they had a casualty. But the cars pulled up not five yards from the wide steps, and Greichin flung the door wide open. He had his revolver out and a bullet snapped from it as he led the rush to the big main doors.

Seven of their nine men got through.

In Greichin's wake, they raced through the spacious corridors.

Up two flights of sweeping marble stairs, past galleries of Old Masters and statues of past rulers, they ran. There were scattered shots as a startled police guard tried to stem the tide, but Greichin's men were undeterred.

Greichin himself was like a madman, now. As they rounded

the last corner, and saw a dozen men grouped like startled statuettes outside a closed door, he snapped an order and a volley of shots rang out. Only one man was on his feet when they reached the door, and his hands were flung towards the ceiling.

'The keys!' roared Greichin, and the man gestured, speechless, towards one of the fallen men, then bent in mortal terror to take them from him. Greichin snatched them from his trembling fingers while he was still trying to rise, and swiftly inserted the only crested one in the lock.

Murdoch, in but not of the attacking party, felt strangely aloof, detached, as he watched them: it was like watching a play. As the door crashed open, he could see five men standing and staring at the intruders in frozen silence. Two old men, three middle-aged; and Murdoch knew from the expression in their eyes that they expected death from this attack. Then Greichin pulled himself up and saluted, and a babble of voices ensued, with the name of Rakken oft-repeated.

The bedlam subsided.

A white-haired man who looked more like a benovelent free church minister than a Field-Marshal—von Eff, leader of the Army Council—murmured something. Greichin turned and others fell back to let Bruce approach a man whom, it was obvious, the rescue-party venerated. Von Eff had a voice in keeping with his appearance.

'You have done Brennia a great service, Herr Morenson.'

'Accurately, Murdoch, sir. I am from London.'

'Ah, that explains your acquaintance with Herr Sanderson. We can converse later, Herr Murdoch. For the moment, we await the arrival of troops from the garrison. It is our intention to visit Herr Rakken . . .' the clear grey eyes twinkled —'as you were doubtless hoping.'

'He has the police, sir, and . . .'

'There are no more than two thousand in the capital, and messengers will by now be on the way to the East and North Garrisons. Have no fear for the capital, Herr Murdoch.'

'Rakken may try to escape—Brennia can be won for the Nazis, outside the capital.'

'Yes.' Von Eff nodded. 'Greichin has told me what is happening, outside. But garrison forces will be despatched to the Government buildings: there is little chance of escape.'

'Thank God for that,' said Bruce, with real feeling.

'I share your sentiments,' von Eff told him, with a grave smile. Bruce found it hard to reconcile that mild voice and courtly manner with the speed with which he had arranged everything.

Certainly von Eff seemed confident that the Army would be in control.

But was that enough? Did Mitzer already have his men on the move and over the border? If he had, this effort was useless. Fifteen minutes—which seemed more like hours, to Bruce—passed by before word came.

A significant factor was that the police guard had transferred their allegiance promptly: further proof that Brennia indeed went where the Army dictated. Half an hour from the time they reached the Palace, Greichin's party was on the move again. And Bruce felt that the sight of a company of mechanised cavalry in the courtyard was one of the most heartening things he was ever likely to see.

The journey to the Administration offices took less than half an hour. As they approached the Chamstrassa, the light from windows in the Government blocks glinted on bayonets and small artillery. And the sight of fully two thousand men and a dozen armoured cars made Murdoch's fears of failure seem absurd.

He was riding with Greichin and three others: von Eff was in the first car. As they pulled up and climbed out, an officer came forward, saluted, and began to speak.

Then Murdoch's fears came back.

Rakken had delivered an ultimatum—and he saw no way in which von Eff dare reject it. Unless the self-appointed Chancellor was acknowledged, he would destroy the Administrative Buildings, the Chamber of Deputies, and all points of communication in the capital. Lest General von Eff think this a bluff, reported the envoy, at the moment of his arrival Rakken proposed to stage a demonstration.

And the message was hardly finished when they heard the

roar of an explosion, saw a sudden, distant billow of flame, and heard the rumbling of falling debris. No one knew what had gone: but within a mile of where they stood, a building had been blown to pieces.

Rakken's message claimed that every building of importance in the capital was mined, and could be destroyed at a touch via a control-board at which he now sat.

.   .   .   .   .

'I do not believe it possible,' von Eff admitted slowly, 'to attack the building without destroying the city. He has been able to prepare for too long. The one chance . . .'

Bruce said harshly:

'Is to get at Rakken!'

Von Eff stroked his beard.

'You are right, Herr Murdoch—and it is impossible.'

'It seemed impossible to get you out of the Palace,' Murdoch reminded him. 'Have I Your Excellency's permission to try?'

27 : Unexpected Encounter

Von Eff's eyes were steady and piercing.

The only others within earshot were two of the Council and Greichin. They waited, tense but uncomprehending, as von Eff hesitated before saying, slowly:

'You have, Herr Murdoch. How do you propose to do it?'

'With one officer as companion,' said Murdoch. 'And a message from you, sir, to Rakken.'

'You propose attacking him under a flag of truce?'

'I propose to trick him as he tricked you, sir.'

'This,' Greichin put in, unexpectedly, 'is not war, Excellency. It is loyalty against treachery.'

'Once inside, what do you propose to do, Herr Murdoch?'

Bruce gave a dry smile.

175

'The circumstances must answer, General. But is should not be difficult to find and destroy this control-panel.'

'You deceive yourself. It will prove extremely difficult. It is just possible that you could contrive it—at a price. But you would hardly be allowed to escape.'

'I don't expect to escape!' admitted Bruce. 'I want just a chance of getting into Rakken's room, with a capable officer—they will not admit more than two men. If my companion can contrive to keep Rakken and his guards occupied while I find the switches . . .'

'You have the necessary technical knowledge?'

'For that, yes.'

Von Eff gave him a long look, then nodded.

'I shall call for a volunteer,' he said, and Murdoch relaxed.

He had been afraid the Field-Marshal would tell him the job was one for Brennians, and that had made him sweat. It was his job: he had been sent out to stop von Romain from creating a situation where armed conflict would inevitably result. The prevention of war was the objective, and if Rakken threatened to succeed where von Romain had failed. . . .

He heard Greichin say:

'I shall be happy to serve, Excellency!'

'We can ill afford to lose you, Kommandor.'

'A responsible officer will make the approach easier, Excellency.'

'Granted. You may go.'

'I shall need a helmet, trench-coat, boots . . .' said Bruce. 'And revolvers . . .'

'They are not likely to let you take them in.'

'They won't expect us to go without them, Kommandor.'

From his pocket, Murdoch took what looked like a circular steel tape-measure. 'This will fit in your hand—thus.' He demonstrated, pointing out the trigger and the 'barrel'— no more than a small hole. 'It is a palm-gun—and effective at close range. If you keep it in your left hand when you surrender your other weapons, you will get it through.'

Greichin shook his head, examining it.

'You're well prepared!'

'I'd give a lot for tear-gas,' Bruce growled. 'But we couldn't hope to get any through.' He was slipping into a trench-coat. Willing hands buckled a helmet beneath his chin and a belt about his waist as he pulled on the leather knee-boots of a cavalry officer. Then he was ready, and von Eff was gripping his hand.

'God be with you, Herr Murdoch. And you, Greichin. We shall remember you!'

It was like a dream.

There was no more than one chance in ten of their succeeding. In all likelihood, Rakken would want to talk through an *aide*. Even if one man was allowed to see him, it was not likely that they would both be favoured. A great deal depended on Greichin, who would do the talking. Murdoch glanced sideways at the man, and knew instinctively that Greichin felt as he did: neither exhilarated nor apprehensive—intent only on a task which might prove futile, but was still their only hope. Escape did not seriously enter their heads: to get to Rakken and locate the switches, was all they asked.

Rakken had been prepared for emergency.

At the main entrances of the police building was a hastily erected barricade of sandbags and barbed wire: crouching behind them, were four machine-gun units. As the two figures emerged from the falling snow, there was a challenge. Greichin answered abruptly, and a police captain appeared from behind the barricade.

'We carry Field Marshal von Eff's reply,' snapped Greichin.

'And that is . . . ?'

'For Herr Rakken!'

The question had been no more than a try-on. The captain called an order and, under guard, they were taken into the building. At the head of the stairs, five armed guards barred the way. Bruce and Griechin were kept waiting while a messenger turned into a room to the left. In three minutes he returned—and behind him came the unmistakable figure of Nortch.

The barrel-shaped body, swarthy, coarse-skinned face and

little porcine eyes reminded Murdoch vividly of Roland Clayton.

'Your message, Kommandor Greichin?' As he spoke, in a harsh, clipped voice, he was looking at Murdoch as though trying to place him.

'It is for Herr Rakken.'

'You may hand it to me.'

'My instructions are definite.' Greichin's manner was perfect; his voice sharp and the contempt in his eyes just what might be expected from a loyalist officer towards a rebel leader.

Nortch's small eyes narrowed.

'You are hardly in a position to dictate terms, Kommandor!'

'My message is for Herr Rakken, or it will not be delivered.'

Nortch shrugged.

'I will see him. Meanwhile, you will be good enough to hand your revolvers to a guard.'

Greichin's lips tightened, but he obeyed. Murdoch followed suit, his heart racing. The opportunity seemed to be coming—Greichin had maintained exactly the right balance.

His mind raced on as the police captain ran his hands lightly over him, checking for concealed weapons. It was no more than a formal gesture: Murdoch knew that neither he nor Greichin were suspected of attempting a 'hopeless' task.

The waiting was interminable.

Greichin stood like a statue: his jaw clenched, his eyes icy. Murdoch did his best to emulate him, but the minutes dragged: he had to keep a firm hold on his nerve.

When a disturbance came, it was not from the room into which Nortch had gone, but farther along the passage.

Voices were raised, there was the clatter of metal, an oath. A policeman rounded a corner, followed by two others who were half-dragging between them a short, thick-set civilian. From the snarled words Murdoch gathered that the prisoner was a spy.

As they passed the door that Murdoch had been watching so tensely, Nortch came out

178

He snapped a question and one of the escort saluted.

'A swine of a Jew, Excellency! He was found attempting to molest the Fräulein.'

'He can wait—there is ample time to shoot him.'

Murdoch's teeth clenched, his hands bunched, every nerve in his body tingled. For he was looking into the sweat-daubed, clearly terrified face of—*Kelorin!*

He felt sick.

Then Kelorin flung himself down on his knees and pawed at Nortch's legs. A stream of abject supplication came from his lips: the great, the just, the all-knowing Herr Nortch must give him a hearing, one brief hearing! It was true he had tried to see the Fräulein—but he had a message of import-ance for her: it was essential that he saw her! He swore by all the Aryan saints, he reviled himself and his race, he begged and pleaded for a word—one word—with the Fräulein Weissman.

Kelorin, who had been so jovial and humorous in the train, so contemptuous of Katerina, *begging* to see her!

'Get away, dog!'

Nortch lifted a heavy boot and Kelorin sprawled back-wards. But he was at Nortch's knees again in a flash; pray-ing for a hearing, swearing that he had news of vital importance for the Fräulein. She would acknowledge him —but his words were for her alone, he must see her. The future of Brennia might be affected by his message!

Nortch stared down at him, hesitating. Then:

'Send for the Fräulein!' he snapped to an officer. 'Let the swine see her here.'

He paid no heed to Kelorin's stream of thanks, but ap-proached Greichin and Murdoch.

'Herr Rakken will see you.'

In a flash Kelorin was forgotten as Murdoch prepared now for the great effort. Steadily, he walked with Greichin, a step behind Nortch and followed by three armed guards, to Rakken's room. The door was opened, and he saw the Nazi leader at a vast desk in the huge, high-ceilinged room. But his greatest interest was in the number of guards inside.

There were four.

The door closed, and Nortch stayed inside. Six in all, then, with Rakken. There was more than a fifty-fifty chance, now! But they had to choose the moment. He had pre-arranged a signal: the first time he spoke, Greichin was to use his palm-gun. . . .

Rakken wore a dark brown uniform. Medals glittered on his chest, most of them insignificant; but the Iron Cross was there. He had a heavy, blue-jowled face and sharp grey eyes, which seemed now filmed with ice.

Nortch snapped out a Nazi salute, but Rakken did no more than nod in return. His eyes were on Greichin.

'Well, Kommandor?'

Greichin's right thumb was hooked in his belt as if in a deliberately insolent attitude, but actually to conceal the palm-gun and be able to use it quickly. His voice had a matching insolence.

'I have been instructed, Herr Rakken, to point out to you the uselessness of defiance.'

Rakken's voice came, harsh and strident.

'Von Eff received my message?'

'His Excellency, Field Marshal Kurt von Eff, received and considered your message, Herr Rakken—together with the members of the Army Council. He instructs me to advise you that only immediate and complete submission to the constitutional Government's forces can be considered. He reminds you that your actions are disloyal to Prince Viktor and his Government.'

Nortch stirred and Rakken's expression was even more wintry.

'The General cannot realise the significance of my message, Kommandor.'

Greichin launched into a long statement of what von Eff had realised; most of it imaginary. Murdoch was looking at the desk: he saw the switchboard with nine small buttons, one of them flat on the panel: that button had been pressed to cause the first explosion. He felt confident, for the first time. It was a temporary switchboard, no doubt rigged up in a hurry: it would take him less than three minutes to cut or disconnect the wires.

They ran along the side of the desk nearer to him, praise be. Behind him, there were two guards: on the other side of Greichin were two more, and Nortch. If he could reach the spot safely, he could probably manage the task—he would be covered by the massive desk.

Greichin's first job was to put the two men on Murdoch's right out of action, while he leapt for the desk. Rakken was wearing a belt and he saw the handle of his gun, only feet away. If he could reach Rakken and grab the gun, it would strengthen their position considerably—the only danger, then, would come from the outside. The stiffness of the guards was in their favour: no one but themselves suspected the coming desperate effort. He satisfied himself of the best move to make, and his lips had actually opened to speak, when a sharp tap came on the door.

It interrupted Greichin's passionate denunciation of the rebels; it made Murdoch turn his head. Rakken's hand slipped to his gun when the door was opened without ceremony—but then his face relaxed in a smile.

While Murdoch found himself looking at Katerina—who would at any moment look into the face of the man who had travelled with her from Dorsh.

28 : Shocks

The shock was so sudden and so overwhelming that the words would not come. The moment she recognised him, she would give the alarm: in the split seconds at his disposal rested the possibility of success—and he could not give the signal. His mind worked lightning fast, but the very sight of Katerina seemed to hold him spell-bound. She was wearing gold brocade, long and flowing, as though she had been attending a State banquet—and even now, when her very existence threatened his own, Murdoch was aware of her still quite unbelievable beauty.

Then she looked into his eyes.

He read something there. And his mind refused to accept it. He read recognition; and warning—warning, from Katerina!

He stood there, hardly breathing, as she approached the desk. Rakken was saying:

'Fräulein—I shall be at your service in a few minutes.'

'Herr Rakken, the matter is urgent. There is a messenger outside. He has matters of vital importance.'

'Fräulein, in thirty secinds . . .'

For the first time, Murdoch saw her really angry. Her tongue lashed Rakken, whose glassy eyes smouldered with resentment. And yet—he gave way. Murdoch was amazed. He was trying to marshal his thoughts: convince himself that she had truly sent that unspoken message. But the fact that she had not denounced him was proof enough.

'Nortch, take these men . . .'

'They can stay!' snapped Katerina. 'Bring the Jew in.'

Rakken shrugged, as if bowing to the inevitable. Nortch snapped an order, and Kelorin was led in. His collar and tie were out of place, his hair ruffled; two buttons had been torn from his waistcoat, and he was breathing hard.

The door closed.

'Well?' Katerina said.

Murdoch *saw* that familiar quirk, the humorous droop of the little Jew's lips, and for the first time he realised that the show in the corridor had been purely for effect.

'The message is "no", Fräulein.'

And Katerina said in English, very calmly:

'*Murdoch, if you have two arms, use them now! Those wires . . .*'

Murdoch knew in a flash that Rakken understood—saw him snatch at his gun. He shouted, but Greichin had also understood, and acted.

And as Katerina darted her hand to the fold of her dress, Kelorin leapt for the door.

Seven shots were fired almost simultaneously: three from the guards, one from Rakken, two from Greichin and the seventh from Katerina. As Murdoch dived for the wires, Rakken reared up, Nortch bellowed for help, and two of the guards collapsed. Kelorin had reached the door and turned the key. Katerina, crouching near Murdoch behind the desk, fired twice again. Greichen swung round, and his third bullet spat out at the same time as Nortch's first. Both men staggered, and Nortch's gun dropped from his hand.

Murdoch was working like a madman.

His only tool was a pocket knife with a wire cutter attachment, and the wires needed individual attention. Only two had been severed when he heard the thud of something heavy on the door, and voices raised in alarm.

The third wire snapped, and the fourth. . . .

Katerina, Kelorin and Greichin—the latter with his right arm hanging useless by his side—were manhandling heavy filing cabinets into position against the door. The only uninjured guard, now without his gun, was helping them.

Five—six—seven. . . .

He straightened up as the last wire snapped and for a moment could not comprehend what was happening. There had been too many shocks. He still could not fully appreciate that Katerina had helped them. But for her and Kelorin. . . .

He wiped the perspiration from his forehead and glanced at Rakken.

The man was slumped over his desk, but his right hand was moving, pulling open a drawer. Murdoch saw the gun in it—and his momentary stupefaction left him. He struck Rakken sharply on the side of the head, then helped himself to the gun as the man sprawled unconscious: the blow had completed the effect of the chest wound.

The thudding on the door was heavier, now, and he turned to pull the nearest curtains aside and flung the window up. Snow eddied in, bitterly cold. He could see little of the courtyard, but the lights of the mechanised units cast a dim light as though from far off. He pushed the gun into his pocket, and climbed on to the sill. Three feet to one side was a drainpipe, camouflaged with stone work, which despite the snow, gave his feet and hands something to grip.

He went down slowly, curbing his impatience, until ten feet from the ground his numbed hands lost their hold. The fall jarred his whole body, but he hardly noticed it.

Scrambling to his feet, he stumbled blindly through the whirling snow across the courtyard to the high iron railings. Hands and feet frozen, mouth and nose painful, eyes burning, somehow he scrambled up them—hardly aware of the pain as a spike stabbed his leg.

He dropped on the other side and sprawled in the snow, and three men ran towards him.

'The—the Field Marshal . . . !' he gasped.

He was hauled before von Eff with little ceremony. But the men sprang to attention at a snapped order from the great man.

'Did you succeed?' von Eff began, incredulous.

'Attack!' gasped Bruce. 'Safe—safe to attack! Second floor—open window—get help to them . . .'

He crumpled, suddenly. But before he had fallen, von Eff was giving orders. And as two men lifted him to carry him to a car, the rattle of machine-guns and rifle-fire had started, and men were scaling the railings of the police building.

.   .   .   .   .

It was Kelorin who saw the open window, and guessed where Murdoch had gone, and why. He spoke quickly.

'We will be safe in five minutes, Katerina—quite safe. Your Murdoch is useful.'

Katerina's lips curved.

'*My* Murdoch!'

'Save your breath!' snapped Greichin. '*Push.*'

The force on the far side of the door was three times the strength of theirs, and with each thud of the heavy wooden settle being used as a battering-ram, the thick panels of the door groaned, and finally began to splinter.

Until the last possible moment, they used all their strength to bolster their makeshift barrier. Then finally Greichin, half-fainting with pain and loss of blood, staggered back.

'The—desk. Get—behind it!'

He would have fallen, but they dragged him with them, the guard playing his part willingly enough. Crouching behind the desk, they waited for the inrush, prepared to fight to the finish. Time seemed to stand still. Then a panel

184

splintered—and Katerina fired as a man's face showed for a moment. He dropped, screeching—just as the rattle of rifle-fire came again from the passage and fusillades from outside. The thud of the falling bodies, the tramp of heavy feet. . . .

Katerina straightened up, and rested a hand on Kelorin's shoulder.

'That's another thing I didn't expect, Joey,' she said in English. 'Bless you.'

'Bless friend Murdoch!' grinned Joachim Kelorin. And even Greichin, weak though he was from loss of blood, was startled by the broad nasal twang of his voice.

29 : Recall

Rakken had known that he would need the Army—and need it at its working best. Thus, the system of communications between the various garrisons had not been disrupted. An hour after the collapse of resistance at Police H.Q., orders were being rushed to the garrisons nearest the Dorshland frontier and the radio was reporting the true state of affairs to the world.

Katerina spoke to Berlin.

Mulke raved like a crazed man, but he knew as well as any that with serious resistance from Brennia, the speedy execution of the *putsch* would be impossible—only with the full help of the German Army could the country be subdued. Martial law had been proclaimed in Dorshland, and Josef was working fast to prevent a rising there. If Berlin persisted, it meant not only war, but a hopeless disadvantage, for the now solid *bloc* of five small states would stem the tide of the Grey Army.

A speech was hurriedly prepared.

So that while raids were being carried out against Nazi cells in Brennia and Dorshland, Mitzer was making the speech, condemning to the world the atrocities in Brennia; reviling the man Rakken who had dared revolt against the true

Government, and reaffirming his own rigid adherance to international laws. Men like Rakken, Mitzer averred, should die horribly, painfully—a lesson to others who might share his barbarian principles. Mitzer was aghast that such men still existed, let alone that they should be able to usurp power. . . .

'And very nice too,' beamed the Pink 'Un, as he listened with eleven members of the Cabinet to a speech which might have precipitated the holocaust of war, and instead preached eternal peace. 'I suppose we'd better have Murdoch back to report in a hurry.'

'Who is this Murdoch?' asked Paddon.

'Cardyce mentioned him,' Dalby offered, affable for once.

'Just one of several thousand,' said the Pink 'Un. 'But I'll recall him. Er—you won't want me any longer, Prime Minister?'

'I don't think so, Holt, thank you.'

'Good!' said Sir Robert, with such emphasis that Dalby's affability was temporarily checked, and Paddon scowled. But Glennister was smiling as he stopped him with a quick:

'A moment, Bob. What news of Clayton?'

'At the moment, he's in Berlin.'

'For what purpose?'

'As he's a friend of some of those present,' beamed Sir Robert, 'I should hesitate to say that he's been trying to work up Berlin, but it wouldn't surprise me. No, don't start an argument now, Paddon—I've got to go and find out.'

.   .   .   .   .

The snow had stopped.

There was frost in the air, but a bright sun smiled from a cloudless blue sky on the rooftops of the capital, the snow-bound side-streets and slush-covered roads. To the north of the city, the *Musse de Brennia* was in ruins: twenty innocent people had died, to demonstrate the thoroughness of Rakken's plans.

Von Eff had startled good-natured old Besra, who had been detained in the Chamber with several other ministers. He had interviewed Katerina Weissman, Kelorin, Murdoch and Sanderson, and had sent compliments to Mary, who was nursing a heavy cold at Sanderson's flat, and had said pleasant things to Katerina and the others. And now Murdoch was in a car driven by Georges' trusted driver, with Katerina on one side of him and Kelorin on the other. His recall to England had arrived late the previous night, and his first reaction had been to put in a request to follow Clayton. The Pink 'Un had refused the request, with a terse:

'Don't worry about him: he's all right.'

With assurance Murdoch confided to Katerina, who shrugged her lovely shoulders, and said in excellent English:

'You can't follow anyone, with a hole in your leg—be satisfied.'

'Hmm,' said Bruce.

'There is a lot to be grateful about,' Kelorin put in. 'I believed we could prevent Rakken winning, but I did not think any of us could escape alive.'

'What puzzles me . . .' began Bruce, but Katerina laughed.

'You promised to wait till we see Miss Dell!'

'Have it your own way,' said Bruce resignedly.

Mary, in borrowed clothes that became her, opened Sanderson's door. And as Murdoch reached the sitting-room, his eyes gleamed. Streaming eyes and a red nose could not disguise Ted Angell, and the two men gripped hands hard.

'Tossed into the snow to die,' grinned Ted, in reply to his unspoken question. 'But the British are a hardy race, and I held up a column of mechanised cavalry to get a lift back. None of which is important,' he added, eyeing Katerina, 'although at least it's credible. Fräulein . . .'

'No,' Katerina corrected. 'Mrs. Kelorin, Mr. Angell.'

'*Well, I'm damned!*' Ted glared at Kelorin. 'I'd been as-suring myself that—no matter, who are you?'

Kelorin laughed.

'Katerina insists, but I don't think it's wise. However—we are from Washington.'

'Joachim is really Joey,' said Katerina, 'and you won't need telling more. We . . .'

Bruce interrupted, as the truth struck home: 'If you didn't arrange the many attacks on our little party, who did?'

Katerina was sober-faced.

'Von Romain, of course. I could have stopped them, but I dared not. I had Berlin happy about me, with . . .' she laughed unexpectedly—'the promise of favours! But until I knew the final effort they would make, I dared do nothing to try to help you. That was why I sent for Joey, Mr. Murdoch. I hoped he would be able to help.'

'He did.'

'Not as I intended. You were, of course, watched and followed in most places. But until Mr. Angell was caught listening to me and Nortch at the Brenn, he and Miss Dell were not suspected: von Romain did not think they had left Malla. So many things don't need discussing. The air crash, the arrests at Malla, the attempts on Cardyce—they all fit in well enough when you know von Romain was desperate to precipitate war.'

'As Berlin's agent?'

'Not altogether. His official mission was straightforward. But he knew, when he lost the first two races, he would have short shrift in Berlin. And then Clayton approached him to foment the trouble and—he fell heavily for graft.'

'Good Lord!' exclaimed Murdoch. 'So Clayton was . . .'

'Very anxious for war,' nodded Katerina. 'Von Romain believed I was with him, when he talked of really big money, and he took me into his confidence. Clayton was convincing the small states—as only a man in his position could—that to join up with Germany would be disastrous: they must unite with Great Britain . . .'

'But . . .' protested Ted.

'Quiet!' said Mary.

'And also assuring Berlin,' went on Katerina, 'that there was no need to fear the British nation: that its state of unpreparedness was no different from what it had been at Munich. Very simple, and very neat.'

'Not to say clever,' murmured Joachim.

'Oh, it was clever. He did not approach Brennia, of course, because von Romain had told him that all preparations for the *putsch* were made. He flew at once to Berlin, when he believed he was no longer being watched, hoping that Dorshland and Mavia would resist, and Brennia be Nazified and attack. Which, in view of the new treaties with Great Britain, would bring the flare-up which, of course, would comsume so many millions of Clayton armaments, and create the need for so many millions more. He has doubtless prepared an alibi: it should be interesting to hear it. But I have *verbatim* reports of von Romain's conversation with me about Clayton, and they are at anyone's disposal.'

'You don't mean,' Ted protested, 'that *you* write short-hand—do you?'

'My dear, I was Debonnet's ultra-private secretary for a year, despite suggestions to the contrary. And I pushed a pencil with some effect in Moscow.'

'Languages no objection?' Mary smiled.

'Joey knows a dozen, and he's taught me most. But to proceed: Let us take some things for granted: my part and Joey's among them. I'd arranged to meet Joey on the train, Mr. Murdoch, and we were extremely annoyed when you turned up—no, I didn't recognise you, at first. It wasn't until I had the message from Berlin, at the frontier, that I really caught-on—you did it perfectly! Well now, I had advised Berlin that von Romain was taking bribes, and of course he was recalled. Berlin left it to me, believing that everything was set, and that Rakken could take over Brennia in twenty-four hours. I was appalled when I found how near the truth that was, and I used all the influence I could to get into the police building. I emphasised the importance of taking my orders as from Berlin, and Rakken submitted—which,' she added sombrely, 'is why the Army Council lived. He wanted to kill them. I told him they were to have the opportunity of joining the regime. By great good luck—and I needed it! —the lines to Berlin were genuinely out of order, because of the snow. He dared not take the chance of defying me.'

'Beautifully done.' Bruce crowed. 'And I thought Mary and I could shout! But how did Joey get in?'

'Through a window,' said Kelorin, promptly. 'I followed Kate...'

'Oh, no...!' Angell implored.

'What's in a name?' Kelorin's lips twitched. 'I'd followed her as far as the police building, and thanks to the snow, managed to get after her—before the alarm had been raised about the Army Council's escape. The devil was that I got into a room and some beggar locked the door on me. I had to raise hell's delight for them to come and catch me, and then I roared that business about an important message for the Fräulein. By then, Kate had learned just what was being planned, but . . .'

He paused, and Katerina shivered.

'There was practically nothing I could do,' she exclaimed. 'Except tell Rakken he had to wait until my messenger arrived. But I wasn't sure that he would. As soon as I heard Joey had been found, I hurried down. The two of us would have made an attempt on the same lines as yours, and the Kommandor's, Mr. Murdoch. It wouldn't have succeeded—nor would yours, on your own. But together, it was comparatively easy.'

'Which is not my word for it.' Kelorin's dark eyes twinkled. 'Cheer up, honey—there's no need to look glum about what might have happened.'

And Katerina laughed.

.   .   .   .   .

Sir Robert Holt was rarely surprised, but Murdoch, two days later, succeeded in startling him when he declared:

'The woman says she's from Washington?'

'She showed me definite proof.'

'Well, I'm damned! Incredible—I'll give Washington credit, there! What had she been doing in Paris and Moscow, then?'

'As far as Berlin knew, working for them. Actually, working for Washington. She lived in Germany for five years— that's where she met her husband. She's an exceptionally lovely woman. Wily old Josef was proof against her.' Murdoch grinned. 'I'd take bets he's the first!'

'How did she manage, on the trip?'

'While von R. was there, she couldn't do much, but she got rid of him eventually—the only time she tried to "help" him was with Josef. But not until he'd made it clear he was coming in with us! It all strengthened her position as an agent from Berlin, of course.'

They talked at some length, and finally reached the subject of Clayton. Holt's Berlin resident agent had been able to confirm in part that Clayton had not only assured Mulke that the British preparations were in the early stages, but had also offered arms from his Belgian factory.

'Clayton,' said the Pink 'Un, 'just wanted a war. Any old war. And I doubt whether he would have supplied them with anything. He knew our position fairly well, knew we'd come out on top. But meanwhile, his factories would be working overtime. Ah, well . . .'

'Where is he?'

'On his way to South America,' growled Holt. 'He'll probably continue to take a rake-off from his companies over here—it's high damn time we stopped private control of armaments! However, not our business; we just have to clear up the mess. You did damn well, Bruce—with Katerina's help or without. And now I suppose you want a holiday?'

'I'll have to lay off for a week or two. My leg . . .'

He had walked in with the help of a stick, but Sir Robert scowled.

'Don't believe there's anything the matter with it! All right, go and waste a fortnight at your perishing cottage—I don't mind. But before you go, Cardyce wants to see you.' Holt chuckled, suddenly, his chins quivering. 'I can believe you helped to kill Rakken, I can believe everything about Katerina, and von Romain—he's been concentrated, by the way; do him good—but I'm damned if I can believe you made Cardyce shave off his moustache!'

Cardyce was affable, and so were many other people. Katerina and Joey were on their way back to the States, and Holt had confirmed their positions from his American opposite number. Greichin's wounds had not proved serious. Young Graham was in London—going through the initial pains of entering Holt's active service. Fuller was back, too, and he drove Bruce and Mary down to Dorset.

The postmistress turned up a disapproving nose as the car passed. Then, as they drew within sight of Cliff Cottage towards evening—with the setting sun bathing everything around them in a soft, rosy glow—they saw a man wielding an axe on the trunk of the fallen elm.

Percy stopped work as the car came up, and beamed.

'Confound you, Briggs!' Bruce protested. 'You're convalescing!'

'Who, me? Take more'n a bullet from a perishin' Hun to stop me workin', Mr. Bruce. Blimey, ain't I glad to see you two again! You know the whole blinkin' show got in the papers? Made a proper song and dance about it, they did, so I'm told.'

'You were told right,' smiled Murdoch. 'After the Enkraine show, most of the cat was out of the bag, and our beautiful Katerina spilled the rest—with the hope that the publicity would make von Romain go slow.' He had told Percy by telephone something of Katerina's story.

Percy nodded.

'Listen—it won't take long, an' the kettle oughter be boilin', time we get in. Wot I want ter know is, 'ow in blazes did they get us three arrested?'

'Haven't you heard of Alsec?'

'Sure—where all them police-dogs come from.'

'Wrong number,' said Bruce. 'Our variety was the police chief—and von Romain found that easy to arrange, once he wondered why you were all on the train with him. Anyhow, Percy—tea's the thing. I hope you've got some cream!'

'Trust me,' Percy assured him. 'Lashin's of it.' He walked alongside the car towards the cottage. 'I dunno, Mr. Bruce,' he mused aloud. 'I don't see the 'alf of it, o' course. But it's all over—every-bloomin'-where yer look, ain't? I mean, I knew you'd fix this lot, once you started. But it never stops, does it?' He shrugged. 'Ah, well—we won't have no war this month, any road.'

'We might even be safe for a year,' Mary murmured, hopefully.

Percy scowled.

'Maybe,' he said. 'And maybe not.'